Three Kisses, One Midnight

Three Kisses, One Midnight

A Novel

ROSHANI CHOKSHI
EVELYN SKYE
SANDHYA MENON

WEDNESDAY BOOKS
NEW YORK

First published in the United States by Wednesday Books, an imprint of St. Martin's Publishing Group

THREE KISSES, ONE MIDNIGHT. Copyright © 2022 by Roshani Chokshi, Evelyn Skye, and Sandhya Menon. All rights reserved. Printed in the United States of America. For information, address St. Martin's Publishing Group, 120 Broadway, New York, NY 10271.

www.wednesdaybooks.com

Designed by Devan Norman
Part-opener illustrations by Rhys Davies

Library of Congress Cataloging-in-Publication Data

Names: Chokshi, Roshani, author. | Menon, Sandhya, author. | Skye, Evelyn, author.
Title: Three Kisses, One Midnight / Roshani Chokshi, Evelyn Skye, & Sandhya Menon.
Other titles: 3 kisses, 1 midnight
Description: First edition. | New York: Wednesday Books, 2022. | Audience: Ages 12–18.
Identifiers: LCCN 2022009006 | ISBN 9781250797230 (hardcover) | ISBN 9781250797247 (ebook)
Subjects: CYAC: Magic—Fiction. | Love—Fiction. | Best friends—Fiction. | Friendship—Fiction. | Halloween—Fiction. | LCGFT: Novels.
Classification: LCC PZ7.1.C54 Th 2022 | DDC [Fic]—dc23
LC record available at https://lccn.loc.gov/2022009006

Our books may be purchased in bulk for promotional, educational, or business use. Please contact your local bookseller or the Macmillan Corporate and Premium Sales Department at 1-800-221-7945, extension 5442, or by email at MacmillanSpecialMarkets@macmillan.com.

First Edition: 2022

10 9 8 7 6 5 4 3 2 1

For Aman, may your Scorpio Sun placement
continue to infuriate me for the rest of my life.

— *RE*

For Reese and her friends—keep being your
brilliant, bold, beautiful selves.

— *ES*

For M, the most magical, creative, wonderful girl I know.
I'm so lucky I get to be your mom.

— *SM*

And for our agent, Thao Le, for all your
wisdom, support, and guidance.

— *From all of us*

IN MEMORY OF RYAN H. STRIPLING

"WORDS CREATE WORLDS."

KISSES TILL MIDNIGHT

THE STAR

pollonia "Onny" Diamante walked into fifth-period biology with magic tucked into the back pocket of her jeans.

Carrying around magic was nothing new to Onny.

At Moon Ridge High, she was voted "Most Likely to End Up as Your Friendly Neighborhood Witch." This was . . . fair. Onny dressed like she was trapped in a Stevie Nicks music video and smelled like the weirdly pleasant love child of a fancy floral boutique and a New Age store that might exclusively sell rare crystals dug up by endangered goats. If she wasn't carrying a tarot card from her daily reading in her pocket—alas, not all dresses cooperated with the universe's divine will—then it was somewhere in her chic leather backpack tucked along with a satin satchel of rose quartz pebbles, a jade carving of a tiger for luck, and, as always, her silver notebook. That notebook, her *lola*'s last gift to her before she moved on from this world, never left Onny's side.

Some people thought Onny's notebook was stuffed full of spells, but it was really full of star charts, astrological predictions, and the occasional documentation of things that *felt* like omens. Onny wasn't so much a witch as she was "witchy adjacent." She didn't want to wield magic so much as know that it was there. She wanted to close her eyes and hear the subtle music of stars shifting in the sky . . . not stare at empty corners and hiss about seeing dead people.

Most of all, she wanted proof that when things felt bleak or when her world felt wildly unmoored, she could find reason in the stars, and she could use that light to find her way out of any dark.

Letting the supernatural guide her was, Onny believed, a family inheritance passed down from her tiny, extremely eccentric Filipina grandmother. Her grandmother used to flaunt her *pamahiin*, or superstitions, as if they were precious diamonds, and she was never seen without her own leather-bound, sometimes-magic-potions-and-sometimes-recipes book. Onny's mom, Corazon, chalked up her grandmother's "magic" to a wild imagination and convincing charisma . . . , but whenever they used to visit Lola's house, Onny noticed the deferential—and sometimes bewildered—looks the neighbors cast her grandmother. Plus, it was hard to miss the tiny presents appearing in her foyer: flowers from a couple who thanked her for curing their colicky baby, a casserole from a local librarian thanking her for adding her "magic touch" to the school rose garden, and, on one occasion, an angry Post-it note from a neighbor convinced that Lola had hexed her boyfriend.

Why'd you do that? Onny had asked.

Because he was noisy, smelly, rude, and her dog didn't like him! Never trust someone your animal doesn't like! her *lola* had said, dismissively tossing the note. *I did that woman a favor.* Hmpf.

All her life, Onny had wanted to be like her *lola*. In the third grade, Onny even brought her own "grimoire" to class, but that just ended with her in the principal's office after she threatened to turn Oliver Bergen into a lizard and he'd started crying about it. The fact that the grimoire was really just her mother's fancy address book might have gotten her off the hook at school, but her grandmother had been furious.

The only true power are words, anak, *and how we make people believe them!* her *lola* had scolded. *We cannot use them lightly! Don't waste your magic words on foolish occasions. Save them for something special.*

What did you use them for? Onny had asked.

Onny would never forget the sly, delighted expression in her *lola's* eyes. They were sitting in her living room. On the nearest table stood one of the many photos of her grandfather. He had passed away long before Onny was born, but she'd grown up on tales of how he'd serenaded her teenage grandmother by moonlight and smuggled love letters to her house disguised in baskets of jackfruit and mango. They were together for fifty years before he died. Her *lola* picked up his picture, smiling at it wistfully.

I used it for love, anak, said her *lola*, winking. *If I could do it again, I would. Magic is never wasted on true love. When you're ready, I'll share the secret with you.*

When her grandmother died six months ago, Onny felt like the world had gone quiet without her. Before she'd passed, she'd given Onny her old spells-and-recipes book. For the longest time, Onny couldn't open it. It was too hard to look at her grandmother's soft, slanting handwriting and not feel a well of grief opening up inside her. But one October morning a few weeks ago, Onny accidentally knocked down the book . . . , and when it fell, she found a letter addressed to her.

There, in her grandmother's beautiful script, these words:

A love potion for my Onny. May it bring you the magic it brought me.

In that second, the air around Onny felt electric, the stars outside drew a little closer, and she imagined the whole world was holding its breath and craning its neck to look at her and find out what she would do next.

Onny had immediately consulted her tarot. With shaking hands, she flipped her card over and found The Lovers card staring back at her. She ran to her astrological journal and read the words that were supposed to capture the entire month of October: *"You're feeling charged with a new idea. Are you ready to accept the universe with open arms?"*

This had to be a sign from the universe. *This* was what those magic words had been waiting for. And *this*, thought Onny with a pang of grief, was her grandmother's last gift to her: love. A love like the kind she and her grandfather had shared. A love that summoned magic into the world.

In a way, it was perfect timing. All Halloweens felt a little magical, but *this* Halloween was a huge deal in Moon Ridge, and not just because of her parents' extravagant midnight "gala." Onny didn't really know why they were calling it that, but the fact that it combined her two favorite things of "bougie" and "spooky" made it an automatic win. This Halloween celebrated the four-hundred-year anniversary of the town's founding.

Local legends said that on every hundred-year anniversary, magic woke up in Moon Ridge and all things became possible, which made the midnight gala the *perfect* opportunity to use her *lola*'s spell.

And of course, like all good magic, it needed to be shared.

The moment Onny started planning, she'd informed The Coven, which consisted of her two best friends, Ash and True. The Coven's nickname was rooted in dark origins, beginning when Onny's boyfriend in seventh grade had dared, over text, to dump her. One night soon after, some of the students saw Onny, Ash, and True in the woods, cackling over a fire. The next day, the ex-boyfriend got mono from the girl he'd kissed at band camp. It was official: The Coven had cursed him.

In reality, the three of them had been toasting marshmallows and trying to rid Onny of her heartache. But no one believed them, and so the nickname stuck.

🍁 🍂 🍁

Five minutes before biology class started, Onny unlocked her phone and scrolled to "THE COVEN" group chat. For weeks, she'd been working on her *lola*'s spell, perfecting its ingredients and recipes and even incantations. Today, exactly one day before Halloween, *everything* was ready.

Onny: DOUBLE, DOUBLE TOIL AND TROUBLE! THE LOVE POTION IS OFFICIALLY BREWWWWWED. Followed all of

Lola's instructions, including stirring in the clippings of a dead man's toenails :D

True: NOPE.

Ash: Please say that's a joke.

Onny: Duh. The potion called for teeth not toenails.

Ash: . . .

True: Well, hopefully he brushed before he kicked the bucket.

Onny: Alright fine. It was calamansi juice, jasmine petals plucked at the full moon, ginger, and alchemical whatnot that I refuse to share because the NSA is watching and I can't risk this becoming government knowledge.

Ash: Idk. Feels kinda wrong to make someone fall in love.

Onny: We are not MAKING someone love us! We are, as the spell says, "awakening" the potential seedlings of love in another person. Like, if it's there, then it'll be love. If not, then NO MEANS NO, even in magic.

True: Wtf. I can't believe I let myself, a future scientist, be talked into this.

Onny: We is making ze magic . . . for science.

Onny: AND ALSO FOR UNDYING LOVE! BECAUSE ANY-
THING CAN HAPPEN TOMORROW! EVEN THE APOCA-
LYPSE! BUT! HOPEFULLY! NOT! THAT! 🖤

Ash: Sigh x 2

True: Brb, brewing up a v humane tranquilizer.

Onny grinned as she quickly typed out a message:

Also, I stole some fancy paper from the art studio and wrote
down the "magic words" on 3 sheets of paper, one for each of
us. Will drop off in your lockers. Get ready to ensorcell ~*~tRuE
lOvE~*~

True: I'm assuming for you that means "Alexander the Great-
Looking."

Ash: 😃 haha.

A dopey grin slid across Onny's face at the mention of Alexander the Great-Looking. True's text was, well, *true.* Alexander
was the apple of her eye . . . and he had just walked into class.

Alexander Abernathy—whom Onny had first dubbed
Alexander the Great-Looking—had the appearance of a missing

Hemsworth brother and sounded—because the universe was a saucy minx and intent on having her fail this class—like a Scottish laird. Sometimes when he talked, she wanted to just fling herself into his arms and proclaim, *Yes, take me away to a heather-strewn moor!*

Alexander was funny, smart, dreamy, and her perfect zodiac companion. Which, to Onny, meant that their love was written in the stars. . . .

At least, it should have been, if not for their disastrous first conversation.

The first time they "officially" met was at last month's Homecoming game. Moon Ridge High's team had just won, and everyone was busy catching rides to the after-party at Cassidy Rivera's house. Ash and True had gone to grab True's beast of a car known as Miss Hocus-Pocus while Onny waited by the curb.

It was right then that all the stars aligned (as Onny knew they would because . . . horoscope), and when Onny turned to her left, she saw Alexander the Great-Looking standing next to her. Onny had noticed him plenty of times during biology class. Mostly: the shoulders. Secondly: the face. Thirdly: the accent. Honestly, if he was just shoulders and face and accent, he'd still be in her top-ten ranking for "Humans I'd Like to Re-populate the Earth with in Case of Apocalypse."

"Looks like the stars aligned, eh?" Alexander had said.

Onny felt the air rush out of her lungs. Did he somehow *know* that was her horoscope reading, too?

"For the game," Alexander clarified.

"Oh," said Onny. "Yes. Totally. Go . . . Moonbears."

It was a sad name for a team, and truly the only way they could get around it was by being an unbeatable athletic force. Pretty smart tactic, actually.

"I can't speak for my own stars, sadly," said Alexander. "My sister put a peculiar zodiac app on my phone, and I think the last thing it said was 'beware of sandwiches.' Deadly stuff, sandwiches."

Onny grinned. "You'd be taking your life into your own hands with a single bite."

"Hang on, now I'm wondering what it's saying about today," said Alexander, pulling out his phone. He swiped the screen, squinted, then read aloud, "'This is the time of love, Sagittarius! Communication for the week is likely to be honest and dynamic. Open your heart and enjoy where the journey takes you.'"

He made a *hmpf* sound. "S'ppose the bit about sandwiches was a lie then."

But Onny was barely listening. He was a Sagittarius? That was a perfect pairing to her air sign!

"I'm an Aquarius," she blurted out.

"Is that so?" said Alexander. He winked, then lifted up his phone. "Well, according to this thing, that means you and I are a perfect match."

It was, in all honesty, a beautiful moment that Onny wished

she could somehow smoosh between glass. The late-September air smelled like woodsmoke. In the distance, she could see the school's apple orchard, where the ripe, shiny fruit hung from dark branches like gems fashioned out of individual sunsets. This was the time of year when Moon Ridge really came alive. In every season, Moon Ridge was a jewel box of a town. Some businesses and farms—like Blush Apple Orchards—had been in people's families for generations, and the city was rich with parks and fountains and kissing benches under the old willow trees. In the winter, Moon Ridge wore the snow like rich buttercream frosting on a cake. In the spring, the flowers on Robocker Avenue swayed like they were dancing. And in the summer, the streets turned hazy in the aftermath of fireworks. But fall was special. In autumn, Moon Ridge crackled with magic: banked fires roared, the trees rippled with gold, and the wind whispered the distant promise of frost in the year's last golden laugh.

At the time, Onny had been leaning against one of the bike racks. Her shoulder-length black hair was waved in a vintage Hollywood style, and she had on a faux-fur shag coat that made her look—and feel—like an underworld queen.

She had completely planned to tilt her chin up ever so slightly, maybe even shoot Alexander a saucy wink (she'd been practicing her winks on True and Ash, and over the summer True had finally conceded that she no longer looked like a creature in its death throes, so hooray), but then . . . of course, Byron Frost had to ruin it.

Onny caught the dark stretch of his shadow right before he shattered her perfect moment.

Oh no, she thought. *No no no no—*

"Looks like your human sacrifice worked, Onny. Congratulations."

Alexander had frowned. "Human sacrifice?"

"She wanted to guarantee the team would win, so, you know, the human had to go. She was quite brutal about it, if I'm being honest."

Onny was seriously considering sacrificing Byron next if he uttered another word.

Alexander's gorgeous smile started tugging downward. "Uh—"

I can fix this! thought Onny valiantly. She flashed him her most dazzling grin, then brushed the hair out of her eyes.

"Ha. Byron is being silly, what he means is—"

But just then, True and Ash rolled up. True, in typical fashion, had smashed the horn twice and hollered out, "C'MON!"

"I'll tell you about it later! It's a really funny story actually—" started Onny, when True honked again.

"CLEARLY I FORGOT THE ROYAL INVITE," shouted True. "THE MAJESTIC MISS HOCUS-POCUS AWAITS YOU, APOLLONIA DIAMANTE!"

It was times like these that Onny desperately wished she had telepathic powers. But by then, Alexander's friends had shown up in their car.

"See you at the after-party?" Onny asked.

"Uh, no, got other plans, actually," said Alexander, looking distinctly disturbed. "See you Monday."

Onny watched Alexander disappear into a sleek car.

Byron waited until that moment to step beside her, a sly smirk on his face as he said, in mock wonder, "Hmm. I wonder if he knew that 'Human' was the name of the tulip we dissected in class last week. Aptly named, and then sacrificed, of course, by you."

Onny could feel the cosmic force of her glare rising up from her toes. Maybe it was a little over the top to imagine a flower being sacrificed to the greater good . . . like the Homecoming game. But Onny had felt kind of bad about tearing apart a flower just to look at its pistils and whatever else, and it sounded so much better in her head to pretend there was a grander purpose to "Human's" sacrifice. Byron, of course, thought she was being ridiculous and had merely stared at her when she began the "funeral procession" to the trash can.

Onny glared at him. "Thanks for ruining that."

"Try sacrificing another flower," said Byron, turning on his heel. "That should fix it."

While Onny eventually explained it to Alexander, who laughed off the whole thing, all of her attempts to get him into another perfect moment had failed. Alexander would smile at her, but it seemed like every time she tried to go over and talk to him, one of his friends would show up and refuse to get the hint. Once, Alexander tried to get her attention, but Onny was already in the car with Ash and True on the way somewhere urgent. Timing was flat out *not* on her side. Fail, fail, fail.

But Onny knew things were bound to change.

She had checked her horoscope for this week, and it had said, *Love is finding you soon, if you let yourself receive it.* And with the Halloween midnight gala and the town's four-hundred-year anniversary, it was bound to be a time of magic and romance. Everyone was coming to her parents' place for the official celebrations, and *everyone* knew Corazon Diamante threw the most epic parties imaginable. Alexander the Great-Looking was sure to be there, and Onny refused to let anything get in the way of their predestined romance.

Plus, this time she had a love potion to seal the deal. She was sure there had to be *something* there, enough between them for a love potion to fan quietly into future flames of love. A flutter of nerves opened up in her chest. *This was it,* she thought, breathlessness stealing through her. All this effort, all the spell work, and everything would line up despite Byron Frost's disastrous commentary.

Ugh, thought Onny. *I hate him.*

As if summoned by her thought, a cold shadow fell over her desk. Onny looked up to see her dreaded lab partner, bane of her romantic existence and destroyer of an otherwise cosmically perfect meet-cute: Byron.

Onny hated admitting it, but the first time she saw him she'd actually gotten butterflies in her stomach. Now when she looked at him, it was a lot more like centipedes.

Byron Frost might have the name and face of a poet, but he had the soul of a mechanical pencil.

He and his mom had moved into Moon Ridge at the beginning of junior year. He'd instantly caused a stir with his young Bruce

Wayne vibe, thick sheaf of cocoa-dark hair, gray eyes, enigmatic-but-sexy-billionaire jawline, and uncannily intense stare.

Sadly, her particular loathing hadn't affected him at all. Byron was not only at the top of their class, but also the darling of every teacher, and he flat out detested anything that reeked of stars and whimsy, i.e., the entirety of Apollonia Diamante. He'd made that clear the first time they met in homeroom, where Onny—in an overture of being nice to the new kid—offered to read his tarot cards.

Beautiful Byron Frost had raised an eyebrow and declared, "I find cosmic bullshit the worst kind of pretension."

From then on, their relationship went as follows:

Swords drawn.

Flags planted.

War declared.

The fact that they were forced to be lab partners was just a cruel quirk of the universe.

"What's this?" asked Byron, dropping into the seat beside her. "Onny Diamante has beat me to class? Will wonders never cease?"

"Hail Satan to you, too," she grumbled at him.

"You usually arrive with the second bell on a cloud of incense smoke."

Onny eyed him suspiciously. Had he been tracking her movements? She looked at him but didn't notice anything out of the usual. Byron looked immaculate as always: formal gray sweater, dark jeans, hair swept away from his forehead. If he could come to school in a three-piece suit, he probably would.

"My meeting with Lucifer ended early," said Onny.

"Tell him I said great work on the polar ice caps."

"Why don't I tell him—" Onny started to say, when their biology teacher swept into the room.

Mr. Brightside—yes, that was his real name—was tall, Black, and looked like a vampire prince reluctantly dragged into the mortal world. And yet even with his penchant for the morbid, his all-black wardrobe, iron rings, dark humor, and unsmiling expressions, Mr. Brightside was somehow married to the round and almost obnoxiously joyful Mayor Ross Grimjoy.

Onny had never seen his husband without a smile. Together, they lived in a Victorian-style house off the town square, where Mr. Brightside supposedly kept a poison garden on the left side of the lawn along with a somewhat morbid lawn "diorama," and Mayor Grimjoy planted sunflowers on the right side. They were . . . quite a pair. *But*, thought Onny as her heart twinged in envy, *they were* ludicrously *happy together*.

"In light of both Halloween and the auspicious occasion of the Moon Ridge's anniversary, let us celebrate with a little pop quiz, shall we?" asked Mr. Brightside as he swept his eyes across the classroom. "First person to answer all ten questions correctly gets five extra points added to their last test."

Everyone in class groaned, but Byron sat up straighter. Onny wasn't sure why he bothered. She'd *seen* his grade on the last test: 97. And he made sure she saw it, because she'd gotten a 96. Jerk.

"How many bones are in the human body?"

Byron's hand snapped up. Mr. Brightside nodded to him.

"Two hundred and six in adults, but two hundred and seventy

for children, since some of their bones fuse together as they grow."

Mr. Brightside's mouth made a small quirk, which looked almost like a smile. "Correct."

"Just want you to know that it's creepy that you know that," whispered Onny.

"Right, I forgot: intelligence is a detriment to my personality."

Onny glared. Byron might be at the top of their whole class, but it's not like Onny was too far behind.

Mr. Brightside continued. "True or false: spiders are insects."

Byron's hand shot up. "False; they're arachnids. All insects have six legs."

Onny whispered, "How'd you get away with just two? You're a miracle."

Byron pretended he hadn't heard her, but Onny saw a muscle in his jawline tighten.

Poor jawline, she thought. *You are utterly wasted on this human.*

Mr. Brightside: "What's the name of the pigment that gives pumpkins an orange color?"

Alexander the Great-Looking raised his hand first. Byron glowered. Onny privately cheered.

"Chlorophyll?" he said.

Mr. Brightside made an *EHHHH!!!* sound.

"Carotene," said Byron smoothly.

Byron got all the next questions right, too, and then came the last one.

"What does 'zodiac' mean?"

Byron blinked, frowning. "I . . . I . . ."

Onny raised her hand, smiling.

"Yes, Ms. Diamante?" asked Mr. Brightside.

"It means 'circle of little animals,'" said Onny.

"Ms. Diamante is correct," said Mr. Brightside. "Since no one got all ten right, no one gets the extra points. Alas. Maybe this upsets you, but I have found that bitterness only enhances the sweetness of existence. . . ."

Mr. Brightside paused to look dramatically out the window.

"Please continue your experiments from yesterday. Lab reports will be due next Monday, and . . ." Mr. Brightside frowned at a sheet of paper on his desk. "It appears we may have an unexpected visitor toward the end of class, so do not be overly concerned if you are unable to complete today's assignment in time."

Onny slowly turned to Byron. "What's this? Byron Frost got a pop quiz wrong? Will wonders never cease?"

Byron coolly flipped open his lab notebook, avoiding her gaze. "Who bothers with knowing useless information like that anyway?"

"People with interesting lives," said Onny serenely. "Looks like my 'intelligence is a detriment to my personality.'"

Onny and Byron spent the next twenty minutes locked in a comfortable, spiteful silence. They passed the microscope back and forth, making notations as they saw fit. Luckily, their findings and answers were identical; otherwise they'd be forced to talk.

Onny had already happily started daydreaming about going home and checking on the love potion. . . . She wondered if her mom had any old perfume bottles so she could use them as vials for Ash and True's share of the potion. She probably could deliver it in a traveling Styrofoam cup, but that was such a depressing aesthetic.

A loud snap interrupted Onny's daydream.

She looked to her right and saw Byron holding up a snapped pencil.

He looked horrified.

Onny raised an eyebrow. "Did you two know each other very well?"

"I hate to ask this, mostly because I'm terrified about what necromancy lurks in your bag . . . but can I borrow a pencil?" he asked.

"What's the magic word?" trilled Onny.

"Please," said Byron flatly.

Onny reached into her bag for her pencil case, then rummaged through it until she found the perfect one for Byron. It was a bright-red mechanical pencil with a sparkly tomato eraser.

Byron stared at it. "A tomato?"

"You got a problem with tomatoes?"

"No, I was just fully expecting something more irritatingly magical, like a unicorn," he said, eyeing the pencil Onny was using that was indeed twisted up like a unicorn horn.

"Tomatoes are very magical vegetables."

"Actually," said Byron, "tomatoes are fruit."

"Whatever," said Onny. "Did you know that the Latin name for tomato is *lycopersicum*, from *lyco* and *persicum*, which means 'wolf peach.' People in Ye Olde Medieval Europe Town used to believe that eating it would turn you into a werewolf. They thought it was poisonous, too, but that was probably because it was related to the deadly nightshade plant."

Byron looked reluctantly impressed. "Your point? Other than tomatoes turned out to be disappointing but nutritious."

"My point is that maybe there's a reason for things seeming magical. . . . Maybe they have an element of truth."

"Further testing is almost always required," said Byron. "Otherwise you end up with people poaching rhinos and turning their horns into powder all because of claims that it might increase male virility."

Onny could sense that their conversation was on a slippery slope toward *strange* territory. It had happened a couple times before. One rainy day last April, Byron had caught Onny covered head to toe in mud after rescuing a frog from a drain. He rolled his eyes and asked whether she was planning to kiss it and turn it into a prince, too. Onny retorted that if that magic worked, she'd kiss him on the spot just to turn him back into a slimy reptile. But the moment she mentioned *kissing,* his expression had changed. She'd once compared his gray eyes to dull pencil lead, but in the rain, they looked silver. Byron stared at her a second too long before his smirk twisted to a tight, angry line. And then he'd turned around and left her in the rain.

The whole thing was just . . . weird.

She wanted to forget all about it, but sometimes the memory snuck up on her.

She should've known better than to egg him on, but it was Friday, and she was punch-drunk on the promise of a love potion and thoughts about the midnight gala, so instead she blurted out, "Oh dear, already researching male virility? I always thought that'd be the case."

"*Always?*" repeated Byron. "Spend a lot of time thinking about my virility, Diamante? Because if you're that curious, we could conduct a thorough investigation." His smile turned wolfish. "You know, for science."

They were teasing words, but they sent a not-completely-uncomfortable shiver through her belly. There was something in the way he said it. The low register of his voice that danced above a growl and the force of his gray eyes.

Fortunately, she was saved from making any comment when the door to the classroom burst open and clouds of dry ice spilled over the threshold. A huge cheer rolled through the room.

"It's the spirit!" yelled someone.

"Oh no," said Mr. Brightside, covering his face with his hands in extreme mortification.

Oh yessss, thought Onny, turning her attention far, far away from whatever that exchange was with Byron.

Every Halloween, Mayor Grimjoy dressed up as the "Lady of Moon Ridge." Sometimes he would pop into the high school classrooms, and if someone correctly told the "Founders' Fable," they'd all be let out early. This year, the mayor had stepped up his costume. And entrance.

When the smoke cleared, he stood before Mr. Brightside's desk, his arms stretched wide. He wore a brilliant, deep-purple cloak that had been superglued all over with golden oak leaves, a wedding dress the color of moonlight, and a crown of roses and tiny pumpkins around his head.

"'Tis I, the benevolent spirit, the Lady of Moon Ridge!"

Mr. Brightside's expression looked caught between actual amusement and genuine horror at his husband. He mouthed something under his breath that looked a lot like *I love you, but why?*

"I have come bearing good tidings of luck and joy on the eve of tomorrow's celebrations!" said the mayor. "I fully expect to see everyone in your best Halloween costume, and if you come with a water bottle, I *will* open it and make sure it's water! So! Don't! Be! That! Person!"

"Can you go now?" whispered Mr. Brightside.

"Oh ho! Who's this, but a fine educator of bright young minds!" Mayor Grimjoy winked. "Very fine indeed."

Mr. Brightside blushed. "I hate this."

"Tell me, young man—"

"We're the same age."

"Dost thou know the tale of our great founding?"

"Can we not do this . . . ?"

"Shouldst thou not answer, the spirit shall follow you home!"

"We live together."

The mayor waved his hand, then turned to the others. "What about you, young pumpkins? Who can tell the tale?"

Almost everyone—except Byron—raised their hand.

"Yes, you there! Tell the tale!"

Onny turned around in her seat and saw Alexander the Great-Looking beaming around at his classmates. His eyes went to Onny's, and the corner of his lips twitched up in a smile. Onny's pulse kicked up a notch.

"Once upon a time—" said Alexander.

"Excellent beginning!" said the mayor, practically bouncing from foot to foot.

"There was a young couple who fell in love, and whose parents forbade them to be together, and so they decided to run away."

"Ah yes; the course of true love never did run smooth," said the mayor, swiveling to his husband.

Mr. Brightside huffed, but the smallest smile touched his face.

"But before they could depart, the girl fell sick and passed away exactly at midnight on Halloween."

Onny's heart squeezed a bit, the way it always did when she thought of the sad tale.

"But Moon Ridge is a place of magic"—Alexander paused to make quotation marks with his fingers—"and the girl turned into the Lady of Moon Ridge. Her beloved waited for Halloween every year. On that day, she'd supposedly come out of the forests and spend the day with him," said Alexander, before winking. "And night, if the poor man was lucky."

The class laughed, and the mayor dramatically dabbed at his face with his wedding veil. "'Tis true! And when the boy died, he joined her in the stars and they became known as the Lovers of Moon Ridge, a celestial pair best glimpsed on Halloween. *Tomorrow* marks the four-hundred-year anniversary of our town's founding! As you know, every hundred years, magic comes alive in our town on Halloween"—the Mayor paused to waggle his fingers—"and mischief and madness shall be afoot! Tomorrow, perhaps the

Lady of Moon Ridge will walk alongside us! Romance shall perfume the air! Autumn shall unleash her golden splendor and—"

Mr. Brightside coughed loudly, then looked pointedly at the clock.

Onny, along with the rest of the class, was already angling toward her backpack, ready to race out of the room.

"Oh. Yes," said the mayor. He took a bow. "CLASS DISMISSED! And Happy Halloween!"

As everyone stampeded out of the classroom, Onny felt strangely aware of the new silence between her and Byron. She glanced at him, and he held out the tomato pencil. His mouth wasn't completely sneering at the moment, which was a change. . . .

Byron shook his head a moment, then said, "Onny, you know—"

But at that moment, someone else stopped by her desk. Onny looked up to see Alexander the Great-Looking grinning down at her.

"So, will I be able to recognize you at the party tomorrow, or is your costume complete and total camouflage?" asked Alexander.

"I don't know about recognizable, but it'll definitely be eye-catching," said Onny, grinning.

"I'd expect nothing less from a girl who performs human sacrifice," said Alexander, winking before he smiled at Byron. "See you later, mate."

Byron looked oddly stiff. A determined look crossed his face as he quickly gathered his things and stood up to leave.

"See you tomorrow," he said briskly.

"What, that's it?" asked Onny. "You're not going to wish me luck on my nightly séance or dancing around a campfire with the rest of The Coven?"

Byron smirked. "I need all the luck I can get, so I'm going to hold on to it for myself."

And with that, he left.

Onny stared after him. Huh. What did that mean?

By then, she was one of the last stragglers. October sunshine spilled through the windows. On the other side of town, her *lola*'s love potion was calling to her, and Onny's blood practically popped and fizzed with dreams.

As she stepped into the crisp, autumn afternoon, Onny's breath plumed into the air. She stared around the honey-cobbled streets of Moon Ridge. Sugar maples and hickory trees lined the streets and swayed in the wind, as if caught up in the unmistakable rhythm of Moon Ridge's Halloween magic. The world seemed to sparkle with enchantments. Perhaps there really were blue-lipped ghosts resting in the shadows of forests, girls with autumn leaves for hair slipping behind buildings, or scarecrows waltzing across fields. It was the kind of magic that promised alchemy and wonder, where a kiss by midnight really could melt into true love. . . .

Tomorrow night, that magic would be hers, too.

True had once described Onny's house as "the kind of place that makes *Gossip Girl* look like it was about peasants." Much as she hated that sentence, it wasn't . . . wrong. Onny's mom had hired an architect who specialized in medieval revivals, so their home looked like a fifteenth-century Normandy castle. Ivy and wisteria wrapped around the gray turrets and hewn stone walls that sat on seven acres of forests and creeks complete with an actual moat and a drawbridge.

When they were kids, Onny, True, and Ash had unleashed a bunch of frogs into the moat because Onny had been convinced one of the frogs would grow up to be a prince. After Corazon Diamante gave up trying to get the frogs off the property, the amphibians' musical belching became the soundtrack to their summers. Sure, the frogs never turned into princes, but their music made Onny believe in magic anyway. The Coven would camp outside, lulled to sleep by the symphony of cicadas and violin-legged crickets, the delicate wind chimes tucked into the branches of the willow trees. The only night-light they needed was the winking shimmer of fireflies. It was a magical childhood, one that Onny knew wouldn't have been possible without the privileges afforded to her by her parents. Despite their wealth—and Corazon's definitively *unsubtle* taste—her parents had always emphasized humility, charity, and the reminder that no riches compared to the love of one's family and friends.

What you have is nothing if you give nothing back, her father liked to say.

Onny thought of the love potion waiting for her in her bedroom and grinned. *You're welcome, friends*, she projected into the universe. Onny could have sworn she heard a growl of thunder that sounded like True and a faint sighing breeze that might as well have been Ash. She'd read somewhere that focusing on what you wanted manifested it in the universe, and so she tried it as she walked up the driveway. She tried to hold, in her heart, the little glass chalice she'd used to make her grandmother's love potion. In her head, she pictured Alexander Abernathy's gorgeous face and bite-me shoulders, but because her brain was insistent on annoying her, Byron Frost's gray eyes kept intruding into her thoughts. He'd looked so weird when he'd left biology class. And then he'd been all brisk and not at all insulting, which almost made her feel like her whole week had been thrown off.

They had a quota of bickering to fill! He'd neglected the quota! He was throwing off her groove! And why? What did that have to do with her parents' Halloween party? Onny sighed, stepped inside the house, and immediately dropped her book bag onto the floor.

"*Hoy!*" hissed her mom. "No bags on the floor! That's bad luck!"

Onny grumbled. For some reason, Corazon Diamante could wave away her grandmother's powers but believe that literally every action summoned bad luck and could only be remedied with a handful of salt circled around her face and thrown over her shoulder. Onny picked up her bag and was on the verge of an extremely dramatic eye roll when she looked up to see her family kitchen . . . demolished.

"What . . . is happening . . . ?" said Onny.

The kitchen was lost under a sea of . . . things. Staff for to-morrow bustled through the kitchen carrying swans and bears carved out of ice, cauldrons covered in gold foil, chalices designed to look like bones, and glitter skulls; and their oak dining table was covered in smoke machines, silver streamers, antique lace, and long blood-red candles sitting inside gold-clawed holders. A man whose shirt said MR. DJ yelled at an assistant: "I have a strict limit on how many times I'm going to play 'Monster Mash,' Karen, so don't start with me."

Corazon Diamante poked her head out from behind several carved pumpkins. Onny's mother was usually impeccably dressed in head-to-toe black, with her pixie-cut hair artfully tousled so that she resembled an elfin *engkanto* from the stories Onny heard growing up. But right now, she looked a lot more like a rabid fairy. Without looking up at Onny, Corazon vaguely gestured to the fridge.

"I made *arroz caldo* for you, and there's cold green tea in the living room," said Corazon. "I love you, I've fed you, now go away; I have a party to decorate."

Onny bit back a grin. "School was great. I mean, the army of cannibals was annoying, but they only ate Byron, so it's fine."

"Mmph," said Corazon, fiddling with a string of popcorn.

"Got my report card, and it looks like I'm flunking, so thanks for immigrating to give me a better life," said Onny casually, as she headed to the fridge.

"Good job, *anak*," muttered Corazon.

Onny took out her food. "And—"

"Apollonia," said a deep voice. "Stop antagonizing your mother."

She spun around to see her father, Antonio Diamante, strolling into the kitchen. Short, dark-skinned, somewhat round, always sporting an immaculate pencil mustache, and currently standing in a black velvet robe, Onny's father looked like a Filipino Gomez Addams even when Halloween wasn't around the corner. He shook a handful of envelopes at her. Tucked under his other arm was a small white box. Corazon looked up, as if she'd sniffed out the promise of a parcel in the air.

"Is that for me?" she asked.

At the same time, Onny said, "Oooh . . . what's that? Mine?"

Antonio Diamante stared in horror at his wife and child. "Not a single soul has asked about my day! Not my wife! Not my child! It—"

"Hi, Dad, how was your day," said Onny, smiling at him.

Corazon was not having it. She shook a pair of scissors at him. "I am telling you what I told *her*. I love you, I fed you, now go away, because I have a party to plan!"

Antonio and Onny exchanged matching glances of: *oh no*.

"Quick! It's from Ash!" said Antonio, dramatically holding out the package. "Take it and run, child! And when they ask what happened to me . . . tell them I battled valiantly against"—he paused to point at his wife—"the beast."

Corazon snarled at her husband. Balancing her food in one hand, Onny grabbed the package from her father, kissed him on the cheek, and darted out of the kitchen toward the staircase that led to her room. In the background, she heard Corazon demanding, "So I'm the beast now, huh?" while her father mildly responded, "It really depends on whether or not you'll share a Halloween cookie with me."

Cue another roar from Corazon. Onny held in her laughter and raced up the stairs.

When Onny opened up the white box from Ash, she literally gasped.

Nestled inside clouds of tissue paper lay a Venetian demi-mask for tomorrow's masquerade. Everyone was coming in costume, but not everyone would have a mask like hers, custom-made by one of her best friends. Onny lifted the piece carefully before turning it over and grinning when she saw the familiar etched initials: AL. Ridiculously tall and ridiculously quiet, Ash might look like a star athlete, but he had an artist's heart and hands, with an eye toward delicacy that seemed to belong to someone far older than him.

"Ash, you outdid yourself," murmured Onny, as she examined the mask.

The pieces framing the eyes swept out like elaborate golden crescents. Delicate whorls of glitter caught what was left of the afternoon sunlight, and small red crystals like shiny drops of blood danced over the top, so that the whole piece looked as sinister as it was beautiful.

Onny: IT'S MAGNIFICENT, ASH. I LOVE IT. I WANT TO WEAR IT ALL THE TIME.

Ash: Glad you like it.

Onny: "Like it." I AM SCREAMING. IF MY SOUL COULD TALK, IT WOULD BE IN CAPS LOCK.

True: Where's mine???

Ash: Should be there when you get home from the junkyard.

Onny paused to roll her eyes. Only True would think an excellent afternoon consisted of scavenging for metal parts to add to Miss Hocus-Pocus. Sometimes True even brought back chunks of metal to hang on her bedroom wall. Onny found it appalling.

Onny: BUT WAIT! THERE'S MORE!

Onny looked up from her phone to the potion that was sitting on top of the mini fridge in her room. True used to *haaaate* the mini fridge, until Onny stocked it up with Dr Pepper, which True was addicted to. It was an effective way to lure her friend to her house. But over the past week, Onny had cleaned the shelves to make room for the three slender glasses of love potion staring back at her.

The drink—although it supposedly worked just by being

in *contact* with the intended, Onny found this aesthetically disappointing—was pretty straightforward: calamansi
juice mixed with something sparkling (*preferably champagne!*
her grandmother had written in the margins of her recipe).
Onny had considered it, but her parents would probably kill her,
so instead she'd mixed the calamansi essence with sparkling
water, which required no small amount of dithering on her part.
She'd texted The Coven last week when she was concocting the
potion to get their opinions, but they were far from helpful.

Onny: This potion demands some sparkle. Do you think it
matters what sparkling water I use? Like . . . is LaCroix good
enough? Maybe Pellegrino?

Ash: . . .

Onny: What? Oh right. Maybe Perrier is the better choice.

True: Eat the rich.

Ash: ^^lolol

Onny: WELL EXCUSE ME FOR CARING ABOUT THE QUAL-
ITY OF OUR SUPERNATURAL LIBATIONS.

The real magic of the potion came from the items Onny
had carefully placed around the glasses. Onny glanced at the

nightstand beside her bed. Ever since she found her *lola*'s journal with the love potion recipe hidden inside, she'd kept it propped up on her nightstand. Her grandmother had written the potion on a cutout of cardboard, perhaps anticipating how flecked and stained it might get, which was true. . . .

Onny had dragged it with her everywhere as she hunted for her grandmother's three *very* specific ingredients for the potion:

1. *A handful of earth that has been joyously and spontaneously danced upon.*
2. *Thorny leaves left to soften in the moonlight for at least one hour.*
3. *A beautiful flower that has witnessed a kiss freely given and joyously received.*

Once those things were gathered and placed around the love potion, it needed an hour *in the presence of such magical ingredients* before its own magic was awakened.

Onny whispered the incantation over the elixir. She could say it in the Waray language her grandmother spoke, but she had given her friends the English translation, which went like this:

"To summon joy and love in another's soul
For a connection that makes two people whole
For laughter and a smile that one can never miss
Sealed before midnight with a truehearted kiss."

And then—and this was the part that made Onny feel as if someone had inflated a balloon inside her chest—*seal it with a kiss by midnight.* Of course, the potion might not work. Her grandmother's annotation at the end of the recipe was simple:

No love can be forced. But this potion will detect the potential for such true affection. And if found, it will fan the flames of that love.

Onny pictured Alexander Abernathy's perfect face, and her heart did a little skip. They *had* to have a soul connection. He was a Sagittarius! Their love was *literally* ordained by the heavens! Her grandmother's potion was simply confirming what the stars already knew:

That they were perfect together.

Maybe all the stuff about love potions and horoscopes seemed silly, but to Onny they felt like safety. They promised her guidance and a soft place to fall should she jump into the unknown. Sometimes, late at night, Onny wondered if she looked to the stars like they were night-lights for all the dark, unexpected corners of growing up, but then she thought of her *lola*, and the magic she summoned with every step, and Onny pushed aside those doubts.

Her phone pinged loudly.

True: HELLOOOO. What happened to the BUT WAIT, THERE'S MORE! This is the worst infomercial. Boycotting this product.

Onny: Sorry! Meant to say that the potions are readyyyy. I can drop them off?

Ash: I thought you failed your driving test.

Onny: No, the lady gave it to me because she felt bad that it was my birthday, remember?

Ash: Very awesome. Much confidence.

True: "Potions." Ew. I hate this.

Onny frowned at the unicorn vomiting rainbows .gif that True sent. Eyebrow arched, she typed out:

Don't knock it till you try it!

True: Try it on who, exactly?

Onny: I leave that to the discretion of the universe.

Onny waited. True was two degrees left of feral, but with that came a ferocious loyalty, one that Onny never doubted. Call it prophetic, but Onny knew exactly what would happen next.

"Three, two . . ." said Onny softly.

Ping!

True: Out of concern for the welfare of Moon Ridge, I'll pick up the ~potions~ myself. See you in 10.

Onny: <3333 lly

True: Grrr.

Ash: Why'd the potions take so long?

Onny: Oooh! Eager, are we?

Ash: No.

Onny: Yes.

Ash: No.

True: Cassidy Rivera.

Ash: NO.

Onny: Methinks Ash doth protest too much.

True began spamming the group chat with heart emojis, and before Onny could respond, she heard her mother hollering up the stairs:

"YOUR FATHER IS EATING ALL THE COOKIES! RE-MOVE HIM FROM MY PRESENCE!"

Onny winced, then put down her phone. *This* was the reason why it had taken so long to get all the ingredients together. The whole "thorny leaves soften in the moonlight" was pretty easy, thanks to her mother's greenhouse in the backyard, which had, of all things, a sarsaparilla plant with thorny leaves. But earth that had been "joyously and spontaneously danced upon"? Onny briefly considered yelling: "IMPROMPTU DANCE PARTY" in the cafeteria, but (1) what if no one danced? and (2) if they *did* start dancing, they'd probably find it weird if she threw a handful of dirt in the air and shouted: "DANCE, MY LOVELIES, DANCE! THY ENERGY SHALL FUEL MY POTIONS!"

So.

Instead, Onny had to play her mother's favorite Janet Jackson playlist in the garden, falsely compliment her father on his dancing moves—Antonio Diamante could do many things, but dancing was not one of them—and then hang out with her parents, offering weak encouragements until they eventually twirled around for a bit. The moment that happened, she had cut the music, shooed them inside, and pulled up some of the grass where they had danced.

The next hurdle was the whole "beautiful flower that has witnessed a kiss."

For a week straight, Onny had carried around a sprig of her favorite *Matthiola incana* in her hair, trying to catch the high school couples in the midst of kissing. One would imagine that it wouldn't be particularly hard, but Mr. Brightside had an uncanny habit of popping up whenever anyone got too close, and True had pointed out that people were beginning to wonder what Onny Diamante was doing awkwardly standing in the middle of dark hallways.

"I'm trying to get us everlasting love!" said Onny.

"Well, it's going to be everlasting creepy if you don't stop," said True.

Thus, Onny was forced to lurk outside the band room trying to catch half the marching band in the midst of a kiss before it turned into, well, a lot more than kissing. Onny had tilted her head, angling up her chin as if she could give the flower sprig in her hair a better view. One couple scooted close together. Onny couldn't remember their real names, but True called them "Scott and Pre-Travis Kourtney" because they were always breaking up. The band room was dark, instruments lined up against the wall. "Scott" grinned, "Kourtney" angled her face, Onny awkwardly inched toward the window door, and—

"Do I even *want* to know what the hell you're doing?"

Onny spun around. A tall, dark, and impeccably dressed Byron Frost stared down at her. Was he wearing a suit? At 3 P.M.? *Why?* He glanced over her shoulder to the band room and raised an eyebrow.

"Voyeurism is a weird pastime," he said. "Can't imagine that looking great on a college app. Oh well, less competition for me."

"I am not . . . voyeur-ing! Voyeurizing? Is that even a word? Whatever," said Onny, flapping a hand at him. "Go away, Byron, or—"

But when she glanced through the window, "Scott" and "Kourtney" were gone.

Byron must have spooked them.

Stupid Byron.

"No!" cried out Onny. "They're *gone*. My poor flower. Cut down in its prime for nothing."

Byron loudly cleared his throat. "I fully accept that I will regret asking this . . . but what are you doing?"

"Practicing my lurking. I'm interning with Krampus for the holidays," grumbled Onny.

"No doubt the Ivy League schools will throw themselves at you."

Onny glared. "What are you doing here, anyway?"

Distantly, Onny heard a woman's musical laugh. It could only belong to Ms. Allegra Frost, the school's warm and friendly music teacher and—by some inexplicable biological quirk— Byron's mother. Onny often saw him driving them to school in their small, bright blue car. It had always struck her how much the car *didn't* suit him. He must be here to pick up his mom.

Byron studied her for a moment. "You're acting weirder than usual."

Onny shrugged. "Did you know the word 'weird' comes from the Old English *wyrd* for 'destiny'? Therefore the fates are guiding whatever I'm doing in this second. Which isn't your business."

Byron looked annoyed, which meant he was somewhat impressed. Onny briefly gloated before she saw his gray eyes flick to the flower sprig in her hair. His mouth twitched. Made sense. Byron Frost would be allergic to the presence of joyous vegetation.

"You don't normally wear flowers in your hair," he said.

"How would you know?" Onny shot back.

Byron opened his mouth, closed it, glared at some invisible spot behind Onny's head, and then shook his head and left her standing in the hall.

Onny had felt strangely caught out by the whole thing. For a bizarre moment, she found herself wanting to explain why she was bothering with flowers in her hair. But why would she want to tell Byron of all people?

When she got home that day, she put the whole situation out of her head. She needed a new plan to complete this step of Lola's potion. It took *days* before it finally happened, which meant multiple hours in which Onny lurked around her parents, waiting for them to think she was out of sight when she actually wasn't, so that they could—revolting as it was—*kiss* in view of the flower.

This, more than anything, was the reason Onny believed love potions were so rare. The ingredients were too awkward and too time-consuming, so that most people probably couldn't be bothered with them. Or they died of embarrassment trying to make them happen.

"ONNY!" shouted her mother up the stairs. "I need your help! You know how important tomorrow is!"

"Trust me," said Onny, with one last glance at the potions. "I know."

🍂 🍂 🍂

The morning and afternoon of Halloween seemed to pass by in a blink. The house was in complete and total chaos, so Onny and her father had hid upstairs in one of the turrets and spent the day reading. Both of them had learned the hard way to stay out of her mother's war path when it came to day-of-event planning.

By 1 P.M., Corazon and her army of decorators had transformed the living room into an autumn fairy's grotto, the ceiling strung with frosted-pendant lights and the pillars wrapped in ivy and golden leaves.

By 2 P.M., the basement became an homage to a ruined

temple worthy of *National Treasure*–level plundering. Grinning skull chalices perched on the bar at the end of the room; smoke machines crouched inside the gaping mouths of eight-foot-tall sphinxes tucked into the corners of the room. The dance floor had been wrapped in a kind of gold foil, while the DJ, already dressed as a yeti, was beginning to set up the sound system.

By 5 P.M., Corazon was hollering that the chef was five minutes late and everything must be set on fire since it was already trash.

Onny and her father peered over the stair railings as Corazon walked in circles, clutching several scheduling binders to her chest.

Onny glared at her father. "Shouldn't you be helping?"

"I'm too scared."

As if sensing her family's presence, Corazon whipped her head up, and Onny and Antonio scrambled backward.

"Did It see us?" he whispered.

"No, I think we're—"

"ANTONIO!"

"Oh no."

At the end of the staircase, Onny heard the slap of her mother's chinelas. Uh-oh. That meant she was heading up the stairs. Onny and her dad squeezed against the wall.

"I thought today was supposed to be magical or something," whimpered Antonio. "Everyone is so happy about this four-hundred-year town's founding anniversary, and what about me? How come 'ghost girl' hasn't spared me?"

"You mean the Lady of Moon Ridge?" asked Onny, raising an eyebrow.

"I can hear you, Antonio," said her mother, taking another step up the staircase. "You can come down now, and I will pretend you always intended to help me, or else."

"I'm going to have a word with this Lady of Moon Ridge," grumbled Antonio. "It's supernatural discrimination."

"*Usa, duwa . . .*" counted Corazon slowly.

When she got to three, they were done for.

"Save yourself!" said Antonio, standing upright. Onny could hear him darting down the stairs. "I'm here, my love!"

"Nice try," said Corazon, but she didn't take another step.

Onny held herself very still and very out of sight.

"I know you're there, Onny," said Corazon darkly. "Do your homework, get ready, and be downstairs by six. Everyone is coming early for the buffet dinner to be served on the lawn."

Everyone, thought Onny with a stray flutter in her chest.

Everyone including Alexander the Great-Looking.

🍁 🍂 🍁

At 7 P.M., Onny inspected herself in the giant vintage mirror propped up against her wall. She'd salvaged it from an antique store in the neighboring town of Twilight Grove years ago, instantly obsessed with the curlicues of bronze, the almost sinister faces of goblins and sprites peeking out beneath the metal foliage. It seemed like the kind of thing a glamorous witch would keep in her house, and right now, Onny felt the part.

She twirled a little in her gown, a red-and-black-silk confection with red beads at the sweetheart neckline. Ash's masquerade mask and a pair of blood-spattered elbow-high white gloves flopped off the edge of her bed, waiting for her to complete the ensemble.

On the makeup vanity beside her mirror sat a single vial of her *lola*'s love potion, expertly poured into a little perfume flask the size of her pinky finger. True had taken the other two vials with her last night, one for her and the other to deliver to Ash. There was also a little incantation written on a piece of hand-made paper. True had inspected the square of parchment paper with an eviscerating eye. It always delighted Onny that while True's personality would loom giantlike above a crowd, the person to whom it belonged was surprisingly itty-bitty. True stood at just five feet tall. She had silky, ink-black hair that was always escaping out of braids and ponytails, rich mahogany skin, and large, dark eyes that seemed to stare out and catch every single detail from a face that was otherwise perfectly doll-like.

"Apollonia Diamante . . . did you torch the ends of this paper?" asked True.

"Yup."

"Why?"

"For the *aesthetics*, obviously," said Onny.

"And what do we do with this potion anyway? Dump it in someone's drink and hand it to them?"

"No!" said Onny, appalled. "No tricking!"

True raised an eyebrow. "So we say, 'Hi, handsome stranger . . . wanna love potion? It's not FDA approved. Cheers.'"

"I mean . . . I imagine you'd do it with more tact."

"Have we met?"

Onny laughed. Honestly, she hadn't given much thought to

how she'd physically *give* the love potion to Alexander. Dressed up in all her Halloween garb, Onny turned to her mirror to practice.

"Beautiful Alexander . . . how would you like to be eternally bound to my soul?" Onny said to her reflection.

Dang.

Even her reflection seemed to cringe.

"Stop judging me," she grumbled, before straightening her shoulders and trying again. "What about . . . 'So remember that one time where we both agreed that we were cosmically perfect together? This is more like cosmic insurance to add to that. Drink?'"

No.

"I indulged in a tiny bit of voyeurism to make this for you. . . ."

Wow.

Worse.

Onny groaned, turned away from the mirror, trudged to her bed, and flung herself on it with a deeply satisfying *oompf.* Then she lifted her head and glanced at her *lola's* letter. When she'd first found the letter, Onny had spent hours tracing the shape of her grandmother's handwriting, a warm kernel of awe slowly expanding in her chest. But she'd stopped the moment she realized how fragile the ink was, and how it had already begun to smudge from the press of her hands. From then on, she'd kept the letter pasted onto its cardboard square close by, but she didn't dare touch it. She didn't want to lose what little she had left of her *lola.*

"What would you do?" Onny asked the letter. "I feel like you'd do something epic, but I'm not you. I don't think I can pull it off."

As if her grandmother were in the room, Onny could imagine her scoffing about the idea of planning. Her grandmother always seized new experiences without a second thought. For her seventieth birthday, she'd gone white water rafting. For her Christmas present last year, she'd demanded a belly-dancing class. And when her mother insisted that she should plan carefully, considering her age, her *lola* had waved an indifferent hand: *Don't lecture me on planning when the best thing in your life was very much unplanned,* she'd said, with a weighted glance at Onny. Corazon had turned an indignant shade of tomato. Lola had winked at her: *Why not let the universe steer you as it wants to,* anak? *You might find yourself pleasantly surprised.*

Onny was all about letting the universe steer her, so maybe that was her grandmother's answer? She would just wait and see what the moment demanded.

"Thanks, Lola," said Onny, grinning.

She pushed herself off the bed, grabbed her phone, pulled on her blood-spattered gloves, tucked the love potion into a little wristlet purse, and headed downstairs.

🍁 🍂 🍁

Onny felt less like she'd walked into a Halloween party and more like she'd stumbled into the pages of the kind of fairy tale that has teeth and just enough shadows to raise your pulse. The white marble floor gleamed, and the string lights twinkled. Servers wearing fox masks and pristine white tuxedos carried platters of

food and balanced drinks pluming with steam, moving grace-
fully through the growing crowd. Ice sculptures of monstrous,
grinning skulls were backlit by long onyx candles. Autumn leaves
and ivy wrapped around the pillar of the living room, and even
though there was nothing cooking, there was a particular scent of
campfires and cinnamon hanging in the air.

The main room forked off into two hallways. Down one
was the dining hall set up with a long table groaning under the
weight of desserts. The other connected to the stairs leading to
the basement's dance floor. It felt too early for dancing, so Onny
searched the crowd for her friends. She thought she'd catch Ash's
tall, lithe frame at the fringes, or True cutting a warpath to a
cooler of Dr Pepper, but she didn't see them at all.

Maybe they hadn't gotten here yet.

The front door was wide open, and her costumed classmates
poured inside. There were the twins—Ali and Cali—dressed like
sleek vampires. An amorous couple outfitted like a dish and a
spoon blocked the hall leading to the basement's dance floor. In
the crowd, Onny caught sight of Mayor Grimjoy and Mr. Brightside. Both wore Ash's Venetian masks and looked . . . like some
sort of regal sun and moon gods? Onny couldn't be sure, because
right then a familiar figure stepped through the front door. Onny
felt a sharp flutter in her chest.

Alexander the Great-Looking Abernathy had arrived dressed
up as a Scottish laird. Kilt, tartan—everything. Drool. He spotted
her from across the room. His eyes traveled up and down her
outfit and then. He. *Winked.*

Onny waved. *Why did she wave?* A wink was not met with a

wave! That was like fist-bumping someone who asked for a high five. Fail fail fail.

On her wrist, Onny felt her purse wristlet carrying the vial of love potion bunch up. She flicked her hand. Across the room, Alexander nodded, mouthing, *One second.*

Onny froze.

Had she . . .

Oh no.

She had summoned him. She looked up and saw that a classmate dressed up as a werewolf had caught him in conversation. That should buy her a couple minutes, right?

Onny whipped out her phone:

Onny: Nbd or anything, but I'm currently dying.

Onny: In case you might be interested.

Onny: You know.

Onny: As my best friends.

Onny: Who are totally . . .

Onny: MIA???

No response.

Curse thee!

What was she supposed to do now?

Alexander was on his way here, and she didn't know what to say, and on top of that—

"Miss, would you like one?"

Onny jolted. She looked up to see one of the servers carrying a platter of blood-red drinks. Onny had taste-tested them with her mom earlier, some kind of fizzy pomegranate juice. Was it her imagination, or was the love potion in her wrist purse *tingling* just then?

"Two please!" said Onny.

Drinks in hand, she walked over to an empty high table and set down the drinks. Her heart pounded as she took out the love potion and poured it into one of the glass flutes.

Here was the moment.

Here was the thing to say:

What would you do if I told you this was a love potion?

She could picture the mock-serious grin on his face as he reached for his drink: "Well, cheers then." It would be the complete opposite response of someone like Byron, whose very presence would probably make the potion curdle on the spot from the sheer power of his condescension. Just then, a tall shadow fell over her. Onny's skin erupted in goose bumps. She'd never noticed how Alexander smelled *really* good. Not swathed in cologne or sweat, but crisp and clean, like freshly laundered silk she wanted to wrap herself in.

"You're blood-spattered," said a familiar voice. "Sacrifice go wrong again?"

Wait a second.

Onny's brain felt like it'd been whiplashed. She looked up to see *not* Alexander standing in front of her . . . but Byron Frost. He was wearing a brown leather apron, tall brown boots, and dark elbow-high gloves, and a pair of steampunk gold-rimmed goggles lay perched in his black hair.

"It must have if you're standing next to me," said Onny.

"Who are you supposed to be?"

Onny sighed, gesturing at her outfit. "I'm Erzebet Báthory, obviously."

"The Hungarian countess who murdered girls and bathed in their blood?"

Onny was temporarily stunned. She had fully been expecting to inform—and in her own intellectual obnoxious way, had been rather looking forward to telling—everyone the obscure historical inspiration behind her costume. Byron knowing who she was felt both weird and satisfying and horrifically timed.

"Well, you know, everlasting youth and all that," said Onny quickly. She drummed her fingers on the table, waiting for Alexander. He met her gaze over the crowd and smiled again.

Byron followed her line of sight and rolled his eyes. "He dressed up as a Scotsman? How original."

"And what are you supposed to be? A butcher?"

"I'm Frankenstein," said Byron, plucking at his leather apron. "Obviously."

"Yeah, super obvious, considering most people wanting to dress up as Frankenstein would go as his monster—"

"Which would be incorrect," said Byron. "Dr. Frankenstein, the scientist, versus Frankenstein's monster, which he created. Huge difference."

"I'll let the news team know," said Onny hurriedly. "Can you badger me later? I'm in the middle of something."

"What, guarding two nonalcoholic beverages that will inevitably be spiked by our enterprising classmates?"

"Yes."

Alexander made his way to her.

"What is this, some kind of pomegranate juice?" asked Byron.

Onny didn't spare him a glance. She was too busy rehearsing the love potion's incantation in her head, her grandmother's words moving through her.

"Smells mildly inoffensive," remarked Byron.

"Uh-huh."

Onny could feel sparkles and witticisms bubbling up on her tongue. Alexander's sandy blond hair caught the lights from overhead. Onny thought she could sense the stars pinwheeling out of sight, the pull of their compatible horoscopes reaching out across—

Slurp.

The sound crashed through Onny's thoughts.

She whirled around to see Byron holding an *empty* champagne flute. He smacked his lips, raising an eyebrow.

"Faintly lime tasting?" he remarked. "Strange—"

"You *drank* it!" said Onny.

"That's normally what one does with beverages."

Horror clawed through her chest.

"But . . . but that wasn't yours to drink!" said Onny.

"I could use a drink?" said Alexander, sidling up to them.

The words were out of Onny's mouth before she realized what she'd done. "I'll get you one! Just, give me . . . a month?"

"A month?" repeated Alexander.

Alexander looked so gorgeous.

And so *confused.*

"Did I say a month?" said Onny, doing her best I'm-completely-stable laugh. "I meant a minute!"

Alexander smiled. "Shall I wait here or . . . ?"

Onny's mind felt a thousand places at once. That was the last of the potion, which meant she'd have to make it from scratch all over again *before* midnight in time to give it to Alexander. What were the ingredients again? A handful of earth danced upon? Something about a flower that's seen a kiss? If True and Ash were here, she could ask them to help her, but they weren't, and honestly this entire mess was due to one person . . . one person who honestly owed it to her to fix this chaos. Onny glared at Byron, channeling her feelings of "you're a life ruiner; you ruin people's lives" at him.

"You're acting strange," said Byron. "Well, strang*er.*"

Onny turned to Alexander, a too-bright smile pasted on her face. "Would you excuse me a moment? I need to have a word with Byron."

"You do?" asked Byron, lifting an eyebrow.

"You do?" asked Alexander, frowning.

"I do," said Onny, grabbing Byron's sleeve. "I'll be back with that drink as soon as possible."

"Um, okay?" said Alexander.

"Great," said Onny, gripping Byron's elbow and steering him expertly through the mazelike crowd, past the dining room and into the laundry closet, where it was blessedly silent. The light bulb had started acting up the other day, and the scant illumination limned Byron's cheekbones and hair, catching on his silver eyes and stern mouth. He looked like some sort of dark angel.

A dark angel among . . . socks.

What a waste of a face, mourned Onny. *Stupid face.*

Byron arched an eyebrow. "Is this the part where you tell me you can't hide your true feelings for me and ravish me in the dark?"

Byron's voice, Onny decided, was also stupid.

It was stupid mostly because it sounded strangely velvety, and even surrounded by socks and the smell of detergent, she noticed it.

"No," said Onny. "This is the part where you make amends after drinking *my* love potion."

Byron frowned.

"Love potion?" he said. Understanding flickered in his eyes. There wasn't a ton of room in the laundry nook, but Byron managed to give off the sense that he'd shoved an entire country's distance between them. "You made a *love potion* for Alexander?"

Why did he sound mad?

"Yes," she said, crossing her arms. "*Some* of us are willing to open our hearts to the universe, but that's not the point. The point is that you drank it and it was for him. Not you."

Byron looked as if he were holding himself very still. "And?"

"And?" repeated Onny, shocked. "And now I've only got until midnight to make a new batch and give it to him, *and* I don't know where my best friends are, *and* since you're the one who took my potion, it's only cosmically right that *you're* the one who will help me remake it."

Onny watched the minute changes taking place on Byron's face. Expressions she couldn't read flickered across his features. His jaw clenched, eyes narrowed. She could almost hear the mockery seething through him, and an answering panic rose inside her.

She'd been working toward this moment for *weeks*.

It was her grandmother's last gift to her.

She wasn't going to let some pessimist with a mechanical-pencil soul steal this from her.

"What will it take to make you help me?" she asked, grabbing the front of his apron. "Seriously, Byron, I'll do anything. Well, almost anything. I draw the line at wearing a T-shirt with your name on it, but I'll agree with your annoying points in class for a full week. Or, I could refuse extra-credit assignments because, let's face it, I don't *need* the extra points on my GPA."

"I'll help you," said Byron.

The words came out so easily, Onny nearly lost her balance.

"I do want something, though," he said.

Onny paused at the way he said it. Soft and thoughtful, not at all like how they normally spoke to each other.

"What?"

Byron watched her. Something else crept into his gaze. Wariness? Amusement? She couldn't tell.

"I'll tell you at the end," he said simply.

"Fine," said Onny. She stuck out her hand. "You're going to help me remake this potion, and I will not be taking questions about the scientific method of how it all works at this time. Deal?"

Byron's mouth twitched. Was that another attempt at a smile?

"Deal."

They shook hands.

Above her head, the dimness of the light bulb flickered brilliantly to life, suffusing the nook in a warm, golden glow. Something deep inside Onny's chest stirred and lifted.

It felt like an omen.

🍂 🍂 🍂

The moment Byron had agreed to help, the plan was simple. All they had to do was gather the three ingredients, put them together, and voilà. Day saved, faith restored, and true love initiated. For some deeply suspicious reason, Byron actually seemed upbeat for once. He didn't bat an eye when Onny met him downstairs with a picture of her *lola*'s love potion on her phone. In fact, he seemed to be taking all of it remarkably in stride, which only made whatever he wanted at the end of this all the more suspect.

Onny stole a glance at him as he followed her through the garden. He hadn't questioned where she was taking him as she led him through the back of the house, past the partygoers, and into the backyard paths that led to the family greenhouse. Torches blazed brightly, and even though there was no one here, Corazon had left out a small banquet table where miniature desserts and quiches and bottles of sparkling water lay beneath lit-up glass terrariums. Byron looked around, a touch of awe on his face. It made him look younger . . . a little more innocent somehow, and Onny turned sharply, feeling as though she'd intruded on something private.

She knew that Byron and his mom didn't come from the same background as she did, and sometimes she felt awkward about how wealthy her parents were . . . like she had to explain that she could take zero credit for it or prove that she'd tried her best to be deserving of the things she'd been given in life. But there was no judgment on Byron's face, and it calmed her. He might think she was utterly ridiculous, but he wasn't going to hold everything against her. It was almost . . . nice?

"I know I agreed not to comment on the scientific method of this, considering that there *is* no science, and I know better than to assume you know what logical rationale is," said Byron.

Welp. Never mind, thought Onny.

"Thanks," she said.

"But how exactly are we supposed to get these ingredients?" asked Byron. He tapped his phone, pulling up the photo Onny had taken of her *lola*'s love potion. "Where are we going to find . . . 'a handful of earth that has been joyously and spontaneously danced upon'? How did you even come up with this?"

"Basement," said Onny, ignoring his other question. "But no one's dancing yet—way too early."

"Don't you think people will notice if we fling dirt at them?"

"I'll mix it with glitter."

Byron was quiet for a moment. "I hate that I believe that will work."

"And then play 'Let's Groove' by Earth, Wind & Fire because you cannot *not* move to that song," added Onny with a grin.

"Earth, Wind & Fire?" Byron sighed and pinched his nose. "Excusing the fact that no one will dance to that unless they're also gearing up for a knee replacement, what about the other . . . ingredients? 'Thorny leaves left to soften in the moonlight'?"

Onny pointed down the lit garden path. "That's why we're on our way to the greenhouse! We can pluck the thorny leaves, put them in a patch of moonlight, and come back to get them at the end."

"And what about our kiss?" he asked.

Onny stopped. Her face burned.

"What do you mean *our* kiss?" she asked, looking up at him.

Byron held up her phone. "We need 'a beautiful flower that has witnessed a kiss freely given and joyously received.'" He looked up at her, the glow of his phone silvering his eyes. His smile turned sly. "What'd you think I meant?"

Onny didn't deign to answer him. "C'mon. We're almost there."

🍂 🍂 🍁

The greenhouse was one of Onny's favorite places on her parents' property. Designed like something out of a haunted Victorian novel, the glass eaves were lined with night-blooming cerus flowers and vines of jasmine, and the end of the greenhouse transformed into a deck, outdoor firepit, and cushy reading chairs that looked out over the creek that ran through the property. Here, the music of the party was faint and fairylike, melting into the October night like woodsmoke.

Recently, Corazon had gone on a full-on floral binge, and the greenhouse was warm and a little humid, exploding with geraniums and petunias, chrysanthemums and orchids, and even a patch of little carnivorous plants. Propped up against one of the windowpanes stood Antonio's telescope. In the night, it looked like a lost, spindly creature from some other world.

Two slender metal tables ran the length of the greenhouse inside, littered with empty pots, packets of seeds, and rusting tools. There was a small trellis for the sarsaparilla vines, its maroon berries and, most importantly, thorny leaves. Now all she needed to find were a pair of shears. . . .

"Can you turn your phone light on? Mom didn't want any electricity in this room."

Byron obliged, and the light of his phone fell on a patch of recently cut flowers that were quickly becoming Onny's favorite. They had globelike heads the color of melted sherbet, and tightly furled petals spiraled like a sea creature's shell.

"I love those flowers," said Onny. "But I can never remember the name. Something complicated. Ronkybonk or something."

"*Ronkybonk?*" repeated Byron. "They're ranunculus."

Onny stared at him. "How do *you* know that?"

"They're my mother's favorite flower," said Byron. "The name means 'little frog' in Latin because it grows near streams. Supposedly, they signify charm . . . and carelessness."

His mouth twisted on the last word like he'd bit into something sour. When he looked up at Onny, his expression turned arch. "What is it now, Diamante?"

"I can't believe you actually *know* the name of a flower," said Onny. "I figured they'd just wither in your presence."

Byron laughed, and once more, Onny was taken by surprise. She wasn't sure she'd ever heard him laugh. Not *really* at least. He could do a great condescending chuckle, but genuine amusement? Never. The sound was disarmingly pleasant.

"You're wrong," he said. "I actually like gardening. In seventh grade, I did master gardening classes with my mom. I even won a prize for my orchid. It was named 'I Want a Dog' because I figured that was the only way to get my parents' attention."

Onny burst out laughing. "That's kinda brilliant."

Byron looked pleased. "Is that an on-the-record compliment?"

"Off," said Onny. "Definitely off-the-record."

A happy silence washed over them for a moment.

"Do you still garden?" asked Onny.

For some reason, the question broke whatever spell was momentarily between them.

"No," said Byron roughly. "No space in the apartment for stuff like that. Plus, mom and I are far too busy these days."

Onny noticed he never mentioned his dad. If his parents were divorced, Byron never seemed to visit him. She'd seen Byron in Moon Ridge for every holiday, either by himself or helping his mother.

"So . . . which of these leaves are thorny?"

"Um, those," said Onny, pointing at the trellis of sarsaparilla. "And then I need to get the rare flower for the, um, kissing part. . . ."

Onny trailed off. For some reason, her brain wandered back to the sound of Byron's voice in the dark. *What about our kiss?* A slight shiver ran up her spine. Why was it so dark in the greenhouse? It felt too private . . . too quiet . . . and it made her all too aware of Byron walking a couple feet behind her.

"What kind of flower do we need?" he asked.

Onny didn't turn, but she could hear the rustling of plants behind her, as if he were trailing his hand down their stems. Onny stopped short before the flower in question. Even in the dimness of the greenhouse, its rich crimson hue demanded notice. It looked like it had once belonged to the ruffled crinoline skirt of an Italian countess, and the red hue was nothing short of sinfully luxuriant. Onny breathed in its heady scent, like cloves rolled in sugar.

"It's called *Matthiola incana*," said Onny.

She heard Byron's tread as he stepped behind her. "You were wearing this in your hair the other day."

Onny startled, before remembering that afternoon when he'd caught her spying on a couple in the band room.

You don't normally wear flowers in your hair.

Since when had he noticed?

Onny heard Byron tapping away at his phone. "Never took you for a fan of hoary stock."

"*Excuse me?*" She whirled around to find him less than a foot away from her.

Byron held up his phone, and Onny squinted against its fluorescent glare. "I thought it was kinda pretentious to call the flower by its Latin name, but now I see that it's a far better alternative than what it's usually called. 'Hoary stock' is possibly the worst name for a flower."

"Trust me, there's worse," said Onny. She turned around,

putting some distance between them before she started poking around through the potted plants looking for the pair of shears.

"Such as?"

"Vegetable sheep? Bastard cobas?"

"You're making that up."

"I'm not!" said Onny, laughing. "My mom has ordered all of it. I made her order two seed packets for 'monkey cups' just for the name, but they haven't gotten here yet."

Byron turned on his phone flashlight, shining it along the tables.

"I still don't quite understand the mechanics of this potion," said Byron. "I drank it, so does this mean that after Alexander drinks it, he's going to start pledging his undying affection for me?"

Onny scowled. Just when she thought they could have a normal conversation without him mocking her, she was proven instantly wrong. "You said you weren't going to question the scientific method. That was our deal, remember? I don't owe you any rationale."

"Oh, I've given up hope of you spouting anything logical," said Byron pleasantly. "I just think I'd be a much more useful assistant in your nefarious spellwork if I actually knew what it's supposed to do."

"One, it's not nefarious," said Onny. "And two, the love potion doesn't work that way. All it does is awaken the potential of love. I'm an Aquarius and Alexander is a Sagittarius, so there's all kinds of cosmic seedlings at work here, okay?"

That seemed to make Byron shut up for a moment. Onny

almost breathed a sigh of relief when he cleared his throat once more.

"And you think those 'seedlings' of love exist only between you and Alexander?" he asked.

"Star charts don't lie," said Onny, turning over a glove.

Darn. Still no shears. She'd used them just last week, so where had they gone?

"And you believe that?" asked Byron.

Here we go again, thought Onny. Here was the part where she told him—for the billionth time—that he couldn't shake the dreamer out of her, and where he told her—for the billionth time—that all the things she believed in were the "worst kind of pretension."

"Haven't we been through this?" asked Onny. "Can't we just skip to the part where you're all 'sneer, you're dumb—'"

"I've never thought you were dumb," said Byron. "Ever."

Onny raised an eyebrow. "Right, well, I'm a dreamer, and yes, I do believe that maybe the world is a little bigger than you might imagine, and maybe you think that's ridiculous, but I believe that a dreamer can only find their way by moonlight—"

"And your punishment is that you see the dawn before the rest of the world," said Byron, finishing Onny's favorite quote by Oscar Wilde.

She stared at him, utterly stunned.

"I like that quote, too," he said.

"Okay, now I know you're lying," said Onny. "Did you eat one of the poisonous plants when I wasn't looking? The Byron I know hates everything to do with the stars."

"Not entirely true," said Byron, taking a step toward her.

He lowered his hand, and the room turned dimmer. Onny held still, her back against a shelf of empty pots. Byron took another step, slowly closing the space between them.

"It's just that I believe there's some danger to spending all your time looking up at the stars."

Now he was standing right in front of her. The glow of his phone picked out the shadows under his cheekbones. Onny fought to find her voice. Her mouth felt dry. She licked her lips. "And that is?"

"I think you forget to see . . ."

He reached out, his hand brushing against her hip. Onny stopped breathing. He leaned forward, his voice low and dark, ". . . what's right in front of you."

When he drew back, a pair of shears dangled from his fingertips.

"Was this what you wanted?" he asked.

Onny snatched the shears out of his hands. Her face felt hot, and she inwardly cursed. What had just happened? It was almost as if she'd *wanted* . . .

Nope.

Nope.

Nope.

The greenhouse was too hot. It was too dark. Her adrenaline was jumbled up from earlier.

"Thanks," she said, before quickly snipping off some of the thorny sarsaparilla leaves and then a sprig of the *Matthiola incana* flower.

Byron lifted his phone light to help her. He didn't move. And he didn't say anything, either, which Onny was more than a little grateful for.

"Now what?" he asked.

"Now," said Onny, handing him the flower, "we leave the leaves in a patch of moonlight."

Onny cast around the room before finding the perfect place. It was right next to her dad's telescope, on a little metal stool perfectly positioned in a slender beam of moonlight. They walked over, and Onny gently placed the leaves in that puddle.

"Now we just need to find someone who's kissing, hit up the dance floor, and we're pretty much done," said Onny.

Byron made a noncommittal *m-hm* sound.

"Do you mind if I look through it?" asked Byron, pointing to the telescope.

"Go for it," said Onny. "Dad positioned it so that people could see the Lovers of Moon Ridge stars, but then Mom didn't want anyone coming into the greenhouse, so . . . waste of time."

Byron peered through the telescope. Onny snuck another glance at him.

"That's weird," he said.

"What is?"

"It's . . . gone," said Byron, stepping away from the telescope. He turned to her. "I thought there were supposed to be two stars for the Lovers of Moon Ridge, but one of the stars is missing. Maybe your dad positioned it in the wrong place or—"

"Doubt it," said Onny. "Dad even had the astronomy professor come and check and adjust everything."

"But the Lady of Moon Ridge's star is gone," repeated Byron, confused.

Truthfully, Onny wondered if maybe Professor Stern *had* gotten it wrong, but a bigger wonder took root in her thoughts. When Byron saw her wide grin, he scowled.

"Oh, you can't be serious, Diamante."

"It's exactly as the legends say!" said Onny, putting down the flower sprig on the nearest table to wiggle her fingers. Finger wiggling when mentioning anything magical was, as she had told True multiple times, *vital*. "Every hundred years, the Lady of Moon Ridge walks among us mere mortals—"

"Why are you wiggling your fingers?"

"—stirring magic into the air and guiding us in love!" continued Onny.

"Stop . . . wiggling. . . ."

"I can't," said Onny, making jazz hands. "It's like a magnet of good vibes."

"She's a ghost."

"A good ghost, too," said Onny.

Byron fell quiet for a moment. "Do you really believe that? In magic . . . not finger wiggling for good-ghost vibes."

As always, there was a faint smirk on his face, but Onny noticed an emotion she hadn't expected in his gaze. *Hope.* Onny bit back her sarcastic response, her hands falling to her side. Yes, she really believed in magic. Not necessarily unicorns and flying broomsticks, but she believed in the alchemy of wonder and hope to create something greater than herself. That was the gift her *lola* had given her. It was that same wonder that gave color richer hues, glittered the rain, limned her whole life in starlight. It made her think of her grandmother's hand in hers, the sometimes-spells-and-sometimes-recipes book splayed across her lap. It was the same wonder that made her believe in horoscopes and love potions, a kind of wonder that made her feel far less lonely and far less scared.

"I do," said Onny quietly. "Or I guess . . . I choose to. I'd much rather prefer a world that was magical."

Onny braced herself for Byron to laugh or smirk, but he didn't do either of those things. Instead, he looked at her, those silver eyes almost glowing in the dark.

"Me, too," he said quietly.

Something changed in that moment. A moment of understanding bloomed between them. It made Onny feel unsettled . . . itchy, even. She found herself speaking just to be rid of the silence.

"I mean, *obviously* I believe in magic if I'm running all over the place for a love potion with the likes of you," she said with an awkward laugh.

The moment she said it, she realized it was the exact *wrong* thing to say.

"Byron—" she started to say, but then he cut her off with an arrogant smile.

He reached past her, plucking the sprig of *Matthiola incana* off the table. "Shall we? Wouldn't want to keep Alexander waiting for his love potion."

The mention of Alexander jolted her. In that second, he

couldn't have been further from her thoughts. And for some reason, *that* annoyed her more than anything.

"No," she snapped. "We wouldn't."

As they left the greenhouse and the thorny leaves to soak in their puddle of moonlight, Onny heard a faint creak behind them. The telescope that was once tilted toward the heavens had swung toward them, moved, perhaps, by the gust of wind when Byron opened the door. Onny told herself it was nothing, but part of her couldn't shake the thought that it was as if they had drawn the attention of something, as if the telescope lens had focused in on them.

As if they might've accidentally caught the gaze of the stars.

🍂 🍁 🍂

And what about our kiss? . . .

For some reason, those words whipped around Onny's head as she and Byron walked in silence up and out of the garden path and back toward the twinkling lights and autumn moon hovering over the Halloween party. If she and Byron walked in together from the grounds, it was going to look . . . odd. What would she say? And then what would they do? They'd have to skulk around the dark corners of her house waiting for people to try to hook up—which, first of all, was gross—all because the flower needed to "witness a kiss"? What if Alexander saw them? What would he think? The thought of Alexander reminded Onny that she had totally left him with the promise of "getting him a drink." How long had it been now? Onny was about to pull out her phone, when Byron held out his hand in warning.

"Do you hear that?" he asked.

Off to the side came the faint sound of giggling and splashing water, which only mean one thing:

"Someone's found the folly house," said Onny.

"What in the world is a *folly house*?"

Onny didn't answer. Instead, she crept down the garden path to the right. The gravel beneath her feet soon transitioned to a slab-stoned walkway that wound past little ornamental pools and toward a tiny ivory pavilion draped in black silk and overlooking the murmuring creek that ran through the property. In the night, the tiny two-person villa looked like a pearl dropped from the slender, careless boughs of the nearby willow trees.

"Wow," said Byron softly.

Wow was right.

The folly house was *utterly* romantic.

And *utterly* isolated.

When they were planning the party, her parents hadn't thought to block off the garden, despite Onny's suggestion.

"That's ridiculous," Antonio had scoffed. "Why would anyone want to be far away from *our* party in some tiny, dark room?"

Yes. What could someone possibly wish to do in a tiny, dark room completely unchaperoned? Onny had thought.

Antonio Diamante was a little innocent about the ways of Onny's classmates.

"Well, let's hope you don't find out," Corazon had said, rolling her eyes.

Now Onny grimaced. She glanced between the flower sprig in Byron's hand and the pathway to the folly house. The last thing she wanted to do was run around her own house looking for people kissing. Which meant there was only one thing to do, and the path to do so was straight ahead. . . .

🍂 🍁 🍂

"Just so I'm understanding this correctly," said Byron in a harsh whisper. "You want us to hide in there to stalk our horny class-mates so that the flower can see a kiss?"

"Yup," said Onny.

"You realize that it is highly unlikely that a *kiss* is what that poor flower will witness."

Onny shushed him.

"Good to see we're really leaning into the 'morally depraved' inspiration behind our costumes," grumbled Byron.

At that second, a couple stumbled out of the dark. Byron and Onny immediately ducked behind a bush.

"There goes our chance," said Byron. "*Now* can we go back to the house?"

"No way," said Onny. "I give it . . . ten minutes, *max*, before some other couple tries to get into the folly house."

And that was how, minutes later, Onny found herself stand-ing inside the silk-draped folly house with Byron. Moonlight sifted through the silk. A faint ring of LED lights around the railings cast the pavilion into a dim glow. A slender knoll of grass surrounded the back entrance of the folly house and was all that stood between them and the stream flowing outside. Onny shuddered from the cold. Last week, the autumn nights had been cool, but not oppressively so. But somehow winter's breath seemed to have snuck in to silver the late-autumn nights.

On the other side of the folly, hardly five feet away, Byron leaned against a pillar with his arms crossed.

"Are you cold?"

"Nope," said Onny. Her teeth chattered. "I'm sweating in this infernal heat; can't you tell?"

Byron sighed and walked to her side. Even this close, he emanated warmth, which was strange, given that up until now, Onny had been sure that his soul was mostly made up of cement. He lifted up his arm in invitation. Onny watched him warily.

"What happened to the whole 'morally depraved' thing?" she asked.

"Who says this isn't part of it?" retorted Byron.

Onny watched him a moment longer. Her ears were beginning to hurt. With a huff, she sidled close against him. Byron carefully placed his arm around her, and warmth flowed into her. Onny shuddered, and Byron tightened his grip. This close, she could smell him, the clean laundry of his clothes, the faint clovelike spice from the flower tucked into his pocket. Beyond the silk screen, the stars looked like crushed diamonds shaken out onto the thick rug of night.

"It's . . . beautiful," said Byron.

His mouth twisted on the last word, like it was reluctantly pulled from him.

"I know," said Onny. "My dad and I had it built for my mom

for their last wedding anniversary." She smiled at the memory. "He loves surprising her with stuff. She acts like she doesn't like it, but she totally does."

"It sounds like you guys are close," said Byron after a moment.

"We are," said Onny. "Are you close to your parents?"

Onny could feel him stiffen under the question.

"My mom, yes," he said. "My dad? Not so much. We essentially stopped speaking once he gambled away all our savings."

"Oh," said Onny, a pit of sorrow opening up in her gut. "I'm so sorry. . . ."

"Don't be," said Byron flatly. "It's for the best. My dad used to have this way of always pulling you in with a story." He didn't look at her, but she could see his profile facing the sky, a new looseness to him, like the dark of the folly room had freed a part of him. "Dad would tell us our lives were going to change because he'd seen something like an omen of a dove on a telephone pole. Or he'd talk about how he finally found the right astrologer to read his horoscope and today was going to be the big day. The day everything became *good*." Byron laughed a little, but it was a hollow sound. "We probably would've believed him forever if we didn't run out of food."

Onny thought back to the first time she'd met Byron . . . the scowl on his face when she'd offered to read his tarot cards. The way his lip curled when he uttered the line that would make him her mortal enemy forever:

I find cosmic bullshit the worst kind of pretension.

At the time, she'd thought it was coldhearted arrogance. Looking at Byron now, Onny felt a strange lump in her throat.

After that first interaction, everything else about him became tainted with condescension. The careful way he dressed, that aura of solemn maturity, even the relentless way he'd brought himself to the near top of their class. *Oh*, thought Onny. She thought she'd understood who Byron Frost was. . . . Now she felt like she'd never really seen him in the first place.

Outside the folly, Onny heard a shushed hissing sound. "I hear something!"

Byron's arm fell from her shoulder, and the two of them dropped to the ground. Onny's heart began to thump wildly. Byron held out the flower sprig to her, and Onny raised it up in the air, getting it ready to witness a kiss between two classmates. She hadn't given much thought to what she would do *after* the flower saw the kiss, though.

1. At best they would be shocked to see Onny and Byron waving up at them from the floor. At worst they would expire on the spot from pure shock.
2. What if they, uh, *didn't* notice Onny and Byron? Would she have to do something like yell: "MAKE ROOM FOR THE HOLY SPIRIT," and split?

But as it would turn out, there was no reason for her to worry about that at all. Because on the other side of the folly curtains weren't her classmates . . . but two adults. Adults that she instantly recognized the moment they started speaking.

"Hello?" said Mayor Grimjoy awkwardly. "Now . . . I . . .

uh . . . I realize the reason for you kids coming all the way out here is *not* to get caught, but um . . ."

"We are screwed," whispered Byron.

"I *know* carnal knowledge is a thing of wonder, but this is very inappropriate," continued Mayor Grimjoy.

Onny cast around in the dark, her heart racing. She would rather set herself on fire than get caught by the town *mayor.*

"*Carnal knowledge?*" scoffed his husband, Mr. Brightside. "Listen to me: whatever you're doing in there, *don't.*"

"I, um, I regret to let you know that you will have to sit down with the principal for a meeting, since this event is technically cosponsored by the town and the school . . ." said Mayor Grimjoy sheepishly. "*And* you'll have to make a formal apology to the Diamante family for trespassing on their grounds in the act of, um—"

"Attaining carnal knowledge?" suggested Mr. Brightside.

"I didn't know what else to call it!"

"Sex?"

"*They're children,*" whispered Mayor Grimjoy in a too-loud voice.

"If they're in there, I'm sure that won't be a shock to them—" said Mr. Brightside.

This could not *be happening,* thought Onny.

Byron elbowed her. She turned around to see him pointing out the back entrance of the folly. Onny shook her head. If they went that way, they'd get cornered on the other side. Byron held a finger to his mouth, then raised his palm, which held a handful of small rocks that must have gotten trapped on the folly floor.

On the count of three, he mouthed. *One . . . two . . .*

Onny gathered the rustling silk of her gown, slowly moving back.

"We can *hear* you in there," said Mr. Brightside darkly.

"They're probably trying to make themselves decent!" hissed Mayor Grimjoy.

Byron lifted the edge of the curtain, flinging out the rocks. They thudded noisily beside the streambed.

"They're trying to escape!" shouted Mayor Grimjoy.

"Oh, just let them—" started Mr. Brightside.

Through the screen Onny saw Mayor Grimjoy tear off in the direction of the rocks. Byron tugged on her arm, and they crept out through the back before sprinting up the path toward the trees. Laughter bubbled up in her throat, and they were halfway up the path when Byron touched her arm.

"Wait," said Byron, his voice low in her ear.

Swiftly, he drew her back against his chest, turning them both so that they were barely concealed behind the thick trunk of an oak tree. Some fifty feet away, Mayor Grimjoy looked distraught, and Mr. Brightside laughed and hugged his husband tightly.

"Can we go back now?" asked Mr. Brightside. "I hate to admit it, but I much preferred haunting the punch bowl to make sure no one spiked it."

"Oh no," groaned Mayor Grimjoy. "We left Wicked Wynona unattended! What if someone steals her?"

"There, there," said Mr. Brightside, patting his back. "We can't be everywhere at once. And I'm sure that, er, frightening doll will be okay. . . ."

Mayor Grimjoy sniffed loudly. "I just want the children to make good choices. And they're not. And I wanted you to have a wonderful time. And you're not."

"Oh, stop that," said Mr. Brightside. "I'm with you, aren't I?"

"And?"

"I'm not saying it."

"Please?"

"No."

Silence. Mr. Brightside sighed loudly.

"And therefore . . . every time is wonderful."

Onny was only somewhat aware of the conversation happening in front of her. The other part was focused on the warm solidness of Byron's chest, the smell of late October curling around them, his voice in her ear, and the way she'd felt it like a finger trailed down her spine.

"Do I have to do everything, Diamante?" asked Byron, leaning forward and curving around her.

His hand reached for her wrist, and he raised it. Belatedly, Onny saw the *Matthiola incana* sprig in her fist. And then, beyond the flower bloom, the silhouette of two figures meeting in the moonlight as Mayor Grimjoy and Mr. Brightside kissed.

On the one hand, Onny thought this was adorable.

On the other hand:

She was watching her *science teacher* kiss someone.

She turned around to tell Byron that they should go, only to realize just how close his face was to hers. And not merely close . . . but startling in its nearness. In the night, his eyes burned. His long lashes cast shadows onto his cheekbones. Byron's hair was so dark that it looked like a rare ink coveted by the same poet who'd given him his name. And then there were his lips. Onny was so used to his mouth positioned in an austere slant or sneer that she was taken aback by how soft they appeared in that moment. It was the kind of terrible, tempting softness that made her want to know if Byron's mouth felt like how it looked.

In the dark, she watched his throat move. Her eyes flew to his. The way he looked at her . . . No one had ever looked at her like that. Like she was something hypnotic, the magical made real.

And then, from behind them, she heard a loud crunching sound.

"Is someone there?" called out Mr. Brightside.

Onny glanced behind Byron, where the pathway wound back up the hill and directly to the lawns outside the basement and dance floor. She grabbed his hand: "RUN!"

Together, they fled up the path.

Behind them, Mayor Grimjoy hollered: "You won't get away with this!"

Beside him, his husband yawned and said, "They already did."

※ ※ ※

By the time they got up the hill and disappeared into the mingling crowd on the lawn, Onny's heart was positively racing.

And she knew it wasn't because of the run.

"Now what?" asked Byron, his voice low.

The partygoers milled around them underneath the

strung-up lights. Santa Claus and Wolverine were locked in an arm wrestle. Jessica Rabbit was glaring at the Joker, and a trio of girls dressed up as the Three Little Pigs were posing for pictures near the ice sculpture of a bear. Some fifty feet away, someone had left the basement doors open. Colorful smoke poured out from the doors, and the DJ was on his third replay of a "Monster Mash" remix. There was so much happening that Onny found it hard to focus. Part of her blamed the moon. Moonlight had a way of turning the world unfamiliar, and right now that's exactly how Byron Frost looked, a completely alien version of the person she thought she'd known.

"Diamante?" asked Byron, waving a hand in front of her face. "Has my beauty stunned you into silence, or are you officially giving up on the ridiculousness of your love potion?"

That snapped Onny back to herself. What time was it? She glanced at her phone:

10:03 P.M.

Shoot. That only gave her two hours to complete the potion by midnight.

"We still have one more ingredient left," said Onny, glancing at the basement dance floor.

Onny reached down, pulling up some of the grass and holding it triumphantly. She reached into the little purse at her side and carefully packed it in. "Voilà! Now we just need people to dance on this and we're done!"

"Done," echoed Byron. "So, what, that would be the end of it?"

His voice sounded flat. He'd turned his head toward the dance floor, and the shadows blocked his expression. Onny felt off. She was this much closer to finishing the love potion and claiming cosmic joy, but somehow it didn't feel like the completion of a grand quest.

"Yup," said Onny in a too-bright voice as she dusted her hands. "You'll have to suffer through *at least* another thirty minutes with me. But then you can exact your diabolical cost, so . . . yay? C'mon! To the basement we go!"

Without another glance at him, Onny marched off to the basement-turned-ballroom. The moment they got inside, Byron's eyebrows skyrocketed up his forehead.

"Diamante, this is *not* a basement."

"It's at the base of the house, ergo, basement," said Onny.

"A good basement has one slightly shitty couch and maybe a Ping-Pong table. Not . . . an ancient crypt . . . and holy crap, does that dance floor have lights in it?"

As Onny had fully expected, Corazon Diamante's Halloween decorations were gloriously over the top. In the swiveling lights, it really did look like a haunted crypt. The wall of windows that would normally look out over the infinity pool and the rest of the property had been curtained off with drapes designed to look like cave walls, and the vaulted ceilings were strung with glowing ivy. The open floor plan had lent itself to a scene that would make Indiana Jones giddy with joy. A huge, toppled skull with its jaws cracked wide held a bar tended to by a werewolf. Statues of Aztec gods peered down from a row of pillars and looked out over a gleaming, golden dance floor that was subtly luminous with tiny LED lights. It was also completely . . . totally . . . empty.

At least a hundred people were milling about the edges, but

no one was moving. Onny glared at the DJ booth directly behind them, which was currently blasting Miley Cyrus's "Party in the U.S.A."

Byron grinned and looked at her. "Fun fact! I'd rather braid my veins than listen to this song."

Onny's shoulders fell. "What am I going to do with my dirt?"

Byron shrugged, hands in his pockets. "You've got two out of the three ingredients. That should be, what, half a love spell? Probably enough to work on what few brain cells Alexander possesses."

Onny glared at him. "What's wrong with you?"

"What's wrong with *you*?" shot back Byron. "You're the one who actually thinks a love potion is somehow going to work, and I'm the idiot indulging this whole mess."

The music blared a little louder, and Onny felt her face warming. She wished she could hold the recipe for the love potion against her heart. She wished, more than anything, that she could pick up the phone and ask her *lola* if she was doing this right, if she was wasting the gift she'd been given or if she really was a colossal cosmic joke. Anything would be better than having to stand here, getting mocked by—

"Whoa, where'd you disappear to, Diamante," said Byron, tapping her shoulder.

Onny looked up. His wide, gray eyes bored down on her and he looked startled for a moment.

"I'm sorry," he said, looking away. "I said I'd help with your love potion—"

"It's not mine," said Onny. "My grandmother wrote it. For me. Right before she died."

Guilt crept into his gaze. He gently touched her shoulder, his hand warm on her skin.

"I know how you two were close," said Byron softly.

Onny looked up at him, confused. "How do you know that?"

"You've mentioned it before, in class," he said. "You used to bring out and show people the amulet she gave you. I forget what you called it."

"An *agimat*," said Onny, shocked that he'd remembered it.

She constantly wore the bright blue *agimat* necklace up until the moment she lost it exactly one day before her grandmother died. She'd been heartbroken, until her mom had comforted her: *You know how your* lola *is about her jewelry. She probably wanted to wear it in heaven.*

"She was the one who got me into all this stuff," said Onny, smiling at the memories. "She used to say my *lolo*'s love for her was something written in the stars and how it all came together with a little luck from a love potion. I mean, they were *totally* made for each other. I guess I wanted something like they had."

When Onny looked up at Byron, an unfamiliar expression flitted across his face. It was there and gone so fast that Onny couldn't quite be sure what she saw, and yet she suddenly felt exposed.

"Um, anyway, there's not much we can do about the last ingredient," she said, looking away from him and gesturing at the golden floor. She studied it for a minute or so. "No one is dancing to this. And no one wants to be the person that's dancing first, soooo . . . what are we going to do?"

Onny turned back to face Byron, but he was gone. She looked

to her right and left, but it was like he'd vanished on the spot. Her face went hot. Was what she said that ridiculous that he'd walked off? What an absolute jerk.

SERIOUSLY? she wanted to yell into the void.

All of a sudden, the music cut off. Onny paused. Slowly, the familiar bass notes of "Let's Groove" by Earth, Wind & Fire spread across the dance floor. All around it, people paused and stared, flat-out bewildered. Behind her, she heard loud footsteps and turned to see Byron walking back from the DJ booth. The light haloed his tall frame, and the moment he was at her side, he flashed that slanting smile at her.

A huge grin stretched across Onny's face. "I thought you said no one was going to dance to this," she said.

"People generally don't like to engage in humiliating acts unless they know they're not alone," said Byron, holding out his hand. "And I did agree to be your willing sacrifice."

Onny stared at him. "*Can* you dance?"

"God no," said Byron, taking her hand and pulling her onto the dance floor. "Which hopefully will only encourage people more."

Onny laughed as he led her to the dance floor and spun her in a circle. She spun against him, her back colliding against his chest. When she turned around, he looked a little dazed. The beat picked up, and Onny grinned as she danced. Byron, on the other hand, was keeping it very safe with a mild side step to the right and left. There was barely a head bob to his movements, but he was there, and he seemed completely unbothered with the fact that half the school was watching them. Somehow, Byron

Frost had a way of making something even extremely awkward look like an intentional power move.

The familiar lyrics washed over her, and Onny threw up her hands. Byron abruptly stopped dancing.

"What in the world are you doing, Diamante?" asked Byron, horrified.

"I'm surrendering my body to the rhythm," said Onny, closing her eyes.

"I hate that sentence," said Byron loudly over the music.

Onny grinned and started shouting the lyrics.

Byron laughed. A true, belly-deep laugh, and when Onny opened her eyes to look at him, it seemed that the party outside them melted away. For a moment, there was only this: the colorful lights like strewn jewels, the eighties bass creeping through the dance floor and into their blood, his hand in hers, and his smile wide and reckless. For the first time, there was a happy looseness to his movements, a rare glimpse of the boy who knew the names of flowers and had remembered what song she'd liked for dancing. Byron moved closer, his silver eyes pinned to hers. A slow flutter swept through her belly.

Right at that moment, Onny heard a loud shriek that could only belong to Corazon Diamante. Corazon appeared at the edge of the dance floor, hopping excitedly and shrieking:

"THAT'S MY SONG!"

Without sparing a glance at her daughter, Corazon pulled a very reluctant Antonio onto the dance floor. In quick succession, the adults pushed through the teenagers awkwardly hovering on the perimeter and flooded the dance floor. Onny reached inside her purse and threw a little bit of the dirt onto the ground. The music changed again, blaring Madonna's "Into the Groove." Onny probably would've kept dancing if Byron hadn't mimed a drink of water. She laughed and nodded, and together they pushed through the dancers and headed toward the bar.

Onny's face felt flushed and warm. She skimmed her hands over the front of her red-and-black gown, aware that Byron's eyes were following her movements. His gaze darkened as he swiped two drinks off a serving platter, not taking his eyes off her the whole time. By now, the music had picked up, jumping from eighties disco songs to upbeat Top 20 hits, which left the darkened skull mouth of the bar almost entirely empty.

Onny knew the music was loud, but it felt quiet here, as if the music couldn't reach them anymore. So quiet that she immediately fumbled for something to say.

"Three ingredients down! Well, sorta. One of us has to go get some of that dirt to finish up the love potion," she said, wrinkling her nose. "But still! Cheers!"

He clinked his glass to hers silently. The whole time, his eyes never left her face. The intensity of his gaze felt like a physical thing.

"Which means I get to ask for my favor in return," he said.

His low voice sent a tickle down her spine.

"Anything," she said lightly. "What do you want?"

"Onny, I—" he started, then shook his head for a moment. He stretched and tightened his free hand, before taking a deep breath and glancing at the dance floor. "You know what? We're actually not done yet. I want you to have all three ingredients before I . . . before I say anything."

He said it more to himself than to her.

"Okay?" she said, fighting back a smile.

He looked at her, something determined flashing in his eyes. "I'll . . . I'll be right back."

Onny raised her glass. "I'll be the one in the blood-spattered gown."

A corner of his mouth lifted in a smile, and then he disappeared onto the dance floor. Onny watched him go, feeling strangely cold in his absence. This whole night was supposed to be about remaking the love potion for her and Alexander the Great-Looking, but now she found herself pausing. When she closed her eyes and imagined the face on the other side of the love potion, it wasn't Alexander's lively green gaze staring back at her, but a pair of smoky, silver eyes. . . .

But that couldn't be right.

This whole day, the stars, the cosmic will of the universe, it was all lining up for Alexander. So why was it that he hadn't crossed her thoughts once? And how come when Byron's face popped up in her thoughts, it wasn't met with revulsion but a sudden softening deep inside her? They couldn't possibly make any sense together . . . could they?

"Onny?"

Her eyes flew open. At that moment, a sinking feeling rooted in her chest. She recognized that voice.

Standing before her and looking more than a little bemused was Alexander the Great-Looking. He held up a glass of punch with a wry smile. Nothing had changed. He was still utterly gorgeous. And yet, Onny didn't feel anything. Not a single flutter in her stomach.

"Apologies, but I got a tad too thirsty and decided to get my own drink," he said.

Oh.

Duh.

Onny wanted to disappear into the ground.

"Listen, about that, I'm so sorry—" she started to say.

"Don't bother," he said, cheerfully. "I found you in the end."

And so he had.

Was this the universe trying to put her strange evening to rights?

"So I've been thinking . . ." said Alexander, moving a little closer. "I think we keep getting the timing screwy, and I'd like to fix that." He took a deep breath. "I'd like to take you out on a proper date."

Onny's eyebrows shot up her forehead. "*What?*"

"A date!" said Alexander. "With food, beverages, conversation. Ideally, some laughter. I know you mentioned astrology stuff, and there's an exhibit at the planetarium."

Onny could only stare at him. Alexander was looking at her, all handsome and hopeful and charming. Maybe a few days ago, she would've leaped at the offer of a date from him. She probably would've said that this was the culmination of all of her astrological hopes and dreams. Instead, she felt the slightest hesitation and, frankly, a great deal of annoyance at the universe. Wasn't it supposed to be on *her* side today?

It was at that exact moment that Onny became fully aware that, *nope*, the universe was definitely not on her side. Because of course—*of course*—at that moment, she noticed someone standing at the entrance of the skull-mouth bar.

Byron.

How long had he been standing there? He was still as a statue. In his left hand he was holding the goggles upright from his Dr. Frankenstein costume. Onny noticed that he'd used them as a kind of container because now they held some of the "danced upon earth." She glanced into his eyes. Moments earlier, she'd imagined they looked like molten silver.

Now they looked like ice.

"So what do you say?" asked Alexander, grinning. "Is it a date?"

Byron's jaw clenched. Without another word, he turned and disappeared in the crowd.

"Onny?" asked Alexander, a frown marring his perfect face.

Onny looked at him and shook her head, her answer leaping from her lips before she could even process them.

"No," she said. "I . . . I'm sorry. You're, like, *perfect*, but I don't think that I—"

Alexander looked a little confused. He opened his mouth, then quickly closed it.

"Right," he said, his voice a little flat. "Well, then."

"I'm so sorry, but I have to go," said Onny, touching his shoulder. "I meant what I said though. . . . I really think you're amazing, and I'm sorry."

Alexander managed a smile, then winked. "Hopefully someone else will think the same."

❧ ❧ ❧

"Hey!" yelled Onny.

The thumping music faded behind her as she raced outside, following after the shape of Byron Frost, who was determinedly walking up the hill and away from the party.

"Where are you going?" called Onny. "What about the ingredients? What about the favor you wanted?"

At this, Byron paused. He turned sharply, not ten feet from her. Her head felt fuzzy. Why had she followed him? Why had she said no to Alexander the Great-Looking and what, *exactly*, did she think Byron was doing?

"I figured you didn't need the ingredients anymore," he said stiffly.

"What do you mean?" asked Onny.

Byron lifted an eyebrow. "You wanted Alexander to ask you out, and so I imagined you didn't need the help of cosmic seedlings of love or whatever this potion does."

"So, what, you just walk away?" demanded Onny. "What about the thing you wanted?"

Byron's expression went carefully blank. "I think it's too late for that."

"Try me," said Onny.

"Isn't it obvious?"

The air between them might've been electric in that moment. They were far away from the other partygoers, and there was nothing around them but the October night and the curl of distant woodsmoke in the air.

Onny's heart raced faster as she shook her head.

Byron's smile slanted again. He exhaled loudly and said, "I want *you*, Onny." In the dimness, his eyes looked molten again, and goose bumps clambered up her spine.

She stared at him, a mixture of heat and confusion prickling through her. "*What?*"

He laughed, but it was without joy.

"Trust me, I didn't want to like you. And I tried not to from the first day we met. Tarot cards, horoscopes—all that stuff," said Byron, shaking his head. "It'd destroyed our lives. And then, just when we're trying to make a new start, *you* show up. And you're . . . beautiful. And funny. And really fucking smart and also kinda weird with your backpack full of crystals and magic stuff, and I just thought that if I let you, you'd ruin my life, too."

Onny felt rooted to the spot even as her thoughts turned back, as if resifting through every time they'd ever interacted. Byron stuck his hands in his pockets, rocking a little on his heels.

"I thought maybe tonight I could convince you to see me differently for a change, but that was ridiculous. I never had a chance if I was competing with the stars." He cast a mocking glance at the night sky before looking back down at her, before his voice dropped to above a whisper: "Did I, Onny? Did I even have a chance?"

Onny tried to open her mouth, tried to *speak*, but she felt caught, trapped between the things that she'd thought she wanted. The things that had felt so safe and all that felt so unknown. For her, walking a path outlined by the stars meant that she was always in the light. That's what pursuing Alexander the Great-Looking felt like: as if she were reaching for some cosmic night-light. And then there was Byron. Infuriating, beautiful, sharp-tongued Byron Frost, who felt less like a starry point and more like the fathomless dark between the stars. Even standing this close to him made her feel like she was peering off the edge of an abyss.

"Thought as much," said Byron softly.

He turned and left her alone in the dark.

🍁 🍁 🍁

So much for the universe being on her side.

It was now half past ten and Apollonia Diamante had no love potion, no cosmically ordained kiss, and no clue what she was doing. She sat on the edge of her bed, her *lola's* love potion recipe clutched tightly to her chest. Tucked away inside her room, it was almost quiet. Here, the sounds of the partygoers and the pulsing music couldn't reach her. Onny checked her phone:

Ash: Where r u guys? Igor got tired of the Mystic Woods. Is there somewhere quiet inside I can bring him? He doesn't like the DJ's music.

Onny almost smiled. Igor was the black cat that lived in the abandoned house behind Ash's. And Ash—being Ash—probably hadn't wanted Igor to feel lonely on Halloween, so he'd brought the ornery cat to the gala.

For a moment, Onny considered going out to the Mystic Woods to find Ash and Igor. But what would she say about everything that had already happened tonight? Once or twice earlier, Onny had almost attempted calling True and Ash, but hadn't for the exact same reason: What would she say? She'd gotten exactly what she wanted, only to find out that . . . maybe . . . it wasn't what she needed? And where was the role of the stars in all this?

Every time she blinked, she couldn't stop thinking about Byron's beautiful face in the half shadows. *I never had a chance if I was competing with the stars.*

All this time, Onny had always thought of horoscopes and magic as a kind of safeguard, a language spoken by the vast universe that promised her a safe place within it. Nothing about Byron Frost felt safe. She didn't even know when his birthday was, which just seemed . . . *wrong.* But then, so did the thought of going on a date with Alexander. She hadn't felt a single spark. With Byron it was something else. When they were arguing, it was like an inferno. And when they weren't? It was like a low, living flame deep in her belly that had always been there whether she liked it or not.

It felt—if Onny was being honest with herself—like magic.

And it scared her.

It scared her because it felt out of control, and she wasn't sure whether it would end up hurting her.

Onny stared at the cardboard square, tracing her fingers over her grandmother's words for the spell:

To summon joy and love in another's soul
For a connection that makes two people whole
For laughter and a smile that one can never miss
Sealed before midnight with a truehearted kiss

"I messed it all up, didn't I?" she said softly. "I wish you were here, Lola. . . . I wish you could tell me what to do."

Onny had only just closed her eyes when she felt a shift in the room. Like a cold, gentle wind curling around her ankles. She jolted upright. Sometimes if she got up too fast, the blood would rush to her head and she'd see spots and lights. But *this* . . . , this was different. At the foot of her bed, there and gone, Onny could've sworn she'd seen the silhouette of a woman in a long white gown. Onny didn't have to see her face to know immediately who she was: the Lady of Moon Ridge.

The only thing Onny could be sure of was that she saw translucent fingers grazing her *lola*'s letter. Time slowed. Onny's thoughts felt like they were racing. Part of her wanted to yell: "SPIRITUAL VISITATION! I AM MAGIC!" And the other part was too stunned, too breathtakingly hopeful about what it might mean. Onny reached for the cardboard square, touching the same spot the ghost had marked.

Onny gently ran her finger along the edge of the cardboard letter, when the pad of her thumb snagged on a corner and slipped into a space she hadn't noticed before. She looked down, shocked when the piece of cardboard cracked down the middle and fell open like the leaflets of a book. How had she missed that there was another part of the letter this whole time? Onny reached out with trembling fingers as she touched her grandmother's fragile handwriting, and the words seemed to dance off the page and spin through her heart:

I know you, anak. *I know you because you're just like me. You'll probably try this immediately, and I hope it works for you as it did for me and your Lolo . . . but here is a secret. Our love didn't come from the stars or a spell, but the choices we made every day. That's where the truest magic comes from. Sometimes I think the bravest thing we can do is to trust in our own magic. I know you will.* Hinihigugma ta ikaw, apo. *I love you.*

When Onny looked up from the letter, she felt something shifting inside her, like a window slowly opening up to let in a light she'd ignored. In the brightness it cast within her, the dark unknown became a little less dark, and Onny saw the choice laid out before her. She still believed in magic. She still believed that the stars illuminated the steps before her . . . but they didn't choose her path. Only she could do that.

Onny glanced at the clock:

10:43 P.M.

There was still time, she thought, shooting to her feet.

There was still time to make her own magic.

Onny found Byron Frost in the half darkness of her mother's greenhouse. Surrounded by the lush, shadowy greenery of Corazon's rare flowers, Byron looked as poetic as his name. He was standing alone, toying with the telescope.

"Boo," she said.

Byron jumped, uttering a curse before he looked up and saw her approaching. "Onny?"

"Nope. Batman," said Onny. "Surprise."

She moved through the aisles in the greenhouse, drawing close enough that she could see the moment when shock melted from his features, replaced with an icy blankness. His jaw clenched, and he raised one cocoa-dark eyebrow imperiously. "What are you doing here?"

"It's *my* house," she said, crossing her arms.

"Fair point. I'll go—" he said, moving past her.

Onny moved without thinking. She placed her hand on his chest, trying to ignore the slow shiver of heat that wound up her arm when she touched him. "Wait."

He stilled. The lights outside the greenhouse had finally turned on, but his back was to it, turning his face almost inscrutable. Even then, Onny could still feel the intensity of those molten silver eyes. And she could feel the rise and fall of his chest, the taut, almost angry stillness that went through him right this second.

"You . . ." started Onny, before faltering. "You still have my love potion ingredients."

Byron made a scoffing sound, then stepped back sharply. "Seriously, Diamante?"

"Those were hard to source!" said Onny. "Obviously I want them back."

"Of course, to seal the cosmic deal with Alexander—"

"It's not for him," said Onny.

Byron stilled. "What?"

Onny took a deep breath before repeating, "It's not for him."

"Strange," said Byron with a faint sneer. "Did the stars change or something? You know they're technically dead, right? One could argue you're being controlled by ghosts."

Honestly, sometimes she really detested Byron Frost. Onny grabbed the front of his Dr. Frankenstein costume.

"Diamante?" he asked, all trace of sarcasm vanishing from his voice as she drew him closer. This close, she could smell the woodsmoke clinging to him. She could see his throat bob uncertainly, his lips parting. "What exactly are you—"

Onny kissed him. At first, it was nothing more than a warm press of her mouth crashing onto his. And then . . . it wasn't. Byron Frost made a sound of impatience. His hands went around her waist, drawing her closer, deepening the kiss. Sensations flitted through her, and it was like the force of Byron's kiss was translating every feeling to a poem. A kiss that tasted like minty Tic Tacs one moment was now a kiss that tasted like silver and snow, and Onny felt lightheaded, breathless with wonder.

Byron drew back, breathing hard.

He clasped her hand to his chest, staring into her eyes. "What was that?"

"Humans call it a kiss," said Onny. "But if you're unpracticed, we can do it again."

"I'm serious, Diamante. I've wanted to do that for so long . . . since, like, the day you glared at me and told me my aura was the color of sad tears," said Byron, laughing a little. "I need to know now if this was a pity kiss or—"

"I meant it," said Onny, leaning against him. "I want to see what happens next . . . with you. And me."

He searched her face, a hesitant smile softening his mouth before he frowned again. "What about the love potion? Or all the magic stuff?"

"Oh, I still totally believe in all of that," said Onny lightly. "It's just that . . . I think I want to make my own magic, too."

"Well, in that case," said Byron, and then he pulled her to him once more.

Out of the corner of her eye, Onny thought she saw something move outside the greenhouse. A whisper of the Lady of Moon Ridge in her long, glowing white dress. Or maybe it was just the bright moonlight blurring across the autumn leaves as Byron kissed her.

KISSES TILL MIDNIGHT

*A*sher Lee was born in the labyrinthine depths of the Louvre in the middle of a thunderstorm, which explained both his love of art and his tendency toward quiet (the security-guard-turned-emergency-midwife had hushed him when he tried to cry his first breath.) His mother—then single and exploring Paris alone—had gasped at the beauty of Leonardo's *The Virgin, the Child Jesus and Saint Anne*, and the shock of the painting had sent her straight into labor. Apparently eager to see the painting himself, baby Ash tumbled out only moments later, with Raphael and Caravaggio as his witnesses.

Eighteen years later, Ash still loved Italian art, although his current infatuation was Venetian mask making. It was a dying art that needed preservation, and its history also fascinated him— masks as disguises had allowed people who normally wouldn't mix to come together. Aristocrats and peasants could eat and drink beside one another, dance under the moon, and even fall in love. All because a mask let them become someone new.

Seven hours before the midnight gala, Ash headed into the backyard toward the garden shed his stepdad had built for him to use as a studio. He had been commissioned by a few people in town to make masks for the party tonight, and he still had finishing touches to put on a couple of them.

As soon as he stepped foot into the yard, though, his neighbors' conversation drifted over the fence.

"Oooh! Look at that smooth move!" Ricky, the thirteen-year-old, said as he tossed a basketball into the hoop with a swish.

"That was traveling, cheater!" Jordan shouted in his squeaky seven-year-old voice.

"Was not," Ricky said.

"Was too."

"Was not."

An older girl's affectionate laugh punctuated their argument. "That was totally traveling, Ricky, and you know it. You ran across the entire court without the ball touching the ground."

The boys devolved into fierce but genial rounds of "I told you so" and "I did not," but all Ash heard was the lingering music of the girl's voice, hanging in the October air like a nightingale's song fading into the sound of falling leaves.

He sighed. Cassidy Rivera. She'd moved in next door during their freshman year and still didn't know he existed. She was a cross-country star—her mom was coach of the high school team—but Cassidy was the athletic type who could play any kind of ball you threw at her. In comparison, Ash had ironically earned the nickname "Yao Ming," like the Houston Rockets player, thanks to being six feet three (and still growing). But Ash knew only as much about basketball as what he'd gleaned from eavesdropping on Cassidy and her brothers next door.

A few weeks ago, Onny had tried to drag Ash to a Homecoming after-party at Cassidy's house. He'd narrowly escaped only by lying and distracting her with a well-placed "Hey, isn't that Alexander the Great-Looking over there?" before ducking away into his house while Onny's head was turned.

"You know, you *could* just talk to Cassidy," his cousin, True, had told him on more than one occasion. "Pop your tall self over the fence and say hi. It's literally one syllable."

But that wasn't going to happen, either. Something about Cassidy's mere presence took Ash's breath away. That sounded corny, but it was actually true. His voice evaporated like smoke any time she was near. So it was a good thing they had the physical barrier of the fence between their houses. Better to stay invisible than be made into a fool.

The basketball began bouncing again next door, and a moment later, a shot slammed violently off the rim, sending a shudder through the backboard and pole. The ball ricocheted over the fence, landed on the grass, and rolled right in front of Ash's feet.

"Wow, Jordan, you're a beast!" Cassidy said on the other side of the fence.

Jordan giggled.

"Let's go next door to see if the neighbors are home and ask for the ball back, okay?" she said.

Ash froze. Cassidy was coming over? No no no . . .

He hurled the ball over the fence as fast as he could.

"Oh, cool. Thank you!" Cassidy called out.

Ash couldn't even get out a "You're welcome." After all, if he'd been capable of speech around her, there were so many other things he'd want to say. He imagined the conversation in his head.

Hi,

I've been eavesdropping on you for the last three years, and even though you don't know me, I feel like I know you.

You always say "Excuse me" when you sneeze, even when you're alone. Your friends like to gossip, but you never participate; you only listen, and their secrets are safe with you. You don't like mustard on your hotdogs. I know this because I once overheard Ricky tell Jordan that the secret to keeping more hotdogs for themselves was to smear mustard all over your share. But you adore your little brothers no matter what tricks they pull, and you'll dote on them—and they'll probably let you—even when they're too big to be doted on.

On second thought, Ash definitely shouldn't say that. *Any* of that. He'd sound like such a creeper.

It was probably better that he couldn't speak around Cassidy.

He shook the melody of her voice out of his head. If he didn't tear himself away from the fence, he could lose the whole morning just soaking in her closeness.

Ash crossed the strip of grass in his backyard without making a sound. He had a knack for being eerily stealthy despite his size. When he was younger, his mom said it was because his father was a ghost. Ash was almost certain she meant that his father had disappeared without a trace. But Ash was only 90 percent sure, because his mom still never shared anything about him. Onny, in particular, kept Ash's 10 percent of doubt alive; she loved the possibility that he really was part ghost.

Ash slid open the latch on his studio. Sunlight streamed in from the glass-paneled ceiling, illuminating the canvases stacked on the shelves, the dozens of masquerade masks hanging on the walls, and the table covered in plastic tarp and paint. Wrapped hunks of pale-gray clay cluttered one corner, and a garment bag hung on a coat hook by the door. This studio may have started out with garden-shed blueprints, but having a carpenter for a stepdad meant Ash got all the natural lighting and work space he needed.

He threw on an apron and sat down to work. These midnight-gala masks had been months in the making. Ash insisted on doing things the authentic Venetian way, which meant first creating clay face models (like mannequin heads), then making plaster molds. He'd ordered *cartalana*, a special wool paper, from a *mascarer* in Venice, and then painstakingly made each mask with layers of the *cartalana* soaked in water and glue. Once heated and dried (which took longer than you'd think, because Ash often messed up and had to start over again), he extracted the mask from its plaster mold, and only then was it ready to be painted.

Ash had already delivered Onny's and True's masks to their houses, and his own was nearly finished and sitting on the windowsill. He spun in his chair to grab his mask and almost knocked over the small vial of love potion Onny had brewed.

Crap! He caught the vial before it toppled over onto a tiny paper crane barely the size of his pinkie.

That would have been bad if the potion had spilled on the

origami bird. Not only because it was the only vial Ash had, but also because he didn't know who had made the crane.

He discovered the miniature origami in random places. The first time—a few years ago, when he still biked to school—Ash had found a thread of them dangling from his bike handle, like a tiny mobile constructed by pixies. Occasionally, one would already be on his lab table when he walked into biology class. Other times, he'd find one in his backpack, unsure when it'd been left. And this past April, after spring break, Ash had opened his locker to be greeted by a flurry of paper cranes, flying out joyfully at his arrival, cascading onto him in a shy but persistent rush of infatuation.

Part of Ash thought it was someone playing a joke on him, toying with his emotions. He wasn't crush-worthy like the athletes or the beautiful, popular crowd. He was just an awkward artist, all long limbs and quiet voice, who didn't fit neatly into high school life, other than in the odd trio of The Coven.

And yet, part of Ash wanted to believe the origami meant that somewhere out there, *someone* liked him, which is why he kept this single paper bird. Maybe that's why he picked up the tiny crane now and put it in his hoodie pocket. It was a soothing reminder that even though Cassidy was mostly unaware of Ash, at least one person (other than Onny or True) might have found him worthy of admiring.

With the crane in his pocket, Ash took a deep breath to refocus himself, then picked up his mask. It was decorated in a patchwork of gold, black, and white rectangles. In keeping with the spirit of the "Founders' Fable," Ash was going to Onny's party tonight as part of Gustav Klimt's painting *The Kiss*. Maybe that was pathetically romantic of him, but he liked the grand gesture of showing up in costume as half of a famous pair of lovers. If magic reawakened in Moon Ridge tonight, maybe his other half would show up, use the love potion with him, and seal their fate before midnight with a kiss.

At that thought, though, Ash laughed softly at himself. He'd be lucky if Cassidy even noticed his existence, let alone requested to be bound to him for eternity.

Shaking off the silly hope, Ash set his mask on the worktable and began to work on reality: affixing spirals of gold filigree to the edges of his mask, the final touches to match Klimt's painting.

Half an hour later, he had just secured the last spiral when a crash echoed through the backyard and shook the glass panes of the studio.

"What the—?" Ash bolted from his chair and ran outside.

The heavy pole holding up the Riveras' basketball hoop had fallen and smashed through part of the fence. Wooden planks and pole and net piled in a heap in Ash's yard. Cassidy lay tangled on top of it all.

And yet, somehow, she looked magical, like a mermaid caught in fishing line. Her hair fanned out all around her in undulating chestnut waves. The morning light glimmered off her sun-kissed skin, and her arms rested in elegant angles, as if she were swimming.

Then she groaned and cradled her elbow.

Ash snapped out of his daydream and opened his mouth to ask if she was okay. But no sound came out.

Right, because his voice disappeared when she was around. Maybe *he* was the little mermaid in this case.

What is wrong with me?

Cassidy opened her eyes and squinted at him. As soon as she realized where she was, her cheeks went bright pink.

Ash still couldn't find his misplaced voice. So he started making panicky mime gestures.

This was why he had no chance with Cassidy Rivera. She was graceful and smart and, by all accounts, a normal human being, whereas Ash was . . .

Well, right now he wished he really was half ghost, because at least then he could vanish into thin air.

But while Ash silently cursed his corporeality, Cassidy had gotten up and was struggling to drag the basketball hoop upright.

He ran over to help.

"I'm so sorry," she said. "I can't believe that happened. Ricky's been bugging me to take him to the midnight gala for weeks, even though he knows it starts way past his bedtime. So I bet him that if I could dunk, he'd have to stop pestering me about the party, and—"

Cassidy suddenly stopped talking and dropped the basketball hoop back on the grass. Her mom had emerged from the house and made her way to the broken fence.

"And you decided to destroy our neighbor's property?" Mrs. Rivera finished for her, arms crossed.

"Coach! I mean, Mom. I can explain. . . ."

"I think this shattered fence and our basketball hoop—which, last I checked, was in *our* backyard—gives me all the explanation I need."

"No, Mom, it was awesome," little Jordan said as he ran over, too pumped up to catch on to the fact that he should not, in fact, be elaborating. "We turned the backboard sideways so Cassidy could get a better angle, and then she took a running jump off the trampoline and hooked onto the hoop, and then—"

Mrs. Rivera arched a brow at him, which was evidently a scary enough hint for Jordan to shut up.

Ricky came over and grabbed his brother's arm. "We should probably go inside for a while."

"I think that's a good idea," Mrs. Rivera said.

The boys were gone in an instant.

She turned to Ash. "I apologize for my children. It's Ash, isn't it?"

"Yes, ma'am," he managed to whisper. "AshLee. I mean, Ash-*space*-Lee. Not Ashley."

Cassidy gave him a funny look.

He felt his skin go pale, and his voice escaped him again. But those were seemingly the only parts of him that were capable of ghostliness.

"Are your parents home, Ash?" Mrs. Rivera asked.

He shook his head. His mom was at work at the library, where they were doing their annual Gentleman and Lady of Moon Ridge history weekend, and Ash's stepdad was at a furniture woodworking class over at Blush Apple Orchards.

"All right, this is what we're going to do," Mrs. Rivera said.

"I'm going to take the boys over to Home Depot to get some replacement boards for the fence, and we'll pick up some nails, too. Cassidy will stay behind and clean up this mess. And then when I get back, she's going to start rebuilding the fence for you."

"I don't know how—" Cassidy began to say.

"You break it, missy, you fix it," Mrs. Rivera said. "It might take you all weekend, but you *will* put the fence back up."

You don't have to do that, Ash wanted to tell her. Honestly, he and his stepdad could easily patch up the fence. But his ghost voice still had a hold on his larynx, so he said nothing.

Mrs. Rivera pulled her car keys out of her pocket. "Ash, sweetheart, I'm sure you're busy"—she looked at his apron (*oh god, he was still wearing his studio apron*)—"so please don't let this interrupt whatever you were doing. Again, I apologize profusely for my kids' recklessness, but don't worry, they will make this right."

Without waiting for Ash's reply—or maybe because she'd figured out he was incapable of intelligent response and she was giving him the gift of a gracious exit from the conversation—Mrs. Rivera turned and shouted for Ricky and Jordan to get in the truck. There wasn't any room in her tone for negotiation.

Suddenly, it was just Ash and Cassidy, alone in his yard.

If only girls were more like paintings, then Ash would stand a chance. He knew how to look at art, how to talk about art, how to melt into art and let it consume you. But Cassidy wasn't a painting; he couldn't just sit at her feet with a sketch pad and stare at her for hours upon hours.

He thought about her for hours every day, though, ever since her family's U-Haul pulled in next door, in the summer before freshman year. Ash had been getting the mail when Cassidy and her brothers clambered out of the truck. His eyes met hers, and his heart palpitated, because Ash was fourteen and terrible with girls, and because she smiled like sunbeams opening up the sky. She waved and said hello, and heat rushed through his cheeks, and he couldn't make a damn noise out of his throat.

So instead of attempting to say hello back, Ash ran into his house, clutching the mail in his hands.

Later that week, his mom came home with a copy of the free local paper. (The *Moon Ridge Gazette* was half news and half gossip, and everyone read it, because what else are you going to do in a small town?) "Looks like we've got a pretty extraordinary new neighbor," she said, setting the newspaper onto the kitchen table in front of Ash. "And she's your age. Maybe you two can be friends."

Ash groaned. Leave it to parents to assume that just because you're in the same grade, you're automatically going to be BFFs.

But Ash still snatched up the *Moon Ridge Gazette* and buried himself upstairs in his bedroom to read it, because he did actually want to know everything about the girl next door.

Cassidy, it turned out, had spent her middle-school years really sick with a degenerative lung condition. Eventually, her lungs failed completely and she had needed a transplant. After the surgery, though, the Riveras decided to move somewhere with fresher air than polluted Boston. Any irritant to Cassidy's fragile new lungs could damage them and turn fatal; even when healthy, she had to take anti-rejection meds for the rest of her life so her body wouldn't attack the foreign organs.

Ash couldn't imagine the courage it took for Cassidy to get through her disease and the transplant. But she apparently never let it get her down. According to the article, Cassidy threw herself back into running as soon as she was done with rehab. Her grandpa had been a member of the Chilean Olympic track team, and her mom was a cross-country coach, so Cassidy had no intention of stopping the family tradition.

It was enough to make fourteen-year-old Ash topple headfirst into a crush on the new girl next door.

And then, as the years passed and Ash learned more about her, he went from superficial infatuation to all-out, lost-beyond-repair, besotted fool.

Cassidy wasn't the fastest, but she was captain of the Moon Ridge High cross-country team because everyone loved her. For every race she ran, she raised money for Donate Life America. And she was funny, often wearing wry tees and sweatshirts about her transplant, like the hoodie with a recycling logo and I'M MADE WITH RECYCLED PARTS on it. Ash's favorite shirt was an outline of lungs, filled in like an iPhone battery indicator at 80 percent power—because Cassidy's lungs functioned at 80 percent of a normal person's (h/t *Moon Ridge Gazette*).

How could anyone *not* fall madly in love with her?

Now, Cassidy began to pull her hair into a ponytail, and Ash found himself doing exactly what he wasn't supposed to—staring. Her every movement was a revelation, from how graceful her arms moved to how deftly her fingers darted in and out of the hair tie. The breeze carried the faint scent of her sunscreen, and the final flick of her ponytail sent a rush of her floral shampoo in Ash's direction. After all these years with a fence between them, this was the nearest he'd ever been to her. He closed his eyes and memorized her scent, imagining what it would look like if he were to render it in oil paints.

When he opened his eyes again, she was watching him, with a lilt of a smile on her face.

"You looked so peaceful," she said. "Like you were meditating. Not like someone whose backyard was just destroyed. Or maybe that's actually *why* you were meditating. I'm really sorry."

Ash shook his head and shrugged, trying to convey without words that it was fine. That it was kind of a dream come true that she was here with him. Even if it was also a nightmare, because he was so completely at a loss as to what to do.

He pointed at the basketball hoop on the ground. "Help?" he managed to force out in a hoarse whisper.

"Oh god, yes, of course I'll help," Cassidy said. "Sorry!"

Ash cursed to himself. He'd meant to offer Cassidy *his* help, not the other way around.

This is why he'd never had a girlfriend.

He scrambled to lift up part of the basketball hoop. It was a miracle Cassidy had managed to knock this thing over. The big plastic base full of sand weighed a ton. Then again, Jordan had said that they'd pivoted the hoop stand, which would explain how it had managed to fall sideways into the fence. The trampoline jump would've provided the momentum, and the pole and stand—well, it was an awful lot of mass.

Together, though, he and Cassidy hoisted it up. Then Ash pushed it back into the Riveras' yard.

Wow. So that's what it was like over here. A "sportopia." Ash stood for a minute and took it all in, because this might be his only opportunity to see—rather than just listen to—how Cassidy lived.

Instead of lawn, the ground was covered in that bouncy sort of bright-blue, space-age tiling. There were white lines painted for a basketball half-court, but there was also a small soccer goal propped up on the other side. A long sand-filled trench took up the length of the opposite fence line—that must be for bocce ball—and then there was the grill where Cassidy and her family barbecued on summer evenings and a wrought-iron patio table with a partially spent citronella candle that kept the mosquitoes away. Ash had smelled the citronella from the other side of his fence, and being able to match the image of Cassidy's candle with the scent gave him a thrill that felt almost illicit.

He flushed and hurried back into his own backyard, just as Cassidy's phone rang.

"Hi, Mom . . . uh-huh . . . okay, I'll go check." She hung up and turned to Ash. "My mom thinks she left the stove on. The cross-country team is coming over for a spaghetti carbo-load later today—you know, to prep for our race tomorrow. I'm just gonna run in to check the stove, but I swear I'll be right back to help you pick up the broken fence boards." She smiled and jogged off.

Ash took advantage of her absence and texted The Coven.

Ash: S-O-S. Cassidy is in my backyard and I lost my voice and I don't know what to do.

Onny: OMG Cassidy as in the girl you've been in love with 4EVA??? (Outkast voice: For-evah! Eva! Eva!)??? SHALL WE CONSULT THE STARS FOR GUIDANCE?!

Ash: No, I need practical advice!

True: Back away from the astrological charts, Onny.

Onny: ~~*~~The stars will never steer you wrong~~*~~

True: Pretty sure the stars cannot do any steering, being as they are inanimate objects.

Onny: I cannot hear this negativity over the sound of the universe and stars aligning. PS, Ash is a Cancer with Pisces moon and Cassidy is a Taurus, so obvz they are PER-FECT!

True: How do you even know her sign?

Onny: Because I KNOW things . . .

Ash: Um hello? If u two are done, still need help over here.

Onny: Talk to her about art.

True: But not too much art.

Ash: I LOST MY VOICE.

True: Right. Prob better that way. You get all insufferable when you're in art professor mode.

Onny: Agreed. Professor Ash is super unattractive.

Ash: I am not insufferable.

True: Professor Ash is insufferable.

Ash: Worst friends ever. You're supposed to be helping me.

Onny: Wanna know what tarot card I flipped for you?

Cassidy reappeared. Ash stuffed his phone back into his pocket and started picking up the broken fence boards.

She joined him but stopped after the second one. "Oh my god!" Cassidy said, holding up a shattered board. "These are all painted different colors." She turned to look at the rest of his backyard. "Your whole fence is a mural, isn't it? And I ruined it."

Her shoulders slouched as she pointed at the entire perimeter of his yard. Each of the three fences was, indeed, painted. Including the one that now had a jagged hole in it.

You couldn't ruin anything, even if you tried, he wanted to say. Cassidy's mere existence negated the broken fence, global warming, the lack of world peace, and anything else wrong in the galaxy.

Aloud, though, he only said—very quietly—"It's fine."

Cassidy crouched on the ground and tried to fit together the broken boards like puzzle pieces, as if she could reconstruct the mural. "Oh wow. These are incredible. It must've taken you ages to paint all this. And each section of the fence is different. Do they mean anything?" She glanced over her shoulder at Ash, and something about how small she looked and the remorse in her frown loosened up his nerves.

Maybe Onny and True were right, that art was a subject he was so comfortable with, he could even talk to Cassidy about it.

"Yeah, each mural represents the neighbor behind it," Ash said. His voice was still scratchy, but it was there.

"What I wouldn't give to be this talented. All I can create are goofy hoodies." She pointed at her I'M MADE WITH RECYCLED PARTS logo.

"You designed that?"

"Pitiful, huh?" The tip of her nose turned pink as she got embarrassed, and it was possibly the cutest thing Ash had ever seen.

"Not pitiful at all," Ash said. He loved the spark in everything Cassidy did, and the fact that she dabbled in art—even though graphic design was different from Ash's painting and mask making—made him tumble even deeper into the rabbit hole of feelings he had for her than before.

Still, she self-consciously crossed her arms over her sweatshirt. "Tell me about the murals?"

"Sure." Ash sat on the ground near Cassidy—but not too close—and pointed at the house on the other side of his. Black-and-white fractals covered that fence, the geometric patterns repeating over and over in tidy and never-ending spirals. "The Johnsons live over there. They're an older couple, and they like things just so."

"What do you mean?" Cassidy settled onto the grass, with the broken boards separating her and Ash.

"Well, for example," Ash said, "the dog is let out every eight hours, at quarter past on the dot, and she gets fifteen minutes, then has to go back inside. Or, like, every spring, Frank starts vegetable seedlings indoors in their sunroom, but the morning after the last frost—usually around the second week of April—he plants them in the raised vegetable beds outside."

"You're really observant," Cassidy said.

Ash shrugged. "I guess?"

"So what does Frank plant? Is that also like clockwork?"

"Yeah." Ash grinned. "It's always kale, cabbage, broccoli, and collard greens, because Maryann loves cruciferous veggies. One year he planted spinach, and he got such an earful, he never did that again."

"How dare he plant something noncarnivorous," Cassidy said.

That made Ash laugh. "Cruciferous! Not carnivorous. They're not meat-eating plants."

"Well, that's not nearly as interesting." Mischief crinkled the corners of her eyes.

Ash memorized the look on Cassidy's face—and the witty conversation (her wit, not his). He might never have a chance like this again.

Oblivious to his pining, though, Cassidy kept talking. "Let me guess: you painted Frank and Maryann's fence with fractals to represent their dedication to order?"

"Yeah. Exactly." Ash smiled. She got it.

Cassidy considered the fractals for a few minutes, and Ash did, too, all the while sneaking glances at her. She was much more mesmerizing than the murals.

After a little while, though, she swiveled to face the back of the yard. "What's in that shed?"

"It's my studio."

"Cool. Can I see?" She rose from the grass.

"No!" Ash lunged and grabbed her wrist.

Cassidy froze and stared wide-eyed where his hand held her arm.

Ash released her as quickly as he'd seized her. He fell backward onto the boards beneath him, holding both arms up in the air in surrender. "Sorry! I'm really sorry. I shouldn't have grabbed you. It's just that my studio . . . it's a super-personal space."

If True were here, she would smack Ash upside the head. She did this often—it was an "affectionate" thing, she said. The first time was when Ash's mom married True's Uncle Neel and afterward, Ash still introduced True to people as his friend. She insisted that she was his cousin, even though they weren't really related by blood, so Ash didn't think it technically counted. But after True smacked him, Ash learned to change his tune, and from there on out, True was his cousin. (She hit hard!)

But True would smack him now, too, for grabbing Cassidy

like that. It had only been a light touch, but still. He was a complete idiot.

Cassidy didn't say anything.

Ash slouched in the grass. "I'm sorry I overreacted. The only way I can explain it is—have you ever had an idea so big that it felt overwhelming, but you plummet ahead anyway and pour your entire heart into it? But then, even though you're pretty sure it's a good idea, you sometimes lose confidence in it along the way, while it's still a work in progress. Like, until you finish making this big *thing*—whatever it is—or before you get to the final goal, you don't want anyone to know yet that you've dared to dream it. Just in case you fail."

Cassidy looked down at him through her lashes. Then she nodded slowly. "Yeah, I get it. I really do."

Ash let out a long exhale, relieved. "That's what my studio is. A home for my ideas, most too fragile yet to share."

She nodded again. But now she wasn't looking at the studio or at Ash. Rather, she gazed off into the sky at nothing in particular. "They'll reveal themselves when they're ready," Cassidy said.

He wondered whether they were talking about the same thing at all.

Cassidy gave him a small smile before sitting back down on the grass.

"Tell me about the fence behind your studio," she said, generously letting him off the hook for the weirdness of the past few minutes.

The mural was of a pastel, Monet-inspired impressionist garden. But behind it, an abandoned shack stood crookedly over-burdened with ivy. A half-dead skeleton of a tree—struck ages ago by lightning—loomed over the roof like a sentient Damocles sword. The back porch sagged, and a rusty metal swing creaked in the wind, even though no one rode it. "That house has always creeped me out," Cassidy said.

"It's harmless," Ash said. "The Coven has gone there since we were little. It was our weird clubhouse, I guess. When we were in elementary school, Onny used to try to conduct séances. She's less into that kind of stuff now, though, and more into astrology and tarot."

"Did you ever . . . contact anyone?"

Ash laughed. "You mean, like, spirits? No. But when Onny gets an idea in her head, there's no stopping her unless you want to get plowed over. I've figured out it's best just to go along."

"You're really close to Onny, huh?" Cassidy asked.

"She's my best friend," Ash answered simply. "And True, too."

"But True's your cousin."

"Yeah."

There was an awkward lull in the conversation. Ash wasn't quite sure why. Had he said something wrong? Everyone knew the three of them were inseparable. Even Cassidy knew that, since she'd brought it up.

But now their conversation had sputtered to a stop. How was he supposed to restart it?

Refocus on art, he told himself. That had been mildly suc-cessful so far.

"So anyway, that fence," he said. "At first I thought it ought to be black, too, like a haunted-house theme. But then two out of three fences would be black, and that's too monochromatic."

"Still doesn't explain the field-of-flowers mural," Cassidy said.

"Not how the house looks right now, in October," Ash said. "But have you seen it in the spring?"

She shook her head. "I try not to look at it at all."

"Next spring, after the rain, check it out. Everything dead and black there gets overrun by green grass and a riot of wildflowers. There are birds and butterflies and, I swear, bunnies frolicking. It's like a grand statement from Mother Nature. No matter how ugly things get, beauty will always find a way to prevail.

"It's also why I chose an impressionist style. It feels spontaneous and unfinished, like nature itself. I mean, I understand that there was no uniform philosophy among the impressionist-era painters, and their beliefs spanned a wide—"

Oh god. He could hear himself. True was right. He *did* sound insufferable.

"Never mind," he said.

"I want to hear what you were going to say."

"No, trust me, you don't," Ash said. "It was boring."

"Nothing you say could be boring."

They both froze as soon as the words were out of Cassidy's mouth.

Did she mean . . . ?

No. Impossible. She was just super-nice to everyone.

But then why did she also seem immobile right now?

Cassidy cleared her throat. "I mean, it's really cool, how

much you know about art history. It's kinda like how I'm a big nerd about cross-country stats."

Oh. Great. So she thought Ash was a nerd.

At least that was more in line with how he understood the world. Ash = blundering geek. Cassidy = sweetest girl on the planet who patiently listens to him blather on and tries to make him feel like he's interesting.

Le sigh.

He could practically hear True advising him: *Back to a safe topic, Ash. Murals. But try not to torture the girl with "fascinating art tidbits." Stick to what's in front of you.*

Right.

"So, uh, about the mural on your fence—"

"Yes!" Cassidy seemed as relieved as he was to change the subject. "I'm dying to know what you think about my family."

Dammit. How had Ash not foreseen how this conversation was going to go? He'd painted—or talked—himself into a corner.

But here's why he couldn't explain the vivid, abstract mural on the fence: it wasn't about the Riveras. It was all about Cassidy.

The bold, luminous colors were the way she tackled life, whether it was the lung transplant or cheering on her teammates or playing with her brothers.

The floating wisps of yellow were how her laughter sounded in the air.

The silver dust was how she made Ash feel whenever she was on the other side of the fence, like every particle within him lit up just because she was near.

"Your family is really . . . lively," was all Ash said aloud.

Cassidy deflated. "Oh. Is that it?"

He realized she wanted more. She *deserved* more. He'd gone on and on about the other houses. But that was talk about art, and this was dangerously walking the line of being about her— and his feelings for her. Ash's voice threatened to flee again.

"Yeah," he croaked. "That's it."

End of subject. One hundred percent awkward. Maybe he should have waited to find out which tarot card Onny had pulled. . . .

It was probably The Three of Swords impaling a heart. Or The Tower, with him falling to his death. Or The Fool. Ash didn't actually know what that card meant, but he did know how stupid felt.

But Cassidy was studying the fence and smiling, and that smile grew bigger and brighter the longer she looked. "I see it," she whispered. "The mural is really happy. There's so much energy and love in it, just like my mom and dad and brothers." She turned to Ash and unleashed her smile on him.

He melted in her radiance. He'd been wrong: girls *were* like paintings, or at least Cassidy was. She made him feel all five senses at once, and the bright light of her spirit consumed him. He wanted to stay here and drink her in for hours, to sketch her, listen to her, learn every angle of the way she thought and the way she breathed and even the way she propped her arms on her knees.

If he were braver, he would ask her to let him do all those things.

Instead, Mrs. Rivera's truck pulled up in the driveway and honked.

"Want to rebuild a fence with me?" Ash asked Cassidy.

It wasn't quite as daring as telling her she was his Mona Lisa.

But she nodded, and that was worth something.

❦ ❦ ❦

Ricky and Jordan were horsing around in the truck bed when Ash and Cassidy got to the driveway. There were two-by-fours and fence planks, as well as pumpkins of all shapes and sizes.

"This big one looks like your belly before you take a dump," Jordan said, giggling at an orange pumpkin with an enormous bulge in the middle.

"Oh yeah?" Ricky picked up a green-and-white-striped pumpkin covered in warts. "This one looks like your face."

"Mom!" Jordan yelled.

"He started it," Ricky said.

"Both of you—shut it," Mrs. Rivera said, coming around from the front of the truck. "And get out of there before you crush all our decorations or break the wood."

Once Ricky and Jordan jumped out of the truck bed, Ash began to unload the planks.

"Oh, sweetheart," Mrs. Rivera said, "you don't need to do that. This is Cassidy's punishment. She'll do it."

"I don't mind," Ash said. "Besides, it'll be faster if we work together."

"I suppose you've probably learned a thing or two about carpentry from your stepdad," Mrs. Rivera said.

Jordan ran over to Ash. "I wanna build things! I'll help!" He tried to pick up one of the two-by-fours, but it was almost as long as he was tall, and he swiveled dangerously.

"Whoa," Cassidy said, catching the end of the two-by-four. "Why don't I take that before you knock someone's knees out?"

He scowled at her. "I had it totally under control."

"I know, buddy. It's just that you're stronger than you realize."

"I'm a superhero," Jordan said to Ash matter-of-factly. "But don't tell anyone, because, you know, I have to keep my identity secret."

Ricky grinned at him. "Don't worry, no one will ever suspect a little shrimp like you."

Jordan chewed on his lip, unsure whether Ricky was making fun of him or complimenting his secret identity. A few seconds, later, though, he nodded, having settled on the latter.

By then, Ash had hoisted all the fence planks in a stack onto his shoulder. Cassidy had the two-by-fours. Ash started toward the gate to his backyard, but Jordan and Ricky trailed them.

"What're we going to do first?" Ricky asked.

"Yeah, what're we going to do first?" Jordan chirped.

Ash's face fell. So much for spending time with Cassidy alone.

But Mrs. Rivera said to her sons, "Cassidy and Ash are going to work on the fence. But you two are going to clean your rooms."

"Aww, Mom—"

"Don't 'aww Mom' me. Those rooms were supposed to be spotless *last* weekend, and they still look like a hurricane blew through a swamp. I want them clean before the cross-country team comes over for the spaghetti carbo-load. Upstairs, now!"

Mrs. Rivera turned to Ash and Cassidy and gave them a wink.

Oh god, was it that obvious that he liked Cassidy? Ash could feel all the blood rush to his face. Maybe he ought to tell her that he would build the fence himself. That would save Cassidy the embarrassment of having to work with him. Enough guys at school had crushes on her; she didn't need to spend her weekend dealing with another one.

But Cassidy just walked up beside him and asked, "You ready?"

He nodded, relieved. Maybe she hadn't seen her mom's wink.

Cassidy set her two-by-fours on the grass in Ash's backyard and clapped her hands together like a team captain ready to pep-talk her runners. "All right! Let's do this thing." But then she paused as she surveyed the broken fence again. "On second thought, maybe I should be a little less enthusiastic. I have no idea what I'm doing."

Ash smiled. He laid his stack of planks on the ground and walked over to the section of fence that had toppled over. Some of the boards were still intact and held in place by the two-by-fours that ran horizontally across. But a good number of the planks in between were either completely shattered or significantly damaged.

"Well, the good news is that the main posts are still fine," Ash said, tapping on one of the solid vertical supports. "If these had come down, we would have to dig up the bases, get new posts, and mix and set new concrete for them."

"But we're pretty much going to have to rebuild everything in between, huh?" Cassidy said.

"Yeah," Ash said. "A couple of the boards on either side of the hole can be salvaged, but we have to replace the rest. We have to put in new two-by-fours that go across, too, since some of the nails on the old ones got twisted or bent."

"Who'd have thunk I was such a wrecking ball." Cassidy smirked, although there was some sheepishness behind her bravado.

It only made Ash like her more.

"Should I get a toolbox?" she asked.

"My stepdad's got everything we need in the garage," Ash said. "Back in a minute."

He started to jog away, then thought better of it. Cassidy was a runner. What if she noticed that he had terrible form or, really, no running form at all? He opted for a casual stroll instead.

As soon as he was in the garage, though, Ash pressed himself against the wall, letting his head drop back for a moment to take stock of everything that had happened so far.

Cassidy fell into his yard.

Cassidy talked to Ash.

Ash somehow managed to talk to Cassidy.

And now he had the entire afternoon with her.

There really was something a little more magical than usual about this particular Halloween.

He took a deep breath and allowed himself a smile. Everything was going fine. Better than fine. And who knew what the next few hours would bring?

Ash got his toolbox off one of the many shelves, a folding stepladder, and some extra nails in case Mrs. Rivera hadn't bought all the types they'd need for the fence. He grabbed a couple sodas from the garage mini fridge, too: a Mountain Dew for himself and a Cherry Coke for Cassidy.

Even weighed down with all the tools and things, Ash still moved near silently. Cassidy had her back to him, and she startled when she realized he was right there.

"You're as quiet as a ghost!" she said, hand over her heart.

Ash laughed. "That's what Onny says, too."

Cassidy's expression shifted, almost imperceptibly, like when a single wisp of a gray cloud touches the puffed edges of white cumulus and blue sky. Most people wouldn't have seen it. But as a painter and an amateur *mascarer*, Ash spent a large portion of his time studying faces, and he noticed. Did Cassidy have something against Onny? Onny *was* a little strange, but it was a quirky, innocuous kind of strange that usually didn't bother anyone, other than the uptight types like Byron Frost.

But then Cassidy saw the sodas in Ash's arms and smiled like blue skies again. "Cherry Coke is my favorite!"

I know, he thought.

They began by prying the bent nails off the two-by-fours that were on the broken part of the fence. Ash stood on the grass while Cassidy climbed onto the stepladder; she could have reached the top two-by-four from the ground, but being slightly elevated gave her better purchase on the nails.

"So why don't you play basketball or volleyball?" she asked. Even on the second step, Cassidy was still about eye level with Ash.

He shrugged. "All of my muscle coordination seemed to end up in my fingers. I'm a lot better at painting than shooting a basketball. Been like that ever since I was little."

"I don't know, you seem pretty coordinated right now." She glanced at the pile of nails he'd already extracted, compared to the one embedded in the wood that she was still working on.

Cassidy was at full-scale war with the nail. The process was supposed to be straightforward—you hook the curved back side of the hammer around the nailhead, yank, and it pulls free. But she'd somehow managed to wiggle the nail into the shape of an iron worm, without it budging from the two-by-four.

"Need some help over there?"

She laughed. "Am I that pathetic?"

"Not pathetic. Just . . . creative in your approach."

"Then, please, Michelangelo of fence building, show me how it's done." She passed her hammer to him with flourish and hopped off the stepladder.

With a smile, Ash wedged the back of the hammer around the nailhead, gave it a slight, rocking nudge, and—*pop!*—the nail came out, and he caught it with his other hand.

"Show-off," Cassidy teased. But her gaze hovered on his biceps for a moment.

Was she flirting?

Don't be ridiculous, Ash thought to himself.

Then again, it *was* the quadricentennial anniversary. . . .

He moved her stepladder back into place, and they returned to work. Cassidy got the hang of it after the second nail.

"Now that you know why I don't play basketball, it's your turn to tell me something about you," Ash said.

"What do you want to know?"

Everything, he thought. But he went for something more basic. "Why do you like running?"

Cassidy paused in her work. Like her little brother, she chewed on her lip as she thought.

"I've always run," she said. "I started when I was five, because Mom's a coach, but it's also kind of a family pride thing. My grandpa actually went to the Olympics with the Chilean team. For the marathon."

"Oh yeah, I sort of remember reading something about that."

Of course, Ash had more than read about it. He had that *Moon Ridge Gazette* article about Cassidy memorized.

He pried out the last nail on the top two-by-four and pulled the beam away from the planks. Cassidy held the other side of the two-by-four, and for a brief moment, Ash and Cassidy were connected—even if it was by a piece of lumber. They set it onto the grass, though, and returned to their separate sides of the fence to work on the two-by-four that ran across the bottom of the fence.

"You still didn't answer my question, though," Ash said. "You told me how you started running, but you didn't tell me *why* you do it."

"I guess I didn't." Cassidy's expression dimmed, and Ash wondered what he'd said wrong. Whatever it was, he wished he could take it back immediately.

But she didn't seem upset, just a little sad. More of that gray storm cloud had moved in.

"When I got sick," she said, "the first horrible thought I had was that I'd never be able to run again."

"Oh god, I'm so sorry," Ash said.

Cassidy barely nodded. Her mind was back in the past. "That was before I realized that the actual worst thing was I might die from my disease. It was looking really bad for a while—I was hooked up to an oxygen machine twenty-four/seven. And since I was only thirteen, the chances of finding a matching organ donor were slim. You can't put adult-sized lungs into a kid's chest."

Crap, Ash thought. *Why did I have to dredge this up for her?*

"After a year of waiting, my lungs failed completely. I lived in the hospital, hooked up to an ECMO machine—basically the most advanced life support that exists. It took all the blood out of my body and oxygenated it for me, since my lungs couldn't do it, then pumped the blood back into my veins."

She started hammering in the nail she was supposed to be extracting from the fence, but Ash didn't think this was the best time to point that out.

"You can't live on ECMO forever, though," she said. "It's risky for a lot of reasons. I kept getting sicker and weaker, and I was literally a few days away from dying when my doctor rushed into my room." Cassidy's mouth flattened into a grim line. She pounded harder at the nail. The wood around it splintered, but she kept hitting and hitting it as her eyes grew watery. "He told me that another girl had died at a nearby hospital. Her last wish was for her organs to go to someone else. And it turned out, that 'someone else' would be me."

Ash was rendered even more speechless than usual.

"It was my second chance," Cassidy whispered, "and I vowed to fill my life with things I loved. So, to answer your question—I run for me because I can, and I run for the girl who died that day and gave me her lungs, because she can't."

"Th-that's a really good reason," Ash said lamely. He was trying not to choke on the lump in his throat.

But then Cassidy's eyes met his, and she seemed to notice the hammer in her hand and the nail smashed into the fence. She blinked away her tears and laughed at what she'd done.

"Anyway," she said, "sorry to get so grim. Definitely didn't mean to get that gory. . . . Must be the Halloween vibes." She grinned at her joke, and just like that, the cheerful girl everyone else knew was back again.

Ash didn't understand how, after all she'd been through, Cassidy could still be one of the sunniest people he'd ever met. Always a smile on her face, and never a cruel word about anybody.

But maybe it was *because* of what she survived that she could cut through to what was truly important.

Cassidy started trying to pry out the banged-up nail.

"Oh!" she said a second later, as if she'd just had an epiphany. "I think I also like running because my family's loud. I love them so, so much, but when I'm running, especially on trails through the woods, I have my own space. Does that make sense? Or maybe you don't need it, because you're an only child."

"No, I get it." Ash's house was generally a placid place: his mom read a lot, and Neel's hobbies were things of soothing rhythm, like sanding pine boards, or the gentle *tap-tap-tap* of wood joinery. But Onny and True—well, they were the definitions of big personalities that took up a lot of any physical—or even mental—space.

"When I'm in my studio," Ash said, "I shut out the world. I turn my phone off. I don't have a clock. It's just me and what's right in front of me. I think everyone needs a place of solace like that."

Cassidy nodded as she tossed the loosened nail onto the pile of others. "Yeah . . . that's totally it. When I'm running, I sometimes pretend I'm the wind. I jump over streams and weave through rocks. The leaves rustle as I blow by, and I sort of lose track of myself. It's like . . ."

"It's like time itself flows over you," Ash said. "You're a small part of a universe that's so much larger than you, and yet, you *are* that universe. You're the wind that's always been, or the color that's always dazzled under the sun. There's no difference between you and what surrounds you; one molds the other, and in that solitude, you disappear and yet you become everything, all at once."

She looked at him with her mouth slightly parted.

Was it pretentious, what he'd said?

Cassidy shook her head at Ash. "That was the most beautiful thing I've ever heard."

"Oh," was all he managed. Ash scrubbed his hand through his hair, bashful. "Um, well, thanks."

"It's exactly how I feel when I run. I've just never been able to explain it. How did you know?"

"That's what it feels like when I make art."

Cassidy turned away from the fence and contemplated his studio for a minute.

"Whatever's in there is lucky to have you," she finally said.

It was a good thing she wasn't looking at him, because Ash

was sure that he flushed red all the way to his ears, and not in a cute way like when the tip of Cassidy's nose tinged pink.

Right then, Jordan sprinted out of his house. "Emergency! Emergency!"

Cassidy whirled around, but her expression was calm. She was used to her little brother's drama. Even Ash was familiar with it from overheard backyard conversations.

"What is it, buddy?" she asked.

Jordan motioned urgently for her to squat. She did, and he whispered something into her ear.

Her eyes went wide. "Ricky did *what*?"

Thinking that she hadn't heard, Jordan explained again, but loud enough for Ash to hear this time. "He took your mask and hid it in the haunted shack." Jordan jabbed his finger in the air in the direction of the abandoned house. "Ricky said you're too much of a scaredy-cat to go get it yourself, but he'll make you a deal to rescue it for you if you take him to the Halloween party tonight."

Ash tilted his head in amusement. "Wow. Ricky's blackmailing you."

But Cassidy didn't seem to find it funny. "Yeah, and it's gonna work, because he's right: there's no way I'm stepping foot in that house by myself. And I have to get that mask back. All the girls on the team bought the same leopard masks online so we could go to the gala together."

Jordan held Cassidy's hand. "I would go with you, but that house is too spooky."

She sighed. "I know, little man. Thanks."

"What if I go for you?" Ash blurted.

Cassidy stared at him for a second, as if she hadn't understood.

Then she shook her head, and Ash's heart plummeted. He was such a moron for thinking he could come charging in like a chivalrous knight.

Cassidy looked from him to the abandoned house, and back to Ash again.

"I'm not going to make you go in there by yourself," she said, her voice shaky. "I'll go with you."

Skeleton Shack. That's what True called the abandoned house when they were kids, because of the lightning-struck tree, standing like a rawboned sentinel. She liked hiding in the shack and making ghost sounds to scare the neighbors. Onny loved Skeleton Shack because the overgrown yard grew strange plants she couldn't find anywhere else in Moon Ridge, like Our Lady's flannel flowers, star-shaped wild garlic, and feverfew. And Ash loved the house because it didn't look like anything special, but it *was*, for those who dared to see.

"Is it safe to go in there?" Cassidy asked, as she and Ash stood at the back porch of Skeleton Shack. She'd sent Jordan home, but they knew he'd be watching with his face pressed to his bedroom window, as if he could guard his big sister from afar.

"It's structurally sound," Ash said, at the same time beating himself up for saying it like such a dork. Who talked like that?

A kid whose stepdad was a carpenter, that's who. Ash rolled his eyes at himself.

At least he was telling the truth, though, and not just feigning bravery for a girl. While other kids had treehouses, The Coven had used Skeleton Shack as their playground. Ash knew every nook and cranny in the place.

The wind stirred the few brown leaves left on the half-dead tree, and that helped Ash get out of his own head. He was standing here with Cassidy Rivera, girl of his dreams. Even though she was scared of the house, Ash swore he could smell the beginnings of Halloween magic in the air—clove and honey with a hint of moonlight to come.

"You know," Ash said, "rumor has it that Mr. Brightside wanted to have his wedding in Skeleton Shack. But Mayor Grimjoy vetoed it."

Cassidy forgot her fear for a moment and laughed. "Whatever witchcraft brought those two together, I want it."

Ash's mind flitted to Onny's love potion, sitting on his desk in the studio.

But it wasn't as if he could use it on Cassidy to make her fall madly in love with him. The potential already had to be there for it to work. This was not, Ash suspected, the same situation that had sparked the romantic smash hit of Mayor Grimjoy and Mr. Brightside.

Better to change the subject now.

"So, about going into the shack . . . ?" Ash stepped up onto the back porch, making sure to skip the rotted stairs.

A black cat peeked at him through a shattered window.

"You've gotta be kidding me," Cassidy said, shaking her head. "A black cat inside a haunted house? I can't go in there."

Ash glanced at the cat. It mewed at him. "Oh, that's just Igor."

"Igor?"

"Yeah, he's, like, the mascot and caretaker of Skeleton Shack." Ash turned to the cat. "Igor, where are your manners? Scowling is no way to greet a guest."

Igor shot Ash the kind of contemptuous look cats are expert at. But then Igor hopped through the broken window and went up to Cassidy, purring as he nuzzled against her legs.

"See?" Ash said. "He's sweet. Don't discriminate just because he looks like an evil witch's companion."

Igor actually paused at that comment to glare at Ash again.

Cassidy laughed.

Ash took the opportunity to try again to coax her into the house. "Come on in. I'm sure Igor's excited to show you around." Ash offered her his hand.

But as soon as he touched her, dizziness swept over him. The feel of her skin against his was like soda drunk too fast, the euphoric bubbles gushing in all at once. He braced himself on an ivy-covered post.

"Are you okay?" Cassidy asked.

Maybe.

Definitely.

In his dizziness, Cassidy was a riotous blur of color, and if Ash were to paint her in this moment, she would be a Kandinsky, wild and bright.

Ash let the image linger for another second, then he blinked and his vision cleared. The Cassidy in front of him was even more beautiful than the deconstructed painting he'd imagined.

"I'm fine," he said aloud.

I've never been better, he thought to himself, his fingers still pressed around hers.

But Cassidy was waiting on him to save the day, so he refocused on the goal of finding her mask—the mass-produced leopard mask that allowed him to be this close to her, to feel her heartbeat beneath her skin. Never had Ash been so happy for cheap, artless products sold in bulk.

She pulled herself up onto the porch and let go of his hand, but when he slipped through the open doorframe into the house, she followed. Igor slunk in on her heels.

The first room was the kitchen. Remnants of a dining table stood beneath a cobwebbed light fixture, an old-fashioned kind made of wrought iron. The bulbs were shattered, and a shallow layer of dirt filled the bottom halves of the glass orbs.

"How could you play here when you were little?" Cassidy asked, frowning.

Ash shrugged. "There was kind of a competitive game among the three of us every time we came. True would challenge us to each find three new things that were eerie. Onny would issue a similar challenge, but for three new plants, so she could use them for her potions."

"And you?"

He felt the color rush into his cheeks. Why did he have to blush so much?

"I'd ask them to find three new things that were beautiful," Ash said softly.

They were silent for a few seconds, and he thought he might die of embarrassment.

Then Cassidy smiled. "I'll take you up on your challenge."

"No, it's okay. You don't have to."

"On the contrary, I do. In the Rivera household, you can't deny a challenge."

"Or else what?"

"Or else you pay the consequences. And in my case, that would mean Ricky sitting on my head and farting or something."

Ash laughed.

"Besides," Cassidy said, "it'll help me not be as creeped out about this place if I'm focused on looking for beautiful things. Plus my mask."

"Okay," Ash said. "But I'll give you a hint. You have to let go of your normal assumptions if you're going to see the beauty of Skeleton Shack. Take these broken light bulbs, for instance." He pointed to the chandelier. "It just looks like dirt in there, right? But if you look more closely, you'll see that there are tiny green blades of grass sprouting from the layers of dust."

Cassidy leaned in. "Oh wow. You're right. That's amazing."

Ash grinned.

"Okay, so what happens if I win?" asked Cassidy.

"Win?"

"If I find three beautiful things. In my family, if you beat a challenge, you get a prize."

"Is the prize Ricky not farting on you?"

Now it was Cassidy's turn to laugh. "That *and* something else. Like you take over one of the winner's chores—dishwashing or unloading the groceries."

"All right . . ." Ash said, thinking. "Then if you beat this challenge, I'll build the rest of the fence for you."

As soon as he said it, though, he regretted it. Working on the fence was the only excuse he had to spend time with Cassidy after they found her leopard mask.

But it was too late. She was already stepping boldly into the dilapidated kitchen, examining the peeled Formica counter and opening cabinets with aplomb. A flurry of moths flew out of one of them, and Cassidy leaped back with a yelp.

"You okay?" Ash asked, at her side in an instant.

She made a face at the cabinets and the stench of rotting wood wafting out of them. "Yeah, I'm fine. But that is definitely *not* beautiful."

Igor snarled at the moths as he put himself protectively between Cassidy and the cabinets.

After the kitchen, there was a narrow hallway, its walls lined with floating bookshelves nailed crookedly everywhere. If Ash's parents ever saw this hall, his stepdad would have a heart attack over the shoddy carpentry—seriously, some of the shelves were attached at angles that made it surprising that books could even balance on them without sliding right off the slope—and Ash's librarian mom would faint over so many neglected books left to the spiders and rats.

Cassidy, however, paused and ran her fingers over the spines of the worn books.

"'I carry your heart with me,'" she said.

Ash froze. "What?"

"It's a famous quote," Cassidy said, poking at a poetry collection. "By E. E. Cummings."

"Oh. Right. Of course," Ash said as casually as he could. But his pulse pounded in his ears without any sense of nonchalance.

"And it's a beautiful thing," she said, smiling at the unexpected find inside such an ugly house.

Ash had to stop himself from saying that her standing there was also a beautiful sight. He was appalled by the depths of his own cheesiness and could only imagine the verbal whipping he'd get from Onny and True if they ever discovered he'd even *thought* it.

He cleared his throat and turned to the other side of the hallway, busying himself with scanning the shelves for Cassidy's wayward leopard-print mask.

"Ooh, I found another beautiful book," she said after a few minutes.

"Doesn't count!" Ash said. "You can't use two of the same category in the challenge. Like I couldn't find another little plant sprouting."

"You didn't tell me that was a rule."

"I'm the gamemaster," Ash said. "That means I get to clarify as we go."

"You're ruthless," Cassidy said, but one corner of her mouth curled up in a smile.

The hall led to the front entranceway, where a rusting coat stand leaned against the door. A shoe rack held only the left shoes of each pair. Ash always wondered what had happened to the right ones.

Cassidy checked in the cubbyholes in case the mask was in there, but she came up empty-handed.

Then she saw a knee-high wooden Buddha statue next to the shoe rack. She bounced in place. "Two beautiful things!" Even though it was dusty, the Buddha's face was still jolly, eyes crinkled in mirth.

Ash brushed off the top of the statue's head. "My mom told me that rubbing his bald spot is good luck."

"Maybe it'll help my missing mask appear faster." Cassidy gave the Buddha's noggin a vigorous rub.

"If you were Ricky," Ash said, "where would you hide the mask?"

Cassidy sighed. "Honestly? Somewhere gross. I love that kid, but he does *not* have the same standards of cleanliness that the rest of us do."

Ash bit the inside of his cheek.

"Oh no," Cassidy said. "What're you thinking?"

"Uh . . ."

"Is it bad? Oh god, it's bad. Just tell me."

He cringed. "The bathroom?"

Cassidy paled, which caught Ash off guard. If she'd looked like she was going to puke, that would be expected—because of dirty old toilets, et cetera. Instead, she was practically breaking out into a cold sweat.

"Th-there's a mirror in the bathroom, huh?" Cassidy asked. "And it's probably dark."

He nodded carefully, not sure where this was going.

"The window *is* small, and it's pretty much blacked out from grime, so yeah, not much light in there."

"Dammit, Ricky." Cassidy clenched and unclenched her fists, like she was trying to calm herself down. "He knows I'm scared of Bloody Mary."

Ash paused as he tried to understand what she was saying. When it dawned on him, he burst out laughing. "I'm sorry," he said, trying to regain composure. "Do you mean that ghost story kids tell?"

Cassidy grimaced. "The one where if you look in a mirror in a dark room and chant 'Bloody Mary,' her spirit will come out and murder you? Yeah. It's really, really ridiculous, I know. But I heard the story when I was in first grade and it scared the crap out of me, and as illogical as it is, I still can't shake it. I have to turn on all the lights anytime I go into a bathroom, because if I go into a dark one, my brain just starts chanting her name."

Ash made a mental note never to tell Cassidy the theory that he was part ghost. However, he couldn't help smiling at her as she paced, still opening and closing her fists. He loved that even though she'd been through real-life horrors, it was a childhood prank that haunted her.

"Tell you what," Ash said. "You stay right there."

"What are you—?"

"Igor will keep watch over you. I'll be right back!" He darted down a different hallway than the one they'd come through, and into what used to be the powder room.

Sure enough, Ash found a pink plastic leopard-print mask in

the bathroom, sitting in a dirt-caked soap dish in the bathtub. Thankfully, Ricky hadn't hidden the mask in the nasty toilet.

Triumphant, Ash ran back to where Cassidy was waiting next to the Buddha statue.

"Was it there?" she asked.

He smiled and presented it to her with a flourish.

Cassidy sighed with relief.

"*Pink* leopard print, though?" Ash teased. He was happy that conversation with Cassidy came easier to him now.

Her nose turned the same color as her mask. "One of the girls bought a dozen of them in a set. She thought the tackiness was funny. Did its hideousness burn your eyes?"

He squinted, pretending to be injured. "Maybe a little. But it's okay. I know something that'll heal them. Come on, let me show you my favorite part of the house."

Ash steered her through the rest of the house, toward the living room. Igor bounded ahead.

Here, the roof had collapsed long ago, and a gaping hole opened over the center of Skeleton Shack like an interior courtyard. Not expecting this, Cassidy walked straight into the vines of ivy dangling from the opening in the roof.

"Help! I'm being eaten by foliage!" she said.

Ash laughed as he untangled her.

When she could see without leaves in her eyes, Cassidy gasped.

The space was like a whimsical autumn scene out of a Miyazaki film. Sunlight dappled in through the missing roof, and green moss grew artfully over the wooden frames of old living room furniture, making them look like garden benches.

When Ash was eleven, he'd brought in a dozen small Japanese maples in ceramic pots and lined them up along the edges of the courtyard; now they were tall and reedy in their adolescence, their long, elegant branches laden with feathery crimson leaves. A large puddle from the recent rainstorm formed a pond in the corner, and red-capped mushrooms clustered around the shore like a miniature candy-colored forest.

"Oh, Ash," Cassidy whispered, awestruck.

The world around him vibrated as if a tuning fork had been pinged, and everything suddenly hit the right key. Hearing her say his name like that, in this place he'd made, was overwhelming and sublime all at once.

"Look!" Cassidy said. "I think there's a bird's nest inside that maple tree." In delight, she wandered deeper into the room.

She didn't notice the iron cauldron Onny had left in the middle of the courtyard, obscured by some ferns that had taken root in the thick dirt overlaying the former carpet. The cauldron was directly in Cassidy's path.

"Watch out," Ash said, lunging after her.

But Cassidy tripped and careened toward the sharp corner of what had formerly been a coffee table.

Ash dove and shoved her out of the way. The mask flew out of her hand. Cassidy ended up on her back on a patch of moss.

And Ash was on top of her.

His gaze met hers. Their breaths ran ragged in time with each other's.

She looked at his lips and seemed to lean in. Did she want . . . ?

Her mouth was so close. Three inches of bravery, that's all it would take to kiss her.

Now or never.

He was just about to do it, to close that impossible distance between them . . .

Then Igor reappeared, stuck his nose right in between Ash's and Cassidy's, and started licking her.

She laughed and turned her face away.

Dammit, Igor! Ash thought. *That was supposed to be* my *kiss, not yours.*

But the moment was broken. Cassidy shifted beneath Ash. Mortified that he had her pinned, Ash scrambled off and helped pull her up so they were both sitting.

She let out a small laugh—was there a nervous tremble in it?—and said, "I guess the challenge is over."

"Huh?" Ash wasn't following. His heart still pounded in his ears from being so close to her.

"The bird's nest. I found a third beautiful thing."

"Oh. Um, right."

"So I guess you owe me a fence now," she said.

Ash wrung his hands. He'd not only squandered the opportunity to kiss her, but also lost the rest of the afternoon with her. He jammed his hands into his hoodie pocket to hide his fidgeting.

But right then a gust of wind swept in through the hole in the roof, and the clove and honey scent of Halloween magic rode in on the breeze's coattails.

He knew what he ought to do.

"Will you go to the party with me?" Ash blurted out, before he had a chance to rethink his audacity.

"The midnight gala?" Cassidy said. "Um, I was supposed to go with the cross-country girls, remember?" She picked up the leopard-print mask, which had a little chip in it from her fall.

It wasn't a yes, but it also wasn't a no.

Ash dared to push onward. "You can still meet them there," he said. "Oh, and I could make you a new mask since that one's damaged!" He flung his hands out of his hoodie at the idea. "I have a few unfinished ones. There's still time for me to paint and decorate them with something that'll dry quickly."

But Cassidy didn't seem to be listening to him. Instead, she was staring at something lying on the moss a few feet away. "Where did that come from?" she asked.

Ash followed her eyes and landed on an origami crane. Oh, for god's sake! The paper bird that he'd put in his hoodie earlier . . . It must have flown out when his hands came out of his pocket. "It-it's nothing. A secret admirer made it for me. I, uh, was going to throw that away. It's not a big deal." He snatched the crane off the ground and made a show of slinging it into the puddle-pond.

But internally, Ash groaned. Why did he say it was from a secret admirer when he had no clue whether that was true? *What am I trying to prove? That Cassidy has to compete for me?*

She was frowning at the puddle, where the crane had sunk from view. A moment later she said, "You know what, I should probably go see if Mom needs help setting up the spaghetti stuff. The cross-country team'll be here soon. Thanks for helping me find my mask. And for building the rest of the fence." Then Cassidy gave Ash a smile, which seemed too bright, even for her. It was . . . artificial.

He hadn't been brave enough to kiss her. Then he'd acted like an asinine alpha male by bragging about the cranes. Now Cassidy was walking away and probably out of his life again.

Ash stood paralyzed in the Skeleton Shack courtyard.

Igor glowered balefully at him.

And the air didn't smell like Halloween magic anymore.

❦ ❦ ❦

Ash: Cassidy's gone. . . .

Onny: Oh no! What happened?

Ash: I dunno. Was all going fine, I thought. Then she just left.

True: What did you do?

Ash: Why do you assume it was my fault?

True: I love ya, Ash, but honestly, you have a v off-putting vibe with the females of the species.

Ash: Gee thanks.

True: Not your fault tho. Love isn't in our blood. Or something.

Ash: We're not even blood-related, T.

True: Don't start with that again.

Onny: Maybe it'll still work out with Cassidy?

Ash: Fence is going back up. All the runners are coming over tonight. That's it. That's who she belongs with, not a weird art guy like me.

Onny: But your zodiac tho!

Ash: I don't know if I believe in your stars anymore. . . .

True: Word.

Ash sighed and set his phone down on the bed beside him. He stared at the ceiling in his bedroom, which was painted midnight blue with a glow-in-the-dark constellation in the center, a project that Onny had spearheaded when they were in third grade. She'd mapped out different parts of the night sky for herself, True, and Ash, and then enlisted their parents to help make her dream-scapes a reality. On True's ceiling was Virgo in the northern celestial hemisphere. In Onny's room, they'd painted Aquarius, one of the oldest of the zodiac constellations. And on Ash's ceiling, Cancer, which was supposed to be a crab but really just looked like an upside-down Y.

"You're just a picture in the sky made up by ancient people," Ash said to the constellation.

But he wasn't grumpy at the stars or the ancients. He was annoyed at himself for half-believing—hoping—that the zodiacs were real, that despite his awkwardness around Cassidy, the stars would still find a way to bring them together.

Ash let his head flop to the side; his pillow partially obscured his face, but not enough that he couldn't see the rest of his room. It was a perpetual mess, and no amount of his mom's imploring could ever get him to tidy it up. One entire wall was a corkboard, covered with charcoal sketches, torn-out notebook pages with stream-of-consciousness brainstorms, and scraps of foil and ribbon and other materials Ash wanted to save for future projects. His desk was no better, buried in so much clutter that he actually had to do his homework on the floor. His closet had an OPEN AT YOUR OWN RISK sign taped to it, and the final wall was claimed by books stacked upon books stacked upon even more books. After all, a librarian's son doesn't fall far from the papyrus plant.

He pulled the covers over his head. Maybe he would just stay in here for the rest of the afternoon and evening. Onny would probably murder him for missing the party, but Ash wasn't going to be good company anyway. Besides, he was bad luck for love. He probably shouldn't be wandering around during a night when fate was trying to matchmake lovers. One glance from Ash would wilt their budding love on the vine.

Only ten minutes had passed, though, when Ash's stomach

began grumbling. He tried to ignore the hunger, but another ten minutes later, it was a full-on protest. He'd skipped lunch, and his stomach had no patience for self-pitying love sickness.

Ash hauled himself out of bed and back downstairs into the kitchen. He microwaved some leftovers—a bowl of braised-beef noodle soup and a couple *gua bao*, aka Taiwanese hamburgers, which were puffy steamed buns stuffed full of fatty pork belly, crushed peanuts, pickled mustard greens, cilantro, and hoisin sauce. It was a "small snack" by his standards. Ash didn't want to eat *too* much, or else he'd grow to seven feet tall and really never be able to shake that "Yao Ming" nickname and questions about why he didn't play basketball.

But as Ash wolfed down the noodle soup and the *gua bao*, he looked out the window into the backyard, and he started seeing Cassidy everywhere again. He'd sat with her right there on the lawn, explaining the murals on the three fences. The memory of taking her hand as he helped her onto Skeleton Shack's back porch, and the giddy dizziness from her touch. And that moment when she first stepped into the courtyard and saw the secret beauty that such an ugly place could hold. . . .

Ash shoved away the remnants of his snack. He suddenly couldn't eat.

He threw some plastic wrap over the leftovers and stuck the food back in the refrigerator. He was about to head back upstairs to wallow in his bed some more, when his phone rang.

Who calls people anymore?

"Um, hello?"

"Hello, Asher?" a man asked.

"Yes, this is he," Ash said, because his mom had taught him impeccable phone etiquette, even though he'd protested that he would never have occasion to use it. Ash supposed this call proved him wrong.

"This is Mayor Grimjoy," the man said, his voice containing more bounce and sunshine than ought to be humanly possible. "Mr. Brightside and I are in the neighborhood, just over on Robocker Avenue. You know, at the park with the old willows and the kissing benches—"

Ash heard Mr. Brightside gasp and whisper frantically, "Don't mention kissing benches! You're talking to my student!"

"Oh, er . . ." Mayor Grimjoy said as he tried to figure out how to execute an awkward conversational pivot. "I mean, we're having a Halloween picnic, and we were wondering if it would be a good time to swing by to pick up our masks soon?"

Oh no, the masks! Ash had gotten so distracted, he'd forgotten he still wasn't done with the ones they'd commissioned.

"Um, yes, sir, I'm actually putting finishing touches on them right now. Do you think you could come by in, like, an hour? At four P.M.?"

"Of course, young Asher." Only Mayor Grimjoy could get away with using a phrase like "young Asher" and have it sound perfectly normal. "We'll see you then!"

They hung up, and Ash whirled around and out the door to go back to his studio.

Two steps onto the lawn, though, and he could hear the boys' and girls' cross-country teams gathered in the backyard next door for their spaghetti carbo-load. Their noise filled the entire outdoors.

Not just Ash's yard, but probably all of humanity could hear their cheering.

"Who's gonna sprint past 'em?"

"Moonbears!"

"Who's gonna punish 'em?"

"Moonbears!"

"Trample the weak! Hurdle the stragglers!"

"Goooo, Moonbears!"

Ash tried not to peek as he crossed the lawn and passed the gaping hole in the fence. But Cassidy was there right in the center of them all, glowing under the sunset's golden caress. Ash's gaze was defenseless in her glory.

One of the girls lifted her up on her shoulders, elevating their captain. At the same time, the boys' team hoisted up their captain, Logan Murray. In the background, someone turned on the speakers and started blasting the Olympic Anthem, and the teams marched Cassidy and Logan around the sport court like athletic royalty.

When they got to the side closest to Ash's backyard, the boys started chanting, "Speech, speech, speech, speech!"

Logan laughed that casual kind of chuckle that seemed to come so easily to jocks and other popular kids. "Ladies first," he said, motioning at Cassidy.

The girls let out a rally of whistles and "woot, woot"s before it was quiet enough for Cassidy to speak. Her back was to Ash at this point, but he could still hear everything she said clearly, thanks to the echo off the sport-court tiles.

"Tomorrow is a big deal to a lot of us," Cassidy said. "The meet takes place on one of the steepest, twistiest trails of the season. North Pointe has been training hard, and they'll have targets on our backs. On top of that, Coach has word that there'll be scouts from Colorado, Oregon State, and University of Michigan."

"All Division One schools!" someone said.

Cassidy nodded. "I know that might make you nervous. But we have no reason to be. We've worked for this, every day. We've earned our place on that medal stand. And most importantly, we're a team. We pace together, we push together, and we *win* together. You hear me?" Her voice rose like a trumpet as she began their cheer. "Who's gonna sprint past 'em?"

"Moonbears!"

"Who's gonna punish 'em?"

"Moonbears!"

"Trample the weak! Hurdle the stragglers!"

"Goooo, Moonbears!"

Even Ash was moved by her speech, and he didn't usually get into sports. But the fire in Cassidy's voice and her ardor for camaraderie were two of the reasons he'd fallen for her. How she spoke to her team was the same way she encouraged Ricky as he practiced soccer footwork, and how she fired up Jordan as he ran shuttle sprints and worked on his dream of being a track star like his sister and grandpa. Cassidy just cared about everyone in her life so damn much.

Logan clapped obnoxiously loudly. "All right, let's give it up one more time for Cap'n Cass!"

Applause erupted across the sport court.

Ash flinched at the fact that Logan had a nickname for

Cassidy. At school, it was pretty obvious that Logan had a crush on her, although she'd never gone out with him. At least as far as Ash knew. And he had pretty good intel—Onny kept up an extensive network of gossipers in Moon Ridge and the neighboring towns. If there was anything to know about Cassidy's relationship status, Onny would have informed Ash ASAP.

So Logan's nickname for Cassidy was probably just from being teammates, right?

"Your turn, Logan," Cassidy said. "What've you got to rile us up?"

"I'm glad you asked," he said. "I was going to give a rousing speech about our race tomorrow, but since you already did such a great job, I'll just go straight to part two." He let out a wolf whistle.

Suddenly, snare drums started up in the driveway out front. Woodwinds began to trill. And trumpets, trombones, and a tuba blared as the Moon Ridge band marched into Cassidy's backyard.

Ash couldn't help it now; he pressed himself to the hole in the fence to watch the scene unfold.

The drum major led the way with his baton, and the rest of the white-and-green-clad band followed in neat lines. Then they transitioned from the entry music to a hyper ensemble rendition of the oldie "Build Me Up Buttercup."

And the whole time, Logan pretended to have a microphone as he sang about how he could be the boy that Cassidy adored, if she let him. He got the whole boys' team in on the chorus, and it was a wall of sound sing-shouting, "DON'T BREAK LOGAN'S HEARTTTTT!"

The girls swooned so loudly, Ash could hear their coos

even over the marching band, and it was a miracle that they didn't faint from Logan's grand gesture and drop Cassidy on the ground.

But Ash couldn't see how Cassidy was taking all this. Her back was still to him.

When Logan finished, the boys—still carrying him on their shoulders—pivoted him to face Cassidy.

"Cap'n Cass, I've asked you out a bunch of times before and you've always said no, but just give me one chance. Go with me to the Sadie Hawkins dance next month. Please?"

Ash cringed. He'd always thought the idea of a girl-ask-boy dance seemed horribly outdated. As if girls needed special permission to ask for what they wanted.

But the girls' team didn't seem to care. They broke out into an urgent mass of "say yes" whispers.

Cassidy laughed. "You do realize," she said to Logan, "that the *girl* is supposed to invite the guy for Sadie Hawkins?"

"Then ask me," Logan said, and his expression was so painfully earnest that Ash momentarily felt for him. He knew what it was like to be hopelessly in love with Cassidy.

"Logan," she began, her voice softer than when she'd given her speech. "Will you go to Sadie Hawkins with me?"

He smiled like a man who'd been wandering the desert and discovered that the oasis he'd seen was real.

"Yes!" Logan shouted, pumping his fist in the air.

Both teams erupted into clapping and congratulations, and the marching band struck up "We Are the Champions."

It was all too much for Ash.

He turned to go to his studio. But a small hand tugged on the hem of his hoodie.

It was Jordan. He must've run over while Ash was watching his prospects with Cassidy plummet off a cliff.

"Do you wanna come eat spaghetti with me?" Jordan asked. He already had tomato sauce on his adorable little face.

Ash gave him a sad smile. "Maybe another time, bud. But thanks for the invite."

"Okay," Jordan chirped. "Because I like you, and I think you'd be a better big brother than Ricky because he farts too much. So I'm gonna wish on a star tonight that you and my sister can be friends, and then we'll get to hang out a lot."

"You do that," Ash said.

Wish for the both of us.

Jordan ran back to the patio table where Cassidy's mom and dad were dishing out massive piles of spaghetti onto paper plates. Ash looked in Cassidy's direction one more time. But she'd been consumed by the huddle of girls, and Logan was waiting at the edge of the crowd for her to emerge.

It's where Cassidy belonged, with the athletes who could persuade entire marching bands to serenade her. She deserved to be showered with attention and adoration and grand gestures. Not stuck with an artist with two left feet, who until today, couldn't even manage to whisper in her presence.

"Goodbye, Cassidy," Ash said.

He trudged alone to his studio and left his heart in the hole in the fence.

❧ ❧ ❧

Ash hunched over his worktable, single-mindedly focused on the masks so he wouldn't think about Cassidy anymore. In front of him were four backup masks that were "naked"—they only had a layer of white acrylic paint on them—and two nearly finished ones that belonged to Mayor Grimjoy and Mr. Brightside. One was a bronze sun with glimmering rays that practically radiated warmth; the other was a moon with dripping black paint all around the eyeholes, like gothic eyeliner, and a mouth full of pointy, *Nightmare Before Christmas* teeth. The masks—and the couple they were destined for—were so different on the outside yet so perfect for each other on the inside. If only Cassidy felt that way about Ash.

He cursed himself for already failing to not think about her. *Focus!*

Ash opened a papier-mâché box. It was slightly lopsided, due to the fact that he'd made it in kindergarten (his first ever project with paper and glue), and it was painted in orange and red fingerprints in the shape of an autumn tree. Now this served as Ash's "miscellaneous" box of sequins, beads, rhinestones, and other trinkets useful for decoration. He picked a handful of silver teardrop gems for Mr. Brightside's mask and glued them on, one by one.

When that was done, Ash attached gold-foil streamers to the sunbeams on Mayor Grimjoy's mask. He had barely finished the last one when his phone rang. He usually turned the ringer off when he was working, but Ash had kept it on this time so that he wouldn't miss the mayor and Mr. Brightside.

"Asher, we're here!" the mayor sang from the phone.

"I'll be right out," Ash said.

He gathered the sun and moon masks and hurried through the backyard.

Do not look through the fence. Do not look through the fence. Do. Not. Look.

To avoid hearing the cross-country team, Ash hummed loudly to himself and miraculously got into the house unscathed by the raucousness next door.

He strode through the living room and opened the front door.

"Hi, Mayor Grimjoy, Mr. Brightside. Would you like to come in?" Ash said, once again deploying the manners his mom had taught him, even though the last thing he wanted was to hang out with his biology teacher and the too-cheerful mayor.

Mayor Grimjoy bounced into Ash's house, practically dragging his husband with him. Even without his midnight-gala mask, Mr. Brightside already looked like the prince of darkness, with his gothic, black velvet coat with tails, blood-red epaulettes on his shoulders, and a black satin cravat at his throat. His pants were black brocade, and his pointed boots were polished to a grim shine. A black cape finished the look.

In contrast, Mayor Grimjoy's Halloween costume was a ceremonial military uniform made of warm yellow fabric and embellished liberally with gold braiding. Polished bronze fasteners served as buttons, and a half cape of fiery orange and red gave the impression that he was composed entirely of the sun's rays.

Internally, Ash sighed. These two really were the epitome of coupledom. Even though the mayor was basically an overgrown camp counselor and his husband was the prince of darkness, they never wavered in support of each other. In fact, Ash had noticed that they were often saying the same thing, even if one version came out like a cheer and the other like a doomsday prophecy.

"We are thrilled beyond belief that you were able to make masks for us!" Mayor Grimjoy said. "Isn't that right, honey?"

"Indeed," Mr. Brightside said, his face as still as stone. "Thrilled as a ghoul during the Hungry Ghost Festival."

Ash didn't know what that was, but it didn't sound pleasant. He let it go without comment.

"Right. So here are your masks." He presented the mayor with the bronze sun, its foil ribbons reflecting the overhead lights, and he passed the crying-moon mask to Mr. Brightside. Supposedly, Mayor Grimjoy had wanted to dress up as the Gentleman and Lady of Moon Ridge (again), but after doing that for who knows how many years in a row, Mr. Brightside had finally prevailed on his husband to try out different costumes this Halloween.

"Oh, Asher, these are divine!" Mayor Grimjoy held the sun mask up to his face and spun toward the mirror in the entryway. (Ash's mom had placed it in just the right place for good feng shui.)

"You look like the Sun King," Mr. Brightside said. Even though most of his face remained as impassive as marble, his eyes lit up as he admired his husband.

"And you are my Moon King," the mayor said. "Together, we rule as equals over the realms of day and night." He spun around and gazed at Mr. Brightside with such tenderness, Ash had to glance away.

Mr. Brightside cleared his throat then, probably remembering that his student was standing there.

"I embarrass him," Mayor Grimjoy said to Ash in a loud, faux-conspiratorial whisper. "But he secretly loves it."

"Please stop," Mr. Brightside said.

"Never." Mayor Grimjoy beamed and pecked his husband on the cheek. "All right, Asher, I believe we owe you for these glorious masks." He counted out a number of bills.

"That's too much, sir," Ash said. "Mr. Brightside already gave me a down payment when he ordered the masks."

"Not at all! You must accept a gratuity on top of the commission fee," Mayor Grimjoy said. "I insist that everyone be paid what they deserve, and you need to know your worth and demand it. Young people—especially artists—too often discount their value. Do not discount yourself, Asher. Do you understand?"

"Yes, sir. Thank you," Ash said, as he accepted the money.

"We'll see you tonight at the Diamantes' soiree?" Mayor Grimjoy asked, as Mr. Brightside edged toward the door.

"Um, yeah. Of course," Ash said.

"But you *must* be more exuberant about it!" Mayor Grimjoy threw his arms in the air. It was part dismay and part rallying cheer. "This is the four-hundred-year anniversary of the founding of Moon Ridge! Magic is stirring as we speak."

"I don't know if I believe in magic."

"Don't believe in magic?!" Mayor Grimjoy turned to Mr. Brightside. "Do you hear what he's saying, darling?"

"As a man of science," Mr. Brightside said drolly, "I might have to side with him."

"Bah!" the mayor said. "Both of you need some Halloween faith. Haven't you heard the saying 'Love found on the darkest day, forever gold it shall stay'? In fact, Jacob and I met on the thirty-first of October!"

Mr. Brightside's first name was Jacob? It seemed so . . . biblical for someone who looked more like a servant of darkness than a bringer of light. Maybe his parents had hoped their son would live up to the name Brightside.

Meanwhile, the gothic prince had opened the front door. He wanted to escape this conversation as badly as Ash did.

"See you at the gala tonight, Asher," Mayor Grimjoy said. "And bring a date. You never know what this mystical evening has in store for you."

Ash involuntarily glanced in the direction of Cassidy's house. It was so quick, though, he didn't think anyone would notice. But Mr. Brightside tilted his head curiously at Ash.

Mayor Grimjoy bounded gleefully out the door. "Thank you again for the glorious masks!" he shouted as he skipped to his car. It was, of course, a bright yellow MINI with headlights and a grill that looked like a giant smiley face.

Mr. Brightside lingered at the door. "Ask her," he said.

Ash frowned. "Ask who, what?"

"Cassidy Rivera. She's the one who lives next door, isn't she? Ask her to the gala."

"I already did and she said no. And then she agreed to go to Sadie Hawkins with Logan Jackson."

"Sadie Hawkins isn't for weeks. But the Halloween gala is tonight. I have an inkling that if you ask again, she'll say yes."

ROSHANI CHOKSHI, EVELYN SKYE, SANDHYA MENON

Ash scoffed. "And how would you know that?"

Mr. Brightside let out a long-suffering sigh. "A little bird told me," he said, with no inflection whatsoever in his tone, and Ash couldn't tell if he was serious—like a raven had come to his window in the middle of the night and divulged this secret—or if he was just annoyed with yet another student not listening to an adult.

With that, Mr. Brightside left without even saying goodbye, his black cape streaming behind him with dramatic finality.

As soon as Ash closed the front door, he flopped onto the living room sofa and whipped out his phone.

Ash: The weirdest thing just happened.

True: You stopped eating like a blue whale?

Ash: Huh?

True: They consume 40 million krill a day. Or maybe you identify more with the hummingbird. Having to eat every 10 minutes.

Ash: What? No. I'm nothing like a hummingbird.

Onny: Hobbit! He eats like a hobbit. Ash, did you have second breakfast today?

True: And elevenses?

Onny: And luncheon.

True: And afternoon tea.

Ash: I hate you guys. Forget it. Not going to tell you anything ever again.

Onny: OK sorry sorry!! What was the weird thing that happened?

Ash: . . .

Onny: True, you have to apologize to him too.

Onny: TRUE!

True: You're not a hobbit. Or a whale or a hummingbird.

Ash: I didn't see the word Sorry.

True: 😠 Fine. S O R R Y. You satisfied?

Ash: I will screenshot this for the archives. True actually apologized.

Onny: TELL US WHAT HAPPENED ALREADY!!!

Ash: Mr. Brightside gave me relationship advice.

True: What.

Onny: Was not expecting that.

True: Also, why are you hanging out with our teacher on the weekend? Nerd.

Ash: Shut up. He and Mayor Grimjoy came by to pick up their masks.

Onny: So what did he tell you? OMG is it true that vampires can hypnotize their victims into falling in love with them???

True: I cannot participate in this conversation.

Ash: He told me I should ask Cassidy to the gala.

Onny: How does he know you like her?

Ash: No idea.

Onny: Vampire telepathy!

True: I'm done here. Goodbye. Have a nice life.

Ash: He's totally wrong, though. Logan got the marching band to come over this afternoon so he could ask Cassidy to Sadie Hawkins. In front of the entire cross-country team. And she said yes.

Onny: I thought girls were supposed to be the ones asking for Sadie Hawkins?

True: I'm back in the conversation, but only to object to the fundamentally anti-feminist nature of the Sadie Hawkins concept. This antiquated idea presupposes that women are docile creatures who need men to initiate any and all relationships. Not to mention the completely outdated notion that there are only two genders.

Ash: Hear hear.

Onny: 100% agreed. But I'd like to go back to Mr. Brightside's advice?

Ash: It doesn't matter anyway. Because Logan already asked Cassidy out.

True: See? Love sucks. Go over to Onny's and be useful instead.

Onny: Oooh, yes. I'm holed up doing homework and then getting glammed up, so I can't see you till the party. But my parents desperately need help setting up the Mystic Woods. A guy from the lighting crew didn't show.

Ash laughed to himself. Onny's parents were so insanely wealthy, they always hired an army to set up their parties. Yet if *one* member of the staff failed to show up, it was suddenly a disaster.

But hey, why not go over and help? Ash didn't have anything else to do anyway.

Ash found Onny's mom outside the greenhouse, in the vast gardens behind their castlelike mansion. She gesticulated frantically with one of the caterers, and Ash waited until she was finished before walking up to her.

"Hi, Mrs. D," he said. "I know Onny's busy and not to be disturbed, but she said you could use some help setting up for the party?"

"Oh, Ash, darling, you're my savior!" Mrs. Diamante drew him into a quick hug. "One of the men from the lighting crew called in sick, and now they're short-staffed. Would you be able to help them string lights through the canopies of the trees?"

"Sure thing." Ash figured he must have been granted his exceptional height for some reason, because it certainly wasn't for playing basketball. Maybe his purpose in life was to help people with things like hanging lights and getting hard-to-reach boxes of cereal from the top shelves at the grocery store.

He jogged out to the copse of oak trees on the other side of the sprawling grounds. When he, Onny, and True were little, they used to call this the Mystic Woods, and they did everything from building forts to attempting to make their own maple syrup (it turns out you can't do that with oak trees) to, of course, charting the night sky for Onny. The Mystic Woods were second only to Skeleton Shack in terms of magic and mystery.

Tonight, especially, as darkness settled like a sorcerer's cloak, the Mystic Woods felt even more enchanted than usual. The crew from Lights Amore! had already been hard at work, and half the trees were strung with mini mason jars full of flickering lights that looked like dancing fireflies. The breeze rustled through the leaves that still hung on the branches, and the radio from the crew's truck played a classical piece full of flutes and chimes that sounded like Halloween sprites gallivanting through the Mystic Woods. In the distance, the frogs in the Diamantes' moat provided extra percussion.

"Hey," Ash said, to one of the guys in the trees. "Mrs. Diamante sent me over. You need a hand?"

"Yeah, man, that'd be awesome. Lemme show you what we're doing."

He gave Ash some quick instructions on how to weave the strings through the branches. The goal was to ensure equal distribution of lights while not making it impossible to take it all down tomorrow. And obviously, don't hurt the trees.

"I think I got it," Ash said, after watching him work through a few branches.

"Cool. Then grab a ladder and some crates from the back of the truck, and you can start on the trees way back there." He pointed to the back of the Mystic Woods, where nothing was lit up yet.

Ash got to work and soon found a rhythm. He'd climb the ladder and wedge himself into the lowest level of branches, then weave the lights in and out, up and down. When he'd exhausted that height, he'd stand on the sturdiest branch and work at waist level. Then shoulder height. Then above his head. If he needed to go any higher than that, he'd climb the ladder again, but for the most part, his six-foot-three frame and corresponding wing-span meant he could pretty much reach as far as he needed.

It was really peaceful, stringing lights by himself as the sun set. The task was almost meditative, and Ash was able to forget about Cassidy and Logan for a while, concentrating instead on placing the lights just so, and making sure his feet were secure in the tree, and stopping every so often to look up at the stars and remember how vast the galaxy was, how small and insignificant his problems were, how beautiful a simple, quiet night could be.

When he finished stringing up all the lights, Ash decided to take a break before turning them on and returning the ladder and empty crates to the truck. He sat at the base of one of the trees and looked up through its lattice of bare branches.

Ash scanned the sky for the Lady and Gentleman of Moon Ridge, the two golden stars that appeared only on Halloween. Although it was barely dusk, they were preternaturally bright and should be easy to see.

But Ash almost missed the Gentleman star at first, because he was used to locating them as a pair. Ash backtracked, and sure enough, there was the Gentleman, exactly where he was supposed to be.

However, the Lady was missing.

What? That couldn't be right. Ash scaled the tree until he was near the top, where he had an unobstructed view of the sky.

But again, the Gentleman of Moon Ridge stood alone, his glimmer weaker than usual, as if he missed his lover and would mope until she returned.

Ash reached for his phone to text Onny and True. He fumbled it, though, and the phone fell.

He lunged after it and smacked his head on a thick branch. His vision blurred, and as Ash sat up and rubbed the throbbing spot, he thought he saw an apparition among the golden oak leaves of the tree next to him.

What the—?

The woman was hardly more than a wisp of fog, a pale figure wearing an old-fashioned wedding dress and a deep-purple cloak.

For a second, Ash thought of Bloody Mary. But this phantom didn't seem murderous at all. Instead, she just watched him with an earnest kind of curiosity.

Then he noticed the crown of roses and tiny pumpkins on top of her long wavy hair, and he remembered there had been stories from past Halloweens of the Lady of Moon Ridge descending to earth to impart lessons in true love. It didn't happen often— maybe on certain anniversaries of the town's founding?—but Ash was pretty sure Onny had mentioned it at some point while she was brewing her love potion.

To be honest, he hadn't paid particularly close attention. As much as he loved Onny, sometimes she went into a little too much detail, and he and True had figured out that if they tuned in at the beginning and end, and otherwise just said "Uh-huh" and "No way!" every so often during the middle parts, they'd still get the gist of Onny's storytelling.

"Are you the Lady of Moon Ridge?" he whispered, as if speaking too loudly might make her disappear.

She held his gaze for a moment, and Ash could feel the cool dampness of her mist around him. Then she nodded, only once.

"Why are you here?" he asked.

The Lady didn't answer, though. She just continued to watch him.

"Am I seeing you for a reason?" Ash asked the Lady.

She smiled gently, as if pleased with him.

Then Ash blinked, the blurriness from hitting his head cleared, and the Lady was gone.

Had he just imagined her?

Or maybe I have a concussion.

Regardless, Ash was intrigued. *If* the Lady was real, then there was a reason she'd appeared before him. And if she was imagined, there was still a reason he'd conjured her.

Her reason for appearing was always related to love.

Ash smiled as he thought of Cassidy—her interpretation of his fence murals. Her nightingale laugh that flitted through the air when she got tangled up in the ivy in Skeleton Shack. The moss, where he'd landed on top of her, and where she'd looked deep into Ash's eyes, but he hadn't been brave enough to traverse the three inches to kiss her.

Would everything have been different if he'd tried?

There was a reason the Logans of the world got what they wanted. They put themselves out there. Whereas guys like Ash always watched from the sidelines, letting others win the race.

Maybe it was time to put himself in the game. Maybe that's why the Lady of Moon Ridge had shown herself to him.

Ash dropped down from the tree and found his phone in the middle of a pile of leaves.

Ash: Remind me how the love potion works again?

Onny: Are you gonna use it?? OMG OMG OMG

True: *eyes pop out of head due to kinetic energy of epic eye roll*

Onny: I think the easiest way is to drink it? But Lola's recipe just says "touch the potion to your intended's body and your own." Whatever that means.

True: *snort* PLEASE can you hurl the potion into Cassidy's face? I'd like to be there to see it.

Onny: LOL. Drinking it is more romantic. But don't forget she also has to kiss you before midnight. That's how your love is sealed.

Ash: OK thanks. Gotta go.

Onny: That's it? You're just gonna leave us hanging like this? I NEED DETAILS!

Onny: Hello? Earth to Ash?

True: Leave him alone. He's flitted off to work his magic.

Onny: Ooooh, so you DO believe in magic.

True: Some days I honestly don't understand how you two dorks are my best friends.

For the third time that day, Ash stepped into the backyard to go to his studio. The bistro lights on the patio next door twinkled, and lively conversation spilled over as the team continued to eat their spaghetti dinner. But Ash was immune to distraction now. He had a plan. Not a loud, showy one like Logan and the marching band, but one that would hopefully work just as well.

He flipped the light switch in the studio and shut the door behind him. Then he turned off the ringer on his phone and set it on the top shelf, where he wouldn't be tempted to check it.

Noise-canceling headphones? Check.

Box of beads, sequins, feathers, and ribbons? Check.

Paintbrushes, palette, and rack of more bottles of paint than an art store? Check, check, and definitely check.

With his setup ready, Ash picked up one of the "naked"

masks—plain white with empty eye holes—and spun in his chair to his worktable. Of course, Cassidy already had a mask, but Ash wanted to make one that was unique to her. He could have decided to give her any of the dozens of finished masks hanging on the wall behind him. But that felt lazy. It was like buying a gas-station rose at the last minute because you just remembered your mom's birthday. Sure, you showed up with a present, but there was nothing of *you* in the gift. If Ash was going to put himself out there and let the girl he'd loved for years know it, he was going to do better than a gas-station rose.

The question was, how to design the mask? On the one hand, he could translate everything he knew about Cassidy into paint. Like the fence bordering her yard. It would be vibrant and gleeful, her exuberance rendered in color, like the Kandinsky he'd imagined earlier when he touched her hand to help her onto the shack's porch.

But there would also be calm, because it underlay everything Cassidy did—how she trained for her races, how she practiced soccer and basketball with Ricky and Jordan, how she lived without fear, despite knowing that her fragile, transplanted lungs could betray her just like her original pair did.

A mask like that would begin with blue at the bottom, a serene ocean. And then it would open up above into a resplendent sunrise, all pinks and oranges and yellows. There would be sapphire tassels beneath the ocean, glitter on the brow, and fans of feathers at the top corners.

Or . . . Ash could make a mask that was the other half of his own costume, the woman in Klimt's painting *The Kiss*.

"No," Ash said out loud, even though he was the only one in the studio. "That's too presumptuous."

But wasn't this whole endeavor presumptuous anyway? Making a mask for Cassidy, asking her to come to the midnight gala after she'd already said no . . . It was all based on the presumption that her answer could be changed. That, even though she'd said yes to Logan for Sadie Hawkins, it was only a dance and not a relationship. That the connection Ash had felt with Cassidy this afternoon might have gone both ways.

He thought back to their conversation outside Skeleton Shack, when they'd talked about Mayor Grimjoy and Mr. Brightside. How, on the outside, it didn't seem like they would work, and yet they did, because even though the sun and the moon appeared as opposites, they were both bright lights, just in their own ways. They were complements who worked perfectly together.

Cassidy was a charismatic athlete who thrived at pep rallies. Ash was an introspective artist who preferred the quiet of shadows to the noise of spotlights. But what drew him to Cassidy wasn't all her trophies or the fact that people carried her on their shoulders while she led cheers. What he loved about Cassidy were her noiseless qualities—her loyalty to her friends, her commitment to her passions, and her devotion to her family. Qualities that Ash liked to think he had, too.

We could be good together. Like the sun and the moon. Like two halves of the same painting.

Ash reached for the gold paint.

His own gold mask shone on the windowsill, reflecting both

the electric lights in the studio and the moonlight streaming in through the glass ceiling. But whereas Ash's mask was covered in rectangles of black and white, along with the gold, Cassidy's mask would match the pattern on the woman's dress in *The Kiss*, with clusters of red, purple, and blue ovals, like pansies springing up in a field of gold.

First, he spray-painted the mask with a layer of gold. Next, Ash double-checked Klimt's painting to make sure he'd get the flowers right. He riffled through his racks of paint until he found close to the correct shades and squeezed out what he needed to custom-mix his colors.

Then Ash reached for the antique perfume vial Onny had given him—sterling silver whorls set over a tapered bulb of glass, like a Christmas ornament from another era.

Please let this idea work.

Ash shuffled through the stuff on his desk until he found the incantation that Onny had included with the love potion. It was ridiculous, and he probably didn't have to recite it since she already had when she made the potion, and yet . . .

He took a deep breath, and chanted the lines:

"To summon joy and love in another's soul
For a connection that makes two people whole
For laughter and a smile that one can never miss
Sealed before midnight with a truehearted kiss."

Ash lifted the stopper and trickled drops of the love potion onto his own mask and then into each color of paint on his palette. When he and Cassidy donned their masks, the potion would be touching both of them.

Stilling his trembling hands, Ash began painting bouquets of abstract oval flowers on the cheeks and the temples of Cassidy's mask. He stenciled on subtle, wavy gold lines. He limned the eyeholes with shimmers of glitter. And the love potion seeped into every painstaking detail of the mask.

Finally, when all that was dry, Ash hot-glued small blue and white crystals to the top edge of the mask, like the blue and white flowers in the hair of the woman in *The Kiss*.

He sat back in his chair and admired his work. Smiling, Ash took his mask off the windowsill and set it next to the new mask. They really did look like they belonged together.

Ash took the noise-canceling headset off. The noise from the cross-country team was gone.

What time was it?

He reached for his phone on the top shelf.

Holy crap, hours had flown by as Ash worked. It was already 9 P.M., and Onny had been texting all the while asking when in Halloween hell Ash and True were going to get to the party.

Ash: Lost track of time, sorry!

Onny: I hope you have a good excuse! I haven't heard from you or True in a millennia! Why aren't you here yet?

Ash: I was working on something.

Onny: Better be a time travel machine so you can get your tardy ass over here.

Ash: I have one more thing I need to do.

Onny: Does this have to do with the love potion???

Ash: Will be at the party as soon as I can. I promise.

Onny: ASHER LEE, I swear on my lola's potions book that if you're not here in half an hour, I will come over there and murder you and use the remnants of your corpse as kindling for my cauldron.

Ash: Wow. Really getting into the Halloween spirit, huh?

Onny: Shut up. And bring Cassidy.

Ash: Working on it.

Onny: Wait. REALLY????

Onny: Ash?

Onny: I take back what I said about the cauldron.

Onny: YOU ARE KILLING ME WITH YOUR STOIC SILENCE BUT I WILL ALLOW IT IN THE NAME OF L O V E.

Onny: Oh btw, the tarot card I flipped for you earlier was an upright Ace of Pentacles. It means new beginnings and prosperity in love. . . .

Ash grinned. He looked one more time at his mask next to Cassidy's.

They belonged together.

Now it was just a question of whether the people who wore them could belong together, too.

There was, however, a flaw in Ash's plan. Cassidy was supposed to go to the midnight gala with some of her teammates. What if he rang her doorbell and Cassidy had already left?

The Ash from this morning would have accepted defeat. Right now. Before he even left his studio.

But this version of himself—the I-think-I-saw-the-Lady-of-Moon-Ridge Ash—was a different guy. It was as if the magic of the "Founders' Fable" had made a cocoon of the day, and Ash had emerged from it no longer a passive caterpillar.

So now I'm an active butterfly? Ash cringed at his own analogy; it was as bad as True calling him a hummingbird or whale. But whatever. The idea was sound. Old Ash would have taken the easy excuse that Cassidy would already be gone, and therefore it wasn't worth going over there to ask her again to go with him. New Ash—emboldened by the dusky orange moon or Onny's love potion or simply the afternoon spent with the girl he loved—was willing to take the risk.

Ash put on his mask and tied the ribbons behind his head.

Then he crossed the studio to the coat hook by the door and unzipped the garment bag.

Inside was the gold robe from *The Kiss*. Ash had sewed on black-and-white patchwork rectangles over most of it and had embroidered gold spirals to match Klimt's painting. It was pretty clever, as far as costumes went—eye-catching, yet incredibly comfortable. The only flaw—which, of course, True had pointed out—was that no one but an art buff would recognize what Ash was supposed to be. But he kind of liked that. It was like a secret handshake for members of a fabulously nerdy club. If you knew what the robe and mask represented, you were in. If you didn't, well, Ash was still happy to be your friend. He would just privately mourn your lack of artistic education.

"No wonder Onny and True say I'm insufferable sometimes." He laughed at himself as he slipped the gold robe over his sweater and jeans.

Ash reached for Cassidy's mask but stopped before picking it up. He didn't want to simply hand it over to her. Logan had brought her an entire marching band. Ash wanted the mask to feel at least a little special.

He opened and closed the drawers in his desk, searching for something to put the mask in. But he didn't exactly have a stash of velvet gift pouches lying around. The only thing Ash could find with the appropriate dimensions was his miscellaneous box, the lopsided papier-mâché from kindergarten, which now contained all the sequins, beads, and rhinestones he'd used to decorate the masks.

That'll have to do.

It was not a traditional gift box, but at least it had personality. Ash lifted out the plastic trays, lined the interior of the box with a nest of gold fabric scraps, and lay Cassidy's mask carefully inside.

Ready? he asked himself as he turned to the studio door.

His nerves threatened to short-circuit.

But Ash plunged into the backyard, and the light of the full, apple-cider moon was so ridiculously Halloween-like that he couldn't help but feel buoyed by an undercurrent of "Founders' Fable" magic beneath his feet.

Ash's original plan was to go to Cassidy's front door. Now, though, he paused in the middle of the grass. Cassidy's second-story bedroom faced his yard, and her light was on.

She was still home. Hope fluttered in Ash's chest.

Come to the window, he thought, as if he could will it to happen.

An unseasonably warm breeze kicked up, flickering through the hem of Ash's robe. The wind sent the dry leaves on the ground scattering, from his backyard through the hole in the fence onto the Riveras' sport court.

And then—almost unbelievably, except that Ash watched it happen—a small tornado swirled, whisking the leaves up into the air and flinging them against Cassidy's window. The dry leaves pattered against the glass like a gentle autumn hailstorm.

The sound brought her to the window. For a moment, Ash could see only her silhouette.

But then the soft light of the moon brought her into focus. She had on pajama pants and a green, long-sleeved T-shirt. Even from this distance, Ash recognized it as the shirt with cartoon stitched-up lungs on it and the words REAL LIFE GHOUL. Appropriately Halloween, even if Cassidy wasn't dressed to go to a party.

Then again, what Cassidy wore wasn't important to Ash. What mattered was the sound of her laugh, the colors of her spirit, the smell of her shampoo, and the smiles that she left in her wake. She was eternally beautiful, in his eyes.

As if she could hear his thoughts calling to her, Cassidy turned her head and saw him.

Ash smiled.

And then he held up the box so she could see it. He hinged open the lid and lifted her mask into the moonlight.

Cassidy's hand flitted to her mouth. Then she pointed her finger at her chest, as if asking, *Is that for me?*

"Yes," Ash said and nodded at the same time.

She stayed at the window, staring at him. He didn't know what she was thinking; she was too far away and it was too dim to make out the expression on her face.

But then Cassidy held up a single finger and disappeared from the window.

It seemed that all the clocks in the world stopped ticking while Ash stood alone in his backyard, holding his breath until she came back.

The Riveras' patio door slid open and latched shut again. Cassidy jogged into view but slowed as she approached the hole in the fence.

"Hey," she said softly.

"Hey back." Ash set the mask back into the papier-mâché box

and carried both with him as he walked over. But he stopped a couple feet shy of the broken boards.

Him on his side, Cassidy on hers.

This was the fence that had separated them all these years.

The fence on which he'd painted the mural of her soul.

And the hole where he'd left his heart this afternoon.

They stayed like that on either side of the fence. Neither said a word.

Finally, though, Ash broke the silence.

"I thought you would've already left for the party with your friends," he said.

Cassidy shook her head. "I didn't feel like going anymore."

"Why not?"

She looked away for a second, and when she looked back at him, she only shrugged.

"I like your costume," Cassidy said, changing the subject. "It's from that *Kiss* painting, right?"

Ash took a step back in surprise. "You know Klimt?"

"Doesn't everybody?"

He laughed. "No, definitely not."

"The other mask you made . . ." Cassidy pointed at the open box that Ash was still holding. "I couldn't see it clearly from my room. It matches your costume."

"Yeah . . ."

"Oh god." The tip of her nose pinked. "I'm an idiot. I thought you meant the mask was for me. But if it matches yours . . ." She wrung the hem of her T-shirt. "It's for Onny. Wow. I'm . . ." Cassidy began to retreat into her sport court. "I should go."

"What?" Ash frowned, confused.

But then he remembered the conversation he and Cassidy had had earlier, when she'd asked if he was really close to Onny, and he'd said yes, and then there had been an awkward pause. . . . "Wait, do you think Onny and I are together?"

"Isn't that why you made her this mask?"

"Onny and True are my best friends, but they're like sisters to me. This mask isn't for Onny."

"Then . . ."

"I made it for you."

She let out a sharp exhale, as if she couldn't quite believe it.

Ash took a step forward into Cassidy's backyard. As he ducked through the hole in the fence, he retrieved his heart that he'd left on the broken boards, bringing it with him.

"It-it's for me?" Cassidy asked.

He nodded. "For you. Do you want to try it on?"

Cassidy looked up at him, the moon illuminating her skin.

"Yes, please," she whispered, as if Ash's presence now somehow stole away *her* voice, rather than the other way around.

Their hearts pounded like thunderstorms, and the air vibrated between them.

Gingerly, Ash brought the golden mask to Cassidy's face. His fingertips grazed her skin, little lightning bolts sparking where they touched. He brushed through her hair—she smelled of blue irises and peonies—and tied the ribbons behind her head.

Her lips were only three inches away.

This time, Ash was brave.

He bent down, just as Cassidy rose on her tiptoes, and his

mouth met hers. The kiss was tender, like velvet brushing against flower petals, and liquid moonlight pouring through their veins.

Ash kept his eyes closed for a long moment. When he opened them, Cassidy was smiling shyly.

"I've always wondered what it would feel like to do that," she said.

He blinked at her. "Always?"

She nodded. "Hold out your hand."

"Why?"

"Just do it. Please."

Ash held his breath and obeyed.

Cassidy reached into the pocket of her pajama pants. Then she uncurled her fist and dropped several tiny origami cranes into Ash's palm.

He gasped.

The pixie mobile flying from his bike handle freshman year. The joyful rush of origami when he opened his locker. The solitary crane that sometimes waited for him on his lab table in Mr. Brightside's classroom.

A little bird told me, Mr. Brightside had said. Cassidy had biology the period before Ash did.

"It was you all along," Ash said.

Cassidy bit her lip and nodded. "But when we were in the abandoned house today, and you threw away the crane and said it was nothing—"

"I'm so sorry." Mortification shivered through Ash's bones. "I said that because the only gifts that could ever mean anything to me would be ones from you, and I didn't think you knew I existed."

Cassidy laughed, the golden mask bouncing on her face with the rhythm.

But then she got quiet and reached tentatively for Ash's hands. Her fingers trembled as they met his. "I thought *you* didn't know *I* existed."

She kept talking, in a rushed whisper. "Ash, I've known about you since the day our U-Haul pulled up in the driveway and you were at your mailbox. I play so much soccer and basketball in my backyard to be closer to you and your studio. At school, I know you always eat with True and Onny under the persimmon tree by the library, and you always give them whatever they want from your lunch, even though it leaves you hungry.

"I know that when you get quiet, you're thinking. I know sometimes your fingers move in midair, because you're sketching or painting something you're imagining. I know you see colors in the world that others don't, just like I see small joys in life that others pass over. I already know you, Ash. And it only makes me want to know you even more."

Ash could hardly breathe. Happiness had a tight hold on his chest.

"But if you knew all that about me," he said, "why didn't you say anything?"

As if he weren't also guilty of not speaking up.

"Because," Cassidy said, "you and Onny and True are just . . . so cool and different."

Ash shook his head. "Believe me, we're different, but definitely *not* cool."

Cassidy shrugged. "Maybe it was the 'Founders' Fable' that brought us together, and it wouldn't have happened before tonight anyway."

Or maybe it was that Ash had finally been bold enough not only to wish, but also to act.

Speaking of which . . .

"Hey," he said. "I know you didn't want to go with me to the midnight gala, but would you consider changing your mind?"

"I might've lied then," she said, "because you threw my crane away."

"I swear I'm going into Skeleton Shack right now and digging that crane out of the puddle."

Cassidy squeezed his hand. "That'll give me time to change out of my pj's then."

Ash grinned. "So that's a yes?"

"That's a yes."

She pulled him down and kissed him, taking her time, as if she weren't afraid anymore that it was all a dream that would evaporate. Ash wrapped her in his cloak and held her closer.

If he could paint this moment, he thought Klimt would approve.

Perhaps there *was* something to the love potion. Or perhaps there wasn't.

But magic had worked its way into Halloween regardless . . . and it wasn't even midnight yet.

KISS TILL MIDNIGHT

*W*hy couldn't boys come with car parts instead of hearts? At the first sign of trouble, True could easily consult the *man*ual, change out the spark plug, and be on her way, every problem solved.

Human emotions, on the other hand, were completely unpredictable, liable to reduce you to a soggy pile of tears at a moment's notice. Case in point: True had had precisely *one* (1) serious boyfriend, and the detonation of that relationship had turned her heart into a nuclear wasteland. If you asked True Tandon, love was a giant scam.

Wait, no. She wasn't supposed to be thinking about Bradley Morris anymore. She'd promised Ash and Onny.

Taking a determined breath, True turned her attention to the transmission under the hood of her three-thousand-year-old Ford Focus. The Focus—or Miss Hocus-Pocus, as she'd lovingly nicknamed her, since she did, after all, cart around The Coven—was always breaking down. But Miss Hocus-Pocus had been close to free, which was what mattered. Her parents couldn't afford to buy her a car, but even if they *had* been able to, True would've wanted to buy it herself. She didn't like handouts.

She yanked on a bolt with too much force, crying out as her forearm jerked backward and hit the raised metal hood. "Ow!" True looked at her grease-coated arm, which would definitely be sporting a bruise by later that night. "I thought we were friends, Hocus." Sighing, she tossed her wrench on the concrete floor of the cool garage—which it met with a ringing, unhappy clang— and checked her phone.

It was well after 10 P.M. Time to get herself to Onny's "epic" Halloween party; any later and she might as well not go at all. True knew her lack of focus had everything to do with the party, in spite of her friends' optimistic rendering of the situation. Onny, being . . . well, Onny, had pontificated about how the quadricentennial only came once every four hundred years, and that it had special, magical properties that would help people—even people like True!—find their one true (pun intended) love.

True, in turn, had tried to explain the concept of time to her somewhat eccentric best friend. Four hundred years happened every four hundred years, thanks to Earth's orbit around the sun and a smart dude named Hipparchus, who proposed the twenty-four-hour day as we know it. It had nothing at all to do with magic or love or dead magical people in love.

Instead of being convinced by this infinitely rational argument, Onny brewed a supposedly magical love potion that she wanted True to drink at the party. Ha. That was never going to happen, not even if Onny and Ash knocked her out and tried to pour the thing down her throat. She'd make sure to swallow her tongue as she lost consciousness.

But the love potion and the party weren't the reason for True's unhappy mood. True lived in a town that was built on the specter of magic, and she accepted the midnight gala every year as a . . . unique part of living in a place like Moon Ridge. She even kinda liked how excited almost everyone—even (especially?) fully grown adults—got this time of year. The "Founders' Fable" may not be her thing, but Moon Ridge was her home, and she was weirdly fond of all its eccentricities and superstitions. Now that she thought about it, Moon Ridge was like that odd great-aunt at Christmas who drank too much and left her wig on the stove, almost setting your house on fire, but who also gave the best, most lavish presents.

This year, though . . . This year was different. This year, Bradley would be at the midnight gala as her *ex-boyfriend*. She could barely stand seeing him in the halls at school. How would she endure his heartbreakingly handsome face at the biggest social event of the year?

Two weeks ago, Onny had pulled True aside and asked if she wanted Bradley's family disinvited, but that had seemed too cruel a solution (though Onny had, of course, offered it only with fierce loyalty). The entire town would be there. True didn't want Bradley left out just because she couldn't handle her own broken heart. No, she'd just have to deal with it somehow. Show her face at the party, paste on a smile that looked somewhat convincing so she didn't ruin anyone's fun, and leave as soon as the clock struck midnight.

Right on cue, her cell beeped. She had a hard time getting to it with grease-stained hands, but after a few seconds of cartoon-level grappling, she opened up her text messages.

Onny: TRUEEEE this is the voice of your destiny summoning yOuUuUuUu! Come hither!!! Also I need you on the dance floor so plz don't bail on me / ily / bye!

Ash: Am I a joke to you? I'm here too.

Onny: Where??? Nm I'll find you laterrrrr.

Onny: True??

True: Sorry, sighed so hard I blew my phone away.

Onny: ARE YOU ON YOUR WAY

True: Almost, Queen Onny! This peasant must first wash the grease off her tired skin, which she acquired from her hard toiling and manual labor on yonder motorcoach

Onny: FINE I'LL ALLOW IT

Ash: Onny bought CASES of Dr P for you. I saw them stacked in the kitchen. Like, at least 6 cases

True: Lol no way

Onny: ~*~Needed to take extra precautions to lure a True beast out of the darkness.~*~

Laughing a little, True walked to the garage door and entered her house, kicking off her work boots and letting down her long black hair as she went. Her parents were already at Onny's party, although they, too, were reluctant participants. Her mom, the fifth daughter of German immigrants, was an accountant's assistant, and her dad, the only son of his Indian American parents, was an insurance agent (which explained True, who'd been born with a calculator for a heart). Needless to say, "magical midnight galas" weren't on the Tandons' list of necessities.

To be honest, True didn't know why her parents went to the Diamantes' parties every year; her mom and dad were as antisocial as she was. Maybe they thought they were setting a better example for her and that they'd inspire her to somehow become a social butterfly.

The thought led to some mirthful snorting as she crossed into the minuscule kitchen. After scrubbing her grease-stained arms off at the sink (good thing her mom wasn't there to see), True walked into her bedroom and reached into her closet for her costume. If she was going to Onny's magical horrorscope of a party and facing the boy who'd broken her heart, she would go as a powerful female scientist.

It was her way of staging a protest.

※ ※ ※

"Oh my god, Truuuuuuue!!! You're here! You're late, but you're here!!"

Onny catapulted into True's arms, nearly sending them toppling into a purple-lit ice sculpture of—what *was* that? A bouquet of flowers? A swan? A woman with an axe embedded in her icy skull? Knowing Onny, any of those were equally likely—of *something* behind them. It was kinda hard to see through the mask Ash had made for her (though the mask itself was beautiful; even True, who had no eye at all for art, could see that).

"Told you I'd come. I mean, the peasant hath arrived." True held Onny away at arm's length and looked her over. She was dressed in Renaissance-era clothing as the serial killer Erzebet Báthory, and looked, as always, like a high-fashion High Priestess from an ornate tarot deck. (True had learned what The High Priestess was through Onny-osmosis. Being Onny's friend probably made her the most enlightened skeptic this side of the Mississippi.)

"You look happier than usual," True continued, her deep-brown eyes narrowing while her mouth twitched with contained laughter. "Did you sage your room and get high off the fumes again?"

Onny chortled. "No! I'm just starting to realize . . . Look, it doesn't matter." Her eyes darted shiftily behind her golden mask to Byron Frost, who was dressed as some sort of snotty English guy and was helping himself to blood-red punch. "Yet." She turned her attention back to True just as Ash came sauntering up dressed in all gold and black as the Klimt man (though True was sure he'd used more poetic phrasing than that when he'd described his costume to her), grinning behind his own mask. "But check this out—Ash and I just noticed."

Onny dragged True over to a nearby picture window and pulled back the heavy gold curtain. Confused, True adjusted her mask to get a better look at the massive garden, all bedecked for the night. Ash ghosted up to them and stood on her other side. "Um . . . nice . . . hedges?" said True. "I really like the net lighti—"

"Not the hedges!" Onny said, a little breathless, while Ash chuckled. "Look up at the sky!"

Not wanting to agitate Onny even more (she was clearly going through something), True dutifully did as she was asked. The full moon shone like a silver ball, flanked by a solitary golden star. "Huh. Pretty."

Onny groaned and clutched her head, while Ash continued to watch in mirth. "No, not pretty!"

Ash cleared his throat. "Maybe I can help. True, do you remember what the legend says about the founders? How they're twin stars in the sky?"

True had a vague memory of Onny talking about that at some point. It winked back into relevance. "Oh yeah. When they died, their love was so strong that they became stars in the sky, watching over the town forever, or something?"

Onny's eyes glinted feverishly behind her mask. "*Exactly*," she said, leaning in close to True. "But look up there." She jabbed her finger at the window. "There's only *one* star—the Gentleman of Moon Ridge. Where, pray tell, is the Lady's star?"

True squinted up at the sky. The mask was obliterating half her field of vision. ". . . Maybe it's hiding behind a cloud or something?"

"No!" Onny shook her head emphatically. "*Absolument* not. You know why? Because of the *other*, rarely spoken-about part of the 'Founders' Fable.'"

True looked from Onny to Ash. "Uh-huh. Which says . . . ?"

"Every so often, on a special anniversary," Ash explained, "the Lady of Moon Ridge is supposed to descend from the skies to impart a lesson on true love to those who need it most. Onny thinks she might be here, walking among us tonight."

Onny nodded frantically. "In fact, I wasn't going to say anything until I was sure, but . . ." She leaned in close to them again. "Guys, I think I saw her. Earlier, me and Byron were outside grabbing . . . air?"

True frowned. Was Onny *blushing*? Innnnteresting. True knew Onny had a hate-hate relationship with Byron (well, usually) but True herself had always had a grudging respect for the guy, though she'd never expressed it out of loyalty for Onny. Any skeptical, scientific mind stood out like a shining centrifuge in Moon Ridge.

"ANYWAY, and I totally saw someone! With a long white dress! And a creepy vibe!"

True composed her facial features so they were perfectly blank. "Someone in a creepy dress . . . on Halloween. What a concept."

Ash twisted his fingers together, his forehead creased above his mask. "No, I . . . I think I saw something, too, True. For real."

True cleared her throat, realizing she wasn't going to win this one. "I totally believe you guys believe you saw her. So, um, yeah. I'll keep an eye out for her, and at any sign of ghostly shenanigans . . . I'll do my most killer Krav Maga move!" She demonstrated said move as best she could in her long dress. "That ghost doesn't stand a chance. Okay?"

Onny and Ash each raised an eyebrow, obviously unimpressed.

True tried again. "Or I'll . . . throw some salt at her? That's a thing people do, right?" She'd seen it on an episode of *Supernatural* once, when she was trying to find something to watch on TV.

Ash laughed. "Well, you get points for trying. You don't have to *do* anything, though, True. We just want you to be aware. You know. In case you see her."

Right. True seeing a ghost tonight was right up there possibility-wise with her seeing a polar bear floating by on a glacier, or Bradley getting down on one knee and proposing to her. But she didn't share her doubts with her friends. "Okay," she said, instead. "Thanks for, um, the warning."

With a knowing look, Onny changed the subject to something else she loved talking about as much as witchy things— True's (nonexistent) love life. "So. You're going to find someone new tonight, yes? That *is* the plan?"

True rolled her eyes and pulled a strand of hair from behind her mask, where it had become trapped. Like her, at this party. "Yeah, I'm going to find someone. Preferably someone who once ate my entire copy of *On the Origin of Species* and then puked it up page by page." She looked around. "Speaking of, where's Igor?"

"Prowling around outside. Igor can't be trusted around the

paper flowers. Or most humans," Onny added thoughtfully. Then, leaning in: "But really, True, you should open your mind—"

"Don't let Onny pressure you," Ash cut in, adjusting the horns on True's bronze mask. "Have I mentioned this looks incredible on you? You're like a sculpture that just walked off Rodin's *Gates of Hell*. Is it comfortable?"

True smiled at her sweet, soft cousin. "Yeah. It's wicked cool, Ash. Thanks again for making these for us. I mean, we all know my usual aesthetic is more gas mask than carnival mask, but even *I* look awesome in this."

"True that." Onny laughed and touched her own mask, the most ornate of all. "I *love* mine, you guys. It just makes all of this seem so much more, I don't know, what's the word?"

"Moon Ridge Madness-y?" True said, at the same time that Ash said, "Moon Ridge Magical?"

They looked at each other and laughed. "Don't worry." Ash, clearly sensing her discomfort, put an arm around her. True was only five feet tall (okay, so she was actually four feet eleven, but she'd like to see anyone stop her from claiming that last one inch), and Ash, at six three, towered almost comically over her. "You'll feel a lot better once you find your magical midnight match. Maybe with some luck from the Lady of Moon Ridge."

True sighed as she looked around the place. "I appreciate your optimism, but I don't think that's going to happen. At least I haven't run into you-know-who yet, though." She paused. "Your house looks really amazing, by the way. You guys really outdid yourselves this year, Onny."

"Thanks," her friend replied, looking genuinely pleased at the compliment.

True wasn't lying: the Diamantes' mansion was all done up, with enchanted, glowing trees blooming in the massive living room, den, and kitchen. Purple and gold spotlights illuminated enormous, vibrant bouquets of flowers (of both the paper and botanical variety) scattered over gleaming surfaces. Glitter lights sparkled and danced where she least expected them, flitting in and out of her peripheral vision like bashful fairies.

The house was steeped in manufactured magic, and as she studied the guests and their borrowed identities—like they'd all shapeshifted for the night—True felt a tingle of superstition that she doused by grabbing the empty test tube in her pocket. Chemistry. Physics. The natural world. *These* were things she believed in. There was no magic present tonight, no matter what everyone else in town might believe.

"But seriously, True," Onny continued, drawing her attention again. "This could be *it* for you tonight. This could be *it* for all of us." Her eyes sparkled with secrets.

True raised an eyebrow. "According to your tea-leaf reading, my soul mate carries the 'moon on his chest'—remember? But considering the moon weighs 7.35×10^{22} kilograms, I'd say I'm screwed. Unless the message was that I'm supposed to fall in love with the universe or something." She narrowed her eyes. "Which I wouldn't put past Onny."

"No, no," Onny said gaily, slinging an arm around True's waist. A pause, and then: "But you *did* bring the love potion with you, right? Just in case?"

Unable to hold back a half smile at her friend's enthusiasm, True reached into her other dress pocket and pulled out a different delicate glass bottle, this one with an ornate silver stopper. Inside, a pale pink liquid undulated like a mini ocean wave. It was a metaphor for her life in Moon Ridge and with The Coven: in one pocket, science, and in the other, magic.

"Yes, Onny," True intoned, like a wayward pupil answering a teacher.

"Good," Onny replied. "Just keep it on you, okay? And only drink it with the one you're sure about. You're definitely going to find a man tonight . . . like, a solid, mortal man. I can feel it in my marrow."

"'A solid, mortal man'?" True threw her hands in the air. "There goes my centaur dream." At Onny's severe look (though Ash was chuckling softly), she rearranged her features into something more serious and slipped the potion back into her pocket. "Okay, fine. Well, clearly people are trying to get your attention," she added, when Ash and Onny's gazes drifted away from her to Cassidy and Byron, respectively. "I'll catch up with you guys later?"

Onny kissed her cheek, under the mask. "Yes, sounds good! Love ya!" She danced away, mingling into the crowd.

Ash squeezed True's shoulder. "Relax." He smiled softly. "Your shoulders are up by your temples."

True shoved him lightly. "Go. Your Cassidy awaits."

Blushing, he drifted off. True watched him for a minute, her heart squeezing with love for both him and Onny. She wanted nothing more than for her best friends—really more like the siblings she'd never had—to find lasting, forever love tonight. Even if the possibility of that happening for her was an absolute, unforgiving zero.

Sighing, her hands wrapped protectively around her torso, True turned and surveyed the laughing, teeming, writhing crowd of people. Onny thought True's soul mate would be here tonight. But True was pretty sure you had to have a soul to have a soul mate, and she was 99 percent sure souls were a fabrication of a prescientific, medievalist society.

But you know what wasn't? Sugar. And also: caffeine. She made her way to the drinks table for a Dr Pepper.

True lounged on the Diamantes' emerald-green tufted sofa in the enormous, high-ceilinged living room currently overrun by teenagers (but thankfully not a Bradley in sight) and a very few unlucky adults. Among them were her cadaverous biology teacher Mr. Brightside, who, much to almost everyone's surprise, had captured the heart of the much happier, sunnier Mayor Grimjoy.

It made sense to True, though. *There were two kinds of people in the world: The Mr. Brightsides and the Mayor Grimjoys,* she thought, as she took a sip of her crisp, cold Dr Pepper. (Bless Onny and her bribing ways.)

Take Lisa O'Malley-Richardson, for instance. She was totally a Mayor Grimjoy. True studied the girl over her can of soda. Lisa was a junior, like True, and was currently bumbling around in the adjoining dining room dressed as a fortune cookie, desperately trying to hand out fortunes she'd no doubt handwritten with a *lot* of thought, to teenagers who couldn't care less. Even True felt a little sad for her.

As if sensing her stare, Lisa looked over at True, her face briefly lighting with a smile. True smiled in return and then, without warning, Lisa was lurching over, a fortune held out in her hand.

"For you," she said, once she was close enough for True to hear. She was still smiling that happy, energetic smile. "A fortune."

"Um, thanks." True glanced down at the strip of paper Lisa had written a message on: *Believe in the magic of possibility.* True's smile grew strained. The only magical possibility she wanted to believe in was that Onny's parents might declare the party over right now instead of at midnight so True's chances of running into Bradley would be reduced to zero.

"Hope it helps you on your journey!" Lisa waved peppily and then stumbled off.

True crumpled up the fortune, tossed it behind the couch so Lisa wouldn't find it later and be hurt, and continued her musings.

The Mr. Brightsides of the world—and True counted herself among them—were skeptical, not easily impressed, and not unlikely to be found digging shallow midnight graves for unknown purposes. The Mayor Grimjoys of the world, on the other hand, tended to be foolishly happy, loved to make friends with strangers, and didn't have a concept of boundaries.

And *sometimes*, defying all reason, the Mr. Brightsides and Mayor Grimjoys got together and things just . . . clicked.

"Hi!"

True looked up at the voice to see a suspiciously handsome guy about her age, with sandy-brown hair, smiling down at her as if she were a pygmy goat at a petting zoo. He had amber-brown eyes, almost golden in the glittering lights of the party, and he was way taller than her—probably close to six feet. He appeared to be dressed like Robin Hood or some other woodsy character, complete with a heavy-looking bow-and-arrow set he held easily in one hand.

If there was one thing history had taught True—and she was a *very* good student—it was that packages that gorgeous were usually filled with all the evils of the world. Kind of a Pandora's box situation in a human-boy suit.

Perhaps misinterpreting her ominous, meant-to-be-discouraging silence as an invitation, Cute Woodsy Boy thrust one big hand at her. "Orion Parker. I go to North Pointe." Which explained why she didn't know him; True went to Moon Ridge High. When she didn't take his hand, the alarmingly friendly Orion Parker flopped down on the couch beside her, so close that their thighs were almost touching. Never mind that the whole entire left side of the couch was empty. "So! Who are you?"

True continued staring straight ahead. She wasn't going to make this mistake again. Bradley had been a lesson—a painful, heinous one—she didn't intend to relearn.

It had been almost a year since they'd broken up. Months and months of being alone and feeling less than, and having the torment of seeing her first and only boyfriend (ugh, *ex*-boyfriend) in the hallway at school holding hands with other girls. He'd moved on, like, instantly after the breakup. And just last week, he'd looked at her pityingly at lunch and said, in front of all his friends, "It's been, what, like a year and a half?" (It had been ten months. Jerk.) "Let me know if you want me to set you up with someone else. You need to move on from me, True."

As if she were pining away after him, sobbing hysterically into her pillow while clutching a tiny plastic model of him (True liked to 3D-print stuff). She'd frozen at lunch but had come up with a million cutting responses later, like, "I've moved on to finally having some peace in my life, douchebag." Okay, so maybe that wasn't very cutting. But still. It was *something*, and something was better than shocked silence, which was all she'd been capable of then.

Now True thought that maybe if she went really quiet and still, this Orion guy would get bored and move on. Like a predator losing interest in prey that camouflaged itself. The seconds oozed awkwardly by, and when True finally cut her eyes sideways at him, he was still looking unabashedly at her, a beautiful, bright smile on his face, as if he just knew she was about to spill all the glorious secrets of the universe onto his lap. An eternal optimist, then.

Sighing, knowing she wouldn't get rid of him easily, True turned to him. "True Tandon. Aria, really, but no one calls me that."

"True." He said the word slowly, his lips drawing into a kiss-shaped pout as he finished. True blinked and looked away. He had nice lips. Bow-shaped. Aesthetically pleasing. But Bradley had once told her she had a "formidable" gaze and that she stared at people too intensely. True had scoffed at him, pretended like it didn't bother her that he'd said that, but it had hurt.

The thing was, she didn't *always* want to be formidable. Sometimes she just wanted to be adored. But the problem was, she didn't have an "off" switch. She was always on, always observing, always sharp. And maybe that had been too much for Bradley. Maybe that was too much for any guy.

"What a fantastic name!" Orion paused. "But I actually meant who are you *tonight*, as in, your costume." He gestured to her mask and then at her old-fashioned, long-sleeved dress.

"Oh." True sat up straighter so he could see more of her costume, wondering if he'd get it. Ash and Onny thought it was very "Trueish" of her, whatever that meant. "Okay, so, I'm wearing a mask that's kind of *scary.* . . ." She pulled the test tube from her pocket and held it out. ". . . And I run a highly specialized laboratory."

"Hmm . . ." Orion turned sideways to look at her fully, his thick blond eyebrows knitting together. He propped an elbow on the back of the couch as he thought. Then, his expression brightening, he exclaimed, "Wait, wait, wait . . . Marie Scary!"

True shrugged, secretly impressed, and slipped the potion back into her pocket. "Pretty close—Marie S-curie."

Orion laughed appreciatively and relaxed against the couch, still turned sideways so he could see her. He pulled his long legs up onto the couch, but even sitting, he towered over her, blocking out the big painting on the wall behind him. It made her feel . . . ensconced. And small. True wasn't sure how she felt about that. "I like that. Marie S-curie. So I'm guessing you're into science, then."

"Science, tech, fixing things . . . anything that's tangible and provable."

Orion pulled back a little, giving her a rakish smile that made her stomach feel like she'd swallowed a helium balloon. Ridiculous. "So you don't believe in the magic of the quadricentennial? The 'Founders' Fable'? Even though the Lady of Moon Ridge's star seems to be magically missing from the sky?"

Before she answered, a group of seniors began suddenly shrieking over something they'd found floating in the pitcher of homemade juice Mr. Brightside had brought. (It was probably just one of his special touches, like frozen grapes made to look like eyeballs, or baby carrots painted with homemade indelible jam to look like decapitated fingers. And yeah, he'd totally put carrots and jam into his juice—Mr. B committed 150 percent when he was going for macabre.)

When the chaos had died down a bit, True spoke again. "Not even a little bit." She leaned forward over her fizzing can of Dr Pepper, her eyes beckoning Orion. He leaned in closer in response, ready to hear whatever she had to say. This close, she could see that his eyelashes were lighter toward the tips, sun-bleached, and she could smell him—citrus soap and a spicy, warm deodorant. True took a breath, turning her wayward thoughts back to the present conversation. "You know what happens every four hundred years?"

Orion's lighter eyes were trained on her dark ones, his lips just slightly parted, as if he were hanging on her every word. "No." True's stomach swooped, actually swooped, as if she were on a roller coaster, at his low, rumbly voice. *Wtf, body?* "What?"

Quietly, True replied, "We can say four hundred more years have passed." She cocked an eyebrow while she waited for that to sink in, and added, in a normal voice, "That's it. Four more centuries have gone by, as they're supposed to, because that's the way time works. Nothing magical, nothing special, just the human need to attach significance to insignificant things. Not that there's anything wrong with that, if it's your thing. It's just . . . not really my thing." She sat back and took a swig of her soda. A moment later, uncertainty hit. She studied Orion's expression while nibbling on her lower lip. This was the exact kind of thing Bradley would've called her out on before telling her to relax.

Orion didn't move. But he didn't look like he was offended or annoyed, either. "Wow," he said after a minute, running a hand through his hair. It flopped back in a perfectly thick, blond wave onto his forehead. "So you don't believe in anything you can't see or prove scientifically?" He seemed genuinely interested in her answer.

A catchy pop song began to play over the state-of-the-art sound system Onny's parents installed a week ago. True, Ash, and Onny had broken it in with an epic karaoke jam session the first night it was put in. Ah, simpler times.

Now True frowned at Orion's question. "Of course not. Why would I?"

"Many reasons." Orion's tone was light as he drummed his fingers on the back of the couch. He adjusted his legs so his knees were pressed very lightly against True's leg, though she didn't think he knew that. Her lab coat and dress were voluminous enough that it was hard to tell where they ended and True began. She considered moving, but . . . didn't. Orion held up long fingers as he listed each reason. "To maintain a sense of wonder and mysticism about the universe. To acknowledge that humans don't have all the answers, even though we like to think we do. To tip our heads back and look at the stars and imagine the magic and havoc they play in our lives."

Uh-oh. Had she offended him? She hadn't meant to, but it was sometimes hard to contain the truth-spouting disease she suffered from. True glanced around at the party happening in full swing around them. People were gyrating to music all over Onny's gigantic living room and kitchen (and more were down in the basement, the official nexus of debauchery); a few were playing various drinking games away from the watchful eyes of adults, and the giant metal wall clock told her it was just past eleven o'clock. She could leave at midnight; Onny had promised her she didn't have to stay beyond that. Less than sixty minutes. That was hardly any time at all. And bonus: Bradley had yet to make an appearance. Maybe they'd miss each other all night and True could go home a happy woman.

She supposed she could get up and go talk to someone else for a bit before she unintentionally offended Orion Parker some more, but she needed to pace herself. If True hurried off every time someone talked to her about magic or the quadricentennial anniversary, she'd run out of people to converse with in about sixteen seconds flat. She could talk to this worryingly cute, albeit thoroughly unscientific dude for a few more minutes before she ran away. The trick was to change the subject to a less controversial topic.

She bobbed her head at his costume, which came with a bow and arrow that he'd set neatly beside him on the couch. "What are you, Cupid?"

A flash of hurt played across Orion's face, like lightning across a stormy sky. "Actually," he said stiffly, gathering his bow and arrow, "I'm pretty intelligent. But I can take a hint. If you want me to go—"

She grabbed his (*wow, strong*) forearm before she could process what she was doing. "No, wait." True leaned toward him and spoke loudly, over the thumping, roiling music. "I didn't call you stupid. I said *Cupid*. You know, your costume." She pointed to his bow and arrow. It occurred to her in the next moment that she could've just let him go. Huh. She didn't know why, exactly, she'd asked Orion to stay. Or why it had bothered her that he seemed hurt, or why she was explaining herself to him.

Orion glanced at the bow and arrow, and then his face relaxed, his eyes turning bright and happy again. "Ohhhh." He shook his head, the bridge of his nose crinkling in mirth. "*Totally* misheard you there."

True found herself staring at him brazenly, her soda forgotten, before she caught herself. Her hand tightened around the cold can, crumpling it a little. *Get yourself together, Tandon. Jesus. Do you want another boy-sized hole in your heart?* No, she did not, thank you very much. She didn't know how much perforation a heart could take before it ceased being a heart completely, and she wasn't in any hurry to find out.

True cleared her throat and took a drink, keeping her voice coolly casual. "So, anyway, what are you?"

Orion gestured to his costume, which was comprised of a brown top, pants, boots, and a brown belt. "I actually took this off because it kept falling off," he said, pulling a pin out of his pocket and pinning it to his chest, "but the costume makes more sense with it on." The pin was the classic Ghostbusters symbol, with a white ghost in the center and a red circle with a line through it.

"Ghost-busting?" True frowned. "But with a bow and arrow?"

"Well, my name is Orion." He smiled and put his hands on his slim waist, his shoulders all broad and pleasing, as if he were posing for a very cheesy but very hot senior photo. "Who, in Greek mythology, is—"

"The hunter," True finished, playing with the tab on her soda can. "And the Ghostbusters pin . . . oh. You're a ghost hunter."

"Ding ding ding!" Orion took a seated mock bow. "You got it."

"But I *don't* get it," True said, shaking her head. "Why are you dressed like—"

The words dissipated from her suddenly dry mouth like fog burning up in the sun. True sat up straighter and blinked, looking into the dimly lit mudroom, which lay beyond the dining room and kitchen to her left.

A female figure hovered there. She wore a crown of pumpkins and flowers, and long blond hair fell in waves to her waist. Her pale skin seemed to glow as if lit from within, and she was dressed in a long wedding dress the color of moonlight. The hem of the dress floated about four inches off the floor.

What?

At first True thought it was a special effect Onny's parents had bought to make the party more Halloween-y. It *had* to be. But then . . . why had no one else noticed the figure? People were standing, like, six feet from her.

There had to be a logical explanation. True's mind flew through the possibilities in .03 seconds: swamp gas, electrical malfunction, northern lights, carbon monoxide poisoning—

And then the figure looked directly at True, her eyes glowing a sudden, intense, manic blue.

True gasped and, without thinking, clutched Orion's hand. "Do you see that?"

"What?" he asked, whipping his head around.

"There, in the mudroom."

But then she blinked, and the figure was gone. Orion turned back to her, frowning. "I don't see anything. What is it?"

Coming to her senses at his words, True quickly yanked her hand away and took a shaky sip of her Dr Pepper. "Nothing. I thought I saw someone but . . . I, uh, obviously imagined it." Moon Ridge Madness was definitely getting to her. Social contagion. Folie à deux. "Just a trick of the light or something."

Orion's lips lifted in a lopsided smile that made True's heart go *thud*. "Or was it a ghost?"

For just a split second, Onny's and Ash's words flashed through her mind, how they said they'd seen the Lady of Moon Ridge tonight. And then she remembered that Onny and Ash had once made themselves sick by drinking a dubious nettle tea they'd bought online that was supposed to "lift the veil and illuminate the presence of fairies in the woodland," and she got ahold of herself.

True gave Orion a weak smile. *Do not truth-spout. Don't be the annoying skeptic at a magical midnight gala.* Before she could think of a suitably diplomatic response to his question, though, she was interrupted.

"OP, my man!"

They both turned at the exuberant male voice. It belonged to Isaiah Akinde, a Nigerian American football player who True knew also attended North Pointe, the private high school Orion went to. True wasn't popular enough to run in the circles that included Isaiah, but she'd witnessed enough Moon Ridge High students swoon over him to know who he was. Plus, he and Onny were good friends.

"Isaiah!" Orion got up from the couch and one-arm hugged his friend, who clapped him on the back. Isaiah was dressed in all black—a tight black T-shirt hugged his muscular frame, while black pants fell from his slim hips, and black boots clad his giant feet. His tongue out as he grinned, Isaiah turned around to show the back of his T-shirt to Orion. A message in glow-in-the-dark letters said GHOST ADVENTURES.

"You went with the Zak Bagans costume!" Orion exclaimed, as Isaiah turned back around. "Nice."

"I like yours." Isaiah nodded appreciatively. "I think our whole group's representing well. Tyler and Priya are around here somewhere, too, dressed like Ed and Lorraine Warren."

"Excellent." Orion laughed, and then his gaze snagged on

True. "Oh, hey. Do you know each other? True, meet Isaiah. He's a senior at North Pointe, like me. Isaiah, this is True, aka Marie S-curie."

"Nice to meet you," Isaiah said, just as True said, "We've already met."

They stared at each other for a second, the air stiff with awkward energy.

"It's okay," True said, finally, releasing Isaiah from the prison of his social faux pas. "I'm Onny's friend; that's how I know you."

Isaiah's face brightened at the mention of their mutual friend. "Oh yeah, Onny's great."

There was a pause while they all smiled at each other in that super-fun, stilted way people do when they don't know what else to say but also don't know how to extricate themselves.

Setting her soda can on the coffee table, True stood; her neck was beginning to hurt from looking up at the two tall guys. Also, it was a way to distract from the cringey silence Isaiah had somehow added to her and Orion's twosome.

Not that, they were, you know, a twosome. Or a couple. Or an anything, really.

"So why are you guys all dressed like ghost hunters, anyway? You mentioned a . . . group? Are you in a band or something?" If they started talking to her about their band, True could kill another twenty minutes easy, thus inching her closer to freedom.

"No." Orion and Isaiah exchanged a laughing look before Orion turned to look down at her. "We're in a group called the Ghost Boosters. We investigate paranormal phenomena. We have a pretty big YouTube following."

"Six hundred eighteen subscribers and counting as of this morning," Isaiah put in, hooking his thumbs in his pockets. "We should get a big bump after we upload our Halloween episode. We spent the night at Moon Ridge Cemetery last night. Got some primo footage of a full-body apparition. We're thinking it's the Lady of Moon Ridge, rising for the quadricentennial. Her star's missing, so it makes sense."

Except it didn't. If her star was missing, shouldn't she have *fallen* from the *sky* rather than risen from the ground? True looked from Orion to Isaiah and then back again. She didn't think they'd appreciate her logic.

"Right," she said instead, in what she hoped was a neutral way.

Ghosts. A paranormal investigator. True may have let herself believe for a moment that she'd seen something inexplicable earlier, but now that her brain had settled down, she knew the figure had to have an explanation based in science. On the other hand, Orion and Isaiah seemed to have no such compunctions about whatever *they'd* seen last night.

It was clear she was out of her depth; kudos to them for chasing their dreams—or spooky nightmares—but she needed to disentangle herself posthaste. A scientific mind could only take so much talk of the supernatural before it combusted spontaneously. Maybe she could sequester herself in Onny's parents' library for the remainder of the evening. *Maybe* she could even find Igor and snuggle with him by the fire (she'd just have to keep an eye on him and make sure he didn't decide to get all dominant and mark Onny's dad's wall of rare books as his territory). For the first time all evening, True felt almost cheerful.

But Orion was still speaking, oblivious to her hatching escape plan. "It's pretty cool. We've even got all the equipment—you know, the EMF meter, the night-vision cameras, the Spirit Box. . . ."

True managed to keep her voice light as she asked the next question, which was kind of amazing, considering she was slowly but surely dying inside. "The Spirit Box? You mean the device that streams radio channels?" She'd read an insightful (and damning) article about those in *Scientific American* recently, though she knew this wasn't the crowd to share that tidbit.

"Yeah! You know it?" Orion looked inordinately pleased that she did.

"I'm . . . acquainted with its properties, yes."

Beaming, Orion continued talking while Isaiah watched their exchange with interest. "Well, the spirits can manipulate the radio frequencies to communicate with us. We've gotten some legit amazing messages from the beyond like that."

True stared at his face—the square jaw, the earnest golden-brown eyes, the effortlessly glorious hair. Maybe he was technically a hottie, but they had literally nothing in common, not even small-talk-level stuff. Unless she wanted to spend the rest of the evening watching videos of ghosts and gargoyles, she should make her escape now.

"That's pretty cool." True made a show of checking her phone. "Oh, shoot!" Looking apologetically at Orion and Isaiah, she hooked a thumb over her shoulder. "I just got a text from Ash, my cousin. He needs me. So I should probably—"

There was a sudden, bone-chilling shriek from the deep

caverns of the den. "Oh my god!" someone shouted. "I found a dead body!"

Mr. Brightside yelled, in response, "Leave her alone! She's mine!"

True raised her eyebrows, turned, and hurried toward the melee, Orion close on her heels.

When she got to the far corner of the den, Mr. Brightside was fussing over what looked very much like the deceased body of a woman, dressed up as a witch. He, in turn, was dressed up as the Moon King, an elaborate silver mask from Ash obscuring half his face. The skin that was visible had been painted the color of bleached bone.

"This is Wicked Wynona," he was saying severely to the gathered group of students, some of whom looked dangerously close to passing out. "She does *not* like to be bothered."

"What *is* that thing?"

The question came from Aiden, a football player and close friend of Bradley's. True's heart thumped erratically as she looked around, ready to catch Bradley's eye, ready to feel the sting of his trademark smirk. What should she say to him? But she couldn't spot him in the throng of students surrounding Mr. Brightside.

Mr. B turned slowly to survey Aiden down the length of his crooked, bony nose, his eyes narrowed. "I got *her* from an antique shop in Twilight Grove. She's a papier-mâché mannequin from the early 1900s. She's surprisingly heavy; the craftmanship is top notch." Stroking the bright-red, very tangled, rat's nest of a mane on the mannequin's head, he added, almost lovingly, "And this is real human hair. Some say she even has actual human teeth, though that's disputed."

There was a gasp from around the room. Some of the girls huddled into their boyfriends, who looked just as freaked out as they did.

Mr. Brightside smiled knowingly. "The reason I got her, though, is because I was told there was a legend attached to her. Apparently, if you brush her hair for ten strokes, you can whisper a wish into her shriveled little ear and she grants it." He looked around the room, and his gaze lit on True. "Aha, True, one of my best students. A true woman of science! Almost didn't recognize you in that mask, but those discerning brown eyes give you away every time. Now I know *you* want to try it, don't you? If only to test this most intriguing hypothesis?"

True exchanged glances with Orion, who looked utterly baffled. She'd have to explain Mr. Brightside's ways to him later. Turning back to her completely loony teacher, True replied, "Well, I'd love to . . . except I don't have a brush."

Mr. Brightside's smile grew even wider. "Well, well, well. Look what I found." His long, wan hand slipped into his jacket pocket and pulled out an old boar-bristle hairbrush, which he held out to True.

The crowd held still, waiting to see what she'd do. Biting her lip to keep from laughing, True walked forward. She had a feeling Mr. Brightside had concocted this entire bizarre story just so he could find gullible people to get Wicked Wynona looking pristine again.

Taking the brush from her teacher, True leaned closer to him and spoke quietly. "Let me guess: you want to add her to that diorama on your front lawn, don't you? That's what this 'getting people to brush her hair' thing is all about?"

Mr. Brightside's Cheshire cat smile grew even wider. He had painted his teeth to look all rotten and gross, and the effect was unsettling. "Whatever do you mean? I don't have a diorama. I'm just storing those things on my lawn . . . indefinitely. And before you ask, what people call my 'poison garden' is simply a botanical repertoire."

True cocked an eyebrow. "Really. So the lifelike wax statue of Lavinia Fisher, the tapir skull, and the supposedly possessed rag doll just happened to fall in a neatly arranged pile around that antique coffin?"

Mr. Brightside chuckled deep in his throat, the sound like a thousand bees buzzing. "My dear True. One day you'll understand why the night calls to me so strongly. Now. Will you do the honors?" He gestured to the mannequin, bedecked in the ugliest green paisley scarf and skull ring True had ever seen.

Snorting, she turned to Wicked Wynona and brushed her ratty red hair ten times. Then she gave Mr. Brightside a slightly admonishing smile. "Only for you, Mr. B. Only for you."

"What? You're not done yet! Go on." He made a shooing motion with his hand. "Whisper your innermost desires into her ear."

The crowd rippled with snickers.

Ugh, gross. Whispering into Wicked Wynona's desiccated ear wasn't on True's bucket list. But she knew Mr. Brightside. If she wanted to get out of this unscathed, she should just do it. Leaning forward toward the mannequin's ear, True whispered, too low for even Mr. Brightside to hear, "I wish the truth about this 'magical night' and the 'Founders' Fable' would come out once and for all." Then she stood back, handed the hairbrush back to Mr. Brightside, and nodded. "There."

As she turned to go, Mr. Brightside called, "That was marvelous, True! I can tell you're meant to be her keeper for the night."

Swinging around, True cocked her head. "Say what now?"

He thrust the hairbrush back into her hand before she could object and addressed the small crowd. "If *you'd* like to make a wish on this most magical evening, I suggest you form an orderly line. True here will be Wicked Wynona's protector the rest of the evening." Patting her once on the back, Mr. Brightside melted away into the farthest recesses of the party, his silver mask glittering like a smattering of stars across his face.

True sighed as the crowd began to move and writhe, people excitedly getting into line, laughing and poking fun at each other. This was *one* way to kill some time without having to make a lot of small talk, True supposed. Igor and the library would have to wait. She'd just give the brush to each person, let them do their thing, and keep the line moving.

"Mind if I join you as co-protector?"

Divested of his bow and arrow now, Orion had reappeared beside her, strong hands clamping around Wicked Wynona's torso and moving her into a more suitable position for the line of teenagers jostling for her to grant their wishes.

True shrugged, tugging at her bun self-consciously. "I mean, sure. If you really want to."

Orion said, solemnly, "It would be an honor to stand here with you, watching inebriated teenagers brush out this decrepit mannequin's human hair."

True snorted, impressed. "Was that a touch of sarcasm? Didn't think you had it in you, to be honest."

He smiled, as bright as his namesake. "I'm a man of multitudes, Miss Tandon. Stick with me, and I'll show you."

She knew he was joking, but still. In that moment, she *wanted* to stick with him, she found, if even just for a little bit longer.

Feeling a little discombobulated by that weird thought, the sheer wattage of his smile, and his familiar manner (it was starting to feel like she'd known Orion Parker for a while, instead of a matter of minutes), True looked away, pretending to need to adjust her mask. She fidgeted a lot around Orion, she noticed. "Ah, so. I guess the 'ghost' I saw was really just Wicked Wynona. She was probably stashed in the mudroom and I got confused about what I was looking at."

"Mm-hmm." Orion gave her an opaque look, as if he wasn't buying it. And truth be told, True's explanation didn't really make a lot of sense—she'd seen the figure glowing and floating; she'd seen its piercing blue eyes looking right at her. Wicked Wynona's eyes were a glassy, dull black, and her hair was red and gnarly. *And* she was wearing a shiny purple dress with a lurid green paisley scarf. The figure True had seen had been wearing a floaty silver dress with a flower-and-pumpkin crown on her blond head. Plus, Wicked Wynona was seriously heavy. She wasn't about to defy gravity anytime soon, like the mudroom figure had done. And lastly, Wicked Wynona had been in the den. True had seen the figure in the mudroom.

It bugged True that she hadn't arrived at a satisfactory explanation yet. If she could get to the mudroom, she might be able to take some soil samples for further testing to see if the intruder had come in from outside—

Her thoughts were interrupted by their first "customer," Jemma, a transfer student from England, who bit her lip as she considered Wicked Wynona. "There are just so many things I could ask for. Gosh, it's a bit intimidating, isn't it? What do *you* think I should wish for?"

True looked around and realized the girl was talking to her. As if she were any kind of expert on the supernatural. "Oh. Um . . . I don't know. Why don't you think about it quietly while you brush." She pushed the hairbrush into Jemma's small hands, and, looking slightly taken aback, Jemma did as True said.

Orion gave True a look she couldn't decipher. To Jemma, he said, kindly, "Usually, people make wishes about the big things in life: love, money, or health. Maybe that's helpful?"

Jemma smiled at him. "Yeah. It is, actually. Thank you."

When she'd brushed, whispered, and gone her way, True raised an eyebrow at Orion. "What?"

He shrugged, big shoulders moving in his costume shirt. "I think you try to push people away on purpose."

A group of seniors was next, all cackling and jostling each other. True handed one of them the brush and turned back to Orion. The seniors weren't paying attention to anything else besides themselves, so she didn't bother lowering her voice. "Duh. I'm not a fan, in case you haven't noticed."

Orion frowned. "Of?"

"Human interaction."

Orion crossed his arms and grinned at her. "See, I think that's just because you haven't met your person yet. The one who holds the key to unlock that heart of yours."

True broke eye contact, her cheeks burning. Not because Orion was semi-flirting with her (she *thought*; of course, she was illiterate in flirting and could be utterly, totally, and devastatingly wrong), but because she thought she *had* met her person, not too long ago. And she'd been—again—utterly, totally, and devastatingly wrong.

A couple she didn't know dressed as Cleopatra and Mark Antony came forward once the cackling seniors had left, and True handed Cleopatra the brush.

Surprising herself, she said to Orion, "That's not entirely accurate. I did meet someone, and I really, really liked him. And it ended hideously. You know why? Because boys suck. Dating sucks. Love sucks. It all *sucks*." Her fists clenched, and to her horror, True felt hot tears pricking at her eyes. Blinking furiously, she looked away.

Mark Antony gave her a look, then took his girlfriend's hand and left.

Orion cocked his head. "Hey." He waited until she met his eye again. The expression on his face was sympathetic, his golden-brown eyes warm and open. "I'm sorry. What was his name?"

"Bradley." She felt goose bumps on her arms just saying his

name out loud. She'd spent so long conditioning herself *not* to talk about him. Onny and Ash would never say it, but she knew they'd gotten pretty tired of hearing her dissect every last expression on Bradley's face when she passed him in the school halls. Now, talking about him felt . . . weird. Almost superstitious, like she was inviting trouble or more heartbreak into her life.

"Why didn't it work out between you two?"

There was no morbid curiosity on Orion's face, just genuine, compassionate interest. A group of students dressed as various Alice in Wonderland characters walked up, interrupting her before she could answer. They were likely from North Pointe; she didn't know them, but they all said hi to Orion, who spent a few moments chatting with them.

Using the distraction as an opportunity, True took a deep breath. In the background and in her chest, happy party music thumped, totally out of sync with how she was feeling.

Did she want to tell Orion the truth? She studied his profile; that sandy blond hair, the strong nose, the five o'clock shadow at his jawline. He was smiling easily, his eyes crinkled. The group of students looked as if they really liked him. Orion Parker, True could tell, was the kind of guy everyone got along with. The kind of guy who'd probably never say something mean and crusty like, "You know, True, you're too much. You might want to take it down a few notches," or "You know what your problem is? You're way too intense about everything. Calm down."

Orion was, in fact, the anti-Bradley. And that's why she decided to be completely honest with him.

When the Alice in Wonderland group was gone and the rest

of the line had mostly dissipated, he turned to her, opened his mouth—and that was it. True unleashed a veritable fire hydrant's worth of information about her and Bradley, without even stopping to consider if it was wise.

"Bradley and I went out for five months. It started out great. He was really smart and he liked fixing cars like I do, and he had this snarky sense of humor that really appealed to me."

If Orion was surprised by her rushed word vomit, he didn't show it. He just nodded, waiting for her to continue. So she did.

"But then, I don't know . . . something changed. The longer we spent time together, the more his snark kind of turned on me. And it wasn't funny snark anymore, it was mean. He rolled his eyes when I got passionate about something. He didn't want to hear my theories about why female mechanics are so rare anymore. He started telling me to stop being so . . ." True searched for the right word and then shrugged. ". . . So *me*, I guess." Her cheeks heated as she said it, remembering the burning humiliation of that moment. "He told me I was too . . . too everything. Too loud. Too opinionated. Too strong-willed. And the worst part was . . ." She swallowed, looking away, wondering if she should say it.

"What?" Orion asked, ducking his head to look at her, thick gold eyelashes framing gentle brown eyes. In the living room, someone broke something made of glass and people groaned. But Orion's attention stayed on her.

She met his eye again, over Wicked Wynona's bony shoulder. "The worst part was, I began to believe him." Taking a deep breath, True blew it out slowly. "I began to censor myself. I became self-conscious about the things I said, the books I was reading, even the way I looked at people. That's when I knew I had to step away. I was losing myself, and that wasn't okay."

Another thing that was so mind-screwy about this whole breakup: *True* had been the one to let go, to step back, to say enough was enough. She'd ended things to protect herself. And yet True was the one who'd been left heartbroken, while Bradley didn't seem to care one iota. It was confusing as hell. Love didn't follow the rules, and True wasn't sure what to do about that.

Orion let her words settle on the air before speaking. "What a shame that would be." When he saw her confused expression, he clarified, "Losing yourself. I mean, I've only known you a short time, but I think you're pretty badass, Marie S-curie." He grinned his lopsided grin, and True's pulse kicked up a beat.

Her cheeks aflame, she adjusted Wicked Wynona's sleeve that didn't need adjusting. "Thanks."

"Besides, I'm glad you broke up with him. 'Bradley'?" Orion did a theatrical shudder. "Ugh. I hate Brads. They're just Chads earlier in the alphabet."

True snorted. "Yeah, I guess that's true. You know, I—" True stopped, feeling someone's heavy gaze on her, as real as a hand.

She turned toward the kitchen. In the corner, behind a group of senior girls who were taking group selfies, she saw *her* again. The pale, glowing woman in the silver dress, with the piercing, unreal blue gaze. Those had to be contacts.

True kept her eyes on her, not wanting the woman to disappear again. "I'll be right back." Already walking away, she handed the hairbrush to Orion.

"Wait. Where are you going?" he called after her.

"Just a second."

True kept walking, her gaze pinned to the woman, who stared back. It was almost like looking at someone through a haze of smoke; the woman shimmered and fluttered, as if a stiff breeze would blow her away. True scanned the kitchen for possible explanations for the shimmer: there was a cauldron in the corner, bubbling away with fake smoke. It was pretty far away, but perhaps enough of the smoke had created a visual barrier?

True had just stepped into the kitchen to get a closer look at the whole situation when the group of senior girls crowded her on their way out. They were all taller than her, and in spite of her best efforts, True lost sight of the woman.

"Excuse me!" She tried to elbow her way through, but then another big group of hungry students stormed the kitchen from behind her and she was swallowed in the melee. By the time she broke free, panting and huffing with the effort, the woman was gone again. The corner was empty.

"Shoot." True poked around the kitchen anyway, trying to find her, but her efforts were in vain. She peeked out the kitchen window at the sky and saw it again—the solitary golden star by the moon. The Lady of Moon Ridge was still missing. A ripple of uncertainty moved through True.

She slipped her phone from her pocket.

True: This is going to sound totally weird, but I saw . . . something. A woman. And she was staring at me with these really creepy blue eyes.

It only took a moment for her friends to respond.

Onny: I told you!! I saw her, too!! It's definitely the Lady of Moon Ridge, you guys.

Ash: But what's she looking for? Did you try to talk to her, True?

True: I walked toward her but she disappeared into the crowd. Keep me posted if you guys see her again, and I'll do the same.

She slipped her phone back into her pocket just in time to hear Orion yell, "Hey! Stop!"

True rushed back into the dining room to see a group of muscular guys making off with Wicked Wynona. "What the hell do you think you're doing?" she yelled.

One of the guys turned to her with a cocky smile, dark hair flopping into his blue eyes. Her heart seized in her chest; it was Bradley, looking almost unbearably beautiful even though his "costume" was his actual football uniform. He knew what he looked good in (even the team name MOONBEARS on the back didn't detract from his muscularity), and he wasn't the kind of person to risk making a fool of himself for a party. Unlike True, who was dressed in the unsexiest costume she could've possibly wrangled up.

"Don't worry, True. We'll bring her back . . . at some point." Bradley laughed and looked her up and down. "By the way, nice dress. Going to a funeral in the 1800s later?" And then he turned and jogged back to his friends, who had melted away with Wicked Wynona.

"I'm Marie S-curie!" True yelled at his retreating back, her fists clenched around her dark, voluminous skirts. "It's a temporally accurate representation of how she dressed!"

Orion was at her side in the next moment. "I'm so sorry." He ran a troubled hand through his hair; it gleamed under the neon lights of the party. "I stepped away for a second to talk to Isaiah, and—"

"We have to get her back," True interrupted, grim determination in her voice. "I promised to keep her safe for Mr. Brightside, and the *last* person who's going to mess with me keeping my word is Bradley freaking Morris."

"That was Bradley? As in, *the* Bradley?" Orion looked after the boys, though they'd long since disappeared.

"Yeah." True cut her eyes at him. She sensed there was more coming.

After a thoughtful pause, Orion raised an eyebrow. "He wore his football uniform as his costume?"

"Bradley likes to present himself in the best light at all times. Someone once told him he looked like the actor Spencer Boldman in it, so . . ."

A muscle twitched in Orion's jaw. He didn't look too impressed. "Right." He turned to look at her. "You know what? We're gonna get Wicked Wynona back. Come on." He grabbed her hand and pushed forward, through the crowd.

True glanced down at his big, warm hand clasped around hers and let herself follow.

"Onny's house is like if the Clue mansion and Cinderella's castle had a baby," Orion said, opening a door on the second floor that led to a darkened bedroom and then closing it again.

"That's a weird sentence, but I totally agree. I've been here countless times and I still get confused. Okay, I need to be able to see clearly for this mission." Divesting herself of her mask and leaving it on a side table to collect later, True walked to the next room, opened the double doors, and saw that it was the library.

It was empty right now, but man, those books called to her. Onny's dad collected first-edition fantasy books—everything from Tolkien to Rowling to Carroll. In spite of her interest in the natural sciences—or maybe because of it—True found fantasy books a welcome, sometimes much-needed escape from reality.

And she had to give that up to look for a mannequin with human hair. And possibly teeth.

"If Bradley hadn't pulled that stupid stunt, I'd love to just curl up in here with a good book and wait out the party." She gazed longingly at the overstuffed armchair by the fireplace.

Orion came up behind her, whistling softly as he took in the decadence of the Diamantes' library—the Tiffany lamps, the Persian rugs, the gigantic floor-to-ceiling windows that over-looked the gardens. Not to mention the bookcases that towered all the way to the sixteen-foot-high ceilings, a ladder perched on one end.

His breath tickled the back of her neck, sending goose bumps prickling over her skin. Startled by her own reaction, True stepped backward, her back pressing along his front. Another shiver played across her skin, and she spun around, her head tipped back as her eyes met Orion's. They were less than a foot away. Kissing distance.

Kissing distance? Why the hell had she thought *that*?

True knew she should step away. But knowing and doing were two different things. Orion's gaze drifted slowly over the planes of her face until he was looking into her eyes again.

"I'm in your way," he said, his voice husky. But he didn't move, either.

"Yes. You are. You just . . . appeared out of nowhere." Her voice had never sounded so breathy, so shaky, before. She wondered if Orion could even hear it over her thumping heart.

The corner of his full mouth moved up just a millimeter. "You're somewhat of a surprise to me, too."

It was obvious they weren't just talking about their current situation outside the library. This was something more.

More than you're ready for right now. Her brain snapped back to attention, throwing up red flags all over the place: Cute boy! Danger! Kissing! Danger! Heartbreak! Never again!

This time, True *did* step back. Clearing her throat, she said, "Um. Yeah, so . . . we should probably keep looking. For Wynona. Wicked Wynona?"

A flicker of what looked very much like disappointment played over Orion's face, but after the slightest pause, he nodded matter-of-factly. True stepped around him quickly, walking back down the carpeted hallway. She heard Orion close the library's doors and follow her.

"I'm not even sure they took Wicked Wynona to the second floor," True said over her shoulder, ignoring her heart beating like a drum in her chest. Suddenly, she was very aware that the second floor was mostly deserted and mostly full of empty bedrooms, and that the sexual chemistry between her and Orion could probably power the entire town of Moon Ridge.

"If this house wasn't twenty-four million square feet, we might have a fighting chance." Orion walked across the hall, opened another door, and stopped short, his mouth popping open. "What the hell?"

Curiosity prickled at True as she picked up her skirts and hurried over to him.

The room he was looking into was covered in dark pools of shadow, broken up only by flickering candlelight. Five ghoulish faces floated in the center of the room, upturned toward Orion and now True, big grimacing smiles spreading across painted lips. True froze, her brain scrambling to make sense of the scene but unable to. The five figures were crouched around something on the floor, something True was very afraid would turn out to be a disemboweled teenager or the head of a teacher or—

"A Ouija board!" Orion exclaimed, a grin splashing across his face. "Cool!"

Ouija board? True blinked, and the room rearranged itself, reality knitting itself back together. Of *course* it wasn't five ghouls perched around a carcass. These were just five teenagers, like her, dressed up as zombies and vampires—and what looked like Mothman—sitting around a Ouija board, probably from Target or somewhere. A *toy*.

True's shoulders relaxed, as did her grip on Orion's elbow. She hadn't realized she'd been digging her claws into him; to his credit, he didn't seem to mind. Still, True flexed her fingers and dropped her hand nonchalantly to her side, just a tad shaky. *Get a grip, True. Just not a grip on Orion.*

A zombie dude in the room spoke, breaking her out of her reverie. "Hey, Orion! This is perfect. We need two more to make seven people. Come join us!"

Orion stepped into the candlelit room, then paused and tossed a rueful glance back at True, who still lingered just beyond the door. "Ah, we can't, man. We're on a mission. Have you guys seen Bradley Morris from Moon Ridge High? He and his buddies were dressed in football uniforms and they had a big witch mannequin with them?"

"Oh, sure," a vampire girl began, her plastic fangs making her lisp. "They went to—"

"Ah, ah, ah." Zombie Boy held up his hand. "We need seven to finish what we're doing here. You help us, we help you."

Orion chuckled. "You're not the debate team captain for nothing, Zach." Turning to True again, he shrugged. "Wanna do a quick round of Ouija before we continue on our search? I think Wicked Wynona will keep."

After just a moment of hesitation True shrugged, picked up her skirts, and followed Orion into the room after closing the door behind her. This would probably only take a few minutes. She sat down on Orion's left, sandwiched between him and Vampire Girl. "So why do you guys need seven people?"

Vampire Girl grinned, her fangs just slightly askew. "*Gabby* believes it's the magic number we need to really get the spirits to engage with us."

Was this girl speaking about herself in the third person? True was just about to say, *And why does* Gabby *believe that?* when a girl across the Ouija board who was dressed as a mummy sighed. "It *is*, you guys. My mom's a medium, and she says seven is the number that unlocks the portal. *Especially* on a night like tonight."

"Okay." Orion rubbed his hands together, looking down at the wooden board. It had numbers painted on in a dark paint, brown or black, True couldn't tell which. The planchette was also solid wood except for the hole on its top and looked heavy, its glossy surface engraved (by hand?) with an intricate fleur-de-lis design. Actually, she could see now, the thing didn't look at all like a toy. To be completely honest, it looked like it belonged in a New Orleans museum, not here in the Diamantes' suburban mansion. Where had these people found it, anyway?

A cold, teasing finger pressed itself into True's spine, and she told herself again to chill. Still, she found herself scooching just a smidge closer to Orion, taking comfort in the way his body heat enveloped her in a firm, solid way, like, *Hey. I will keep you safe.* Not that she needed a guy to keep her safe. It was, you know, like health insurance. Smart to have, just in case.

"Okay, now we all have to put our index fingers on the planchette." Gabby's dark eyes glimmered in the candlelight. "We have to convey our energy through our fingers into the wood." True glanced surreptitiously around as Gabby spoke. Onny's house's layout was hella confusing, but she was pretty sure this was a rarely used—yet tastefully furnished—guest room. Hopefully this group wouldn't burn it to the ground by midnight.

Everyone began placing their fingers on the planchette, and True followed. Her slender index finger, she suddenly realized, was pressed against the side of Orion's much bigger one. Their eyes met for just a moment longer than necessary, memories of the moment they'd shared out in the hallway dancing in True's brain. But then she blinked and looked away, her heart hammering.

"Who's going to ask the first question?" Zombie Boy looked around at them all, a really unsettling grin on his face.

No one said anything.

Orion spoke after five seconds of silence. "I will." His voice was sure and confident, not a trace of the unease present that she'd detected in Zombie Boy's voice in spite of his outward bravado. Orion spoke in a rich, authoritative baritone True hadn't heard yet. "If there is a spirit among us, please tell us your name."

She might just have to watch all his YouTube videos if he always spoke to perceived ghosts this way.

Everyone's gazes swiveled down to the planchette. It was stony-still for a good long moment, and then slowly, very steadily, it began to move.

"D . . ." Gabby read, her voice breathy, her eyes wide in the near dark. The planchette moved again. True tried not to roll her eyes; it was obvious someone was pushing it. "R . . . I . . . B."

"Drib." True raised an eyebrow. "Interesting name."

"Oh my god, that's 'bird' backward!" Vampire Girl pointed out, totally serious. "Maybe there's a bird's spirit here."

Mothman spoke up for the first time. "Didn't Onny used to have a parrot that died?"

The girl next to him, dressed as an evil mermaid, nodded vigorously, her scales flashing in the candlelight. "Yes! I think its name was Feathers. Maybe that was too long to spell."

"Or too difficult," Zombie Boy said thoughtfully.

Oh, for the love of science. True squeezed her eyes shut to gather herself. When she opened them, Orion was studying her again and, this time, she could see the laughter in his eyes. He knew this was breaking her brain.

"Let's ask another question," he interjected, before the conversation could go even deeper down the deceased-pet-bird hole. "Does someone else want to go next?"

Evil Mermaid Girl took a deep breath. "I will." True caught the quicksilver glance she threw Mothman's way before asking, "Who among us will be the next to be kissed?"

The planchette moved an inch to the left, then to the right, and then to the left again. True guessed multiple people must be pushing it to say their names, whether they were aware of it or not. She bit her lip to keep from laughing.

A moment later, the planchette began to tremble and shudder under their fingers. True frowned down at it. It was as if a mini earthquake had seized it somehow; it was practically vibrating. People couldn't make it do that.

"What the . . ." Mothman let out a high-pitched shriek as the vibrations intensified, flinging off all their fingers.

And then the planchette launched itself into the air, its tip pointed right at True. Orion shot out his arm, as if to block it from hitting her, but he wasn't quick enough. The planchette caught True right in the diaphragm before falling into her lap and lying there, sedate and well-behaved once more.

True—and everybody else—stared at it for a good five seconds in complete silence before Gabby screamed and scrambled up to her feet. The group's paralysis broke, and there was a chorus of voices, everyone wanting to know what the hell had just happened, how it had happened, why it had happened.

A moment later, the lights in the room blazed on; Gabby stood by the light switches, about as far away from the Ouija board as she could get, her mummy wrappings coming undone and exposing the black leggings she wore underneath.

"What . . . the *hell* . . . was that?" she gasped, pointing at True and the planchette she now held in her hand.

True looked at Orion, waiting for an explanation. He was the resident ghost expert, was he not? Plus, if she were being honest, she was really just as dumbfounded as anyone else and needed a moment to think of a plausible scientific hypothesis. Orion might as well present his ideas while she thought.

He cleared his throat, looking just as thrown as her. "It's . . ." He shook his head. "This is remarkable, you guys. And that it would happen tonight, of all nights, I mean . . . that's what we'd expect, right?"

"So, which spirit was that?" Zombie Boy shook his head, his eyes still riveted to the Ouija board. "Clearly not the bird."

"Did Onny's family have a bigger pet that died?" Vampire Girl asked. With the lights on, True could see the girl was younger than True had originally thought, probably no older than fifteen. "Maybe a . . . rottweiler?"

True spoke up before anyone else could answer, her thoughts finally coalescing into logic and science once again. "That wasn't a spirit, you guys. I'll admit it was a little weird. But come on. It's pretty obvious to me that someone in the group did it." She looked around at them all, especially Zombie Boy, who, she'd decided, was the most sketch. "Right?"

No one spoke. They all looked at True like *she* was the one speaking nonsense (except Orion, who just looked unconvinced by her solid reasoning). What alternate reality had she entered tonight? "Okay, look." She tried again, holding up the planchette. "It's not doing anything now. Why would it suddenly go dormant if the spirits were really speaking through it?"

"Because we already got our response," Evil Mermaid Girl replied, looking more than a little miffed. "*You're* the next one who's going to be kissed tonight."

True couldn't help it; her gaze flew immediately to Orion. Their eyes met with an almost audible crackle. He was hot, he was sweet, and, True was beginning to think, he was into her.

But I am not into him, she told herself sternly. She couldn't be. Her heart had enough fissures in it. Turning back to the rest of the group, she shook her head and put the planchette back on the board. "I don't think so. This is clearly a case of mass hysteria or delirium or something. Everyone was touching that planchette, which means none of us can be ruled out—"

She was interrupted by the lights in the room flashing

suddenly, on and off and back again, as if someone had activated strobe mode. Except, of course, that the lights didn't have strobe mode.

Gabby, who was standing near the light switches, was the first to react. Screaming, she leaped away from the light switches in a move that would have made any track star proud. That set Mothman off, and soon the room was in chaos and panic once again.

"It's the spirit!" Mothman shrieked, looking at True. He lunged to his feet, clutching at his wire antennae. "It's mad because you doubted!" Turning to the empty air of the room at large, he bellowed, "We're sorry, Drib! We believe! *I* believe!"

"Everyone, remain calm!" True yelled. She looked at Orion, who'd pulled what looked like an EMF meter out of his pants pocket and was holding it up in the air, his movements appearing jerky because of the pulsing lights.

"It's on red!" he announced, half gleeful, half nervous. His cheeks were flushed, his eyes bright in the strobing lights. Kind of hot, actually. "There is some *insane* energy in this room!"

"That's not helping!" True said, and he looked at her all dazed, as if he'd forgotten for a minute where he was. Then, looking abashed, he nodded.

"Freaking out is not helping anything!" he called, in his deep baritone. "Let's see if we can make contact!"

As if on cue, the lights came on and stayed on. The room quieted, everyone holding their breath, it seemed. Except for Mothman, who was in danger of hyperventilating himself into an early grave.

Orion held up his EMF meter again. "It's on green. What-ever was in here is gone now."

True stood, walked over to the light switches, and began to turn them off and back on. The lights obeyed. "There." She turned to the room, hands on her hips. "All good now."

"Yeah," Evil Mermaid Girl said. "But what the hell was that?"

True waved her hands around, though she was beginning to feel a little less sure now. Was this groupthink in action? "You know . . . a little of this, a little of that. There could be a thou-sand, a *million* reasons."

Gabby raised her eyebrows. "Uh-uh. Such as?"

"A fluctuation in the current or some kind of malfunction . . ." True shrugged. "I'm not an electrician, but I'm sure there are multiple other explanations besides 'spirit.'"

"Huh." Vampire Girl ran her tongue over her fangs. "Actu-ally, now that you say that, I *did* hear Mr. and Mrs. Diamante telling my parents that the sound system they installed was giving them electrical issues. But I could've sworn they said it was just blowing the circuits and not doing the strobe-y thing. . . ."

True felt a whoosh of relief go through her body like a wel-come breeze on a hot day. "There you go. That's probably it." What had she been *thinking*, allowing herself to be swayed, even temporarily? "Electrical issues." She turned to Orion. "Okay, so we've checked mass hysteria off the list. I think that leaves Bradley and Wicked Wynona." They had important business, which she'd forgotten due to a séance-gone-wrong. What would Marie Curie think?

Nodding seriously, Orion slipped the EMF meter back into

his pocket. "Yeah, sorry. We have to get to chasing a mannequin, guys. You were going to tell us where Bradley headed off to?"

Zombie Boy blew out a candle near him. "Yeah, I guess you earned that info. They were on their way to the movie-theater room, last we saw."

Orion and True thanked him and then they left, closing the door behind them.

In the cool, quiet hallway, they looked at each other and, after a moment, burst out laughing.

"I can't believe I actually let myself think for a minute that—"

"That was such clear evidence of activity!"

They'd both spoken at the same time and both stopped abruptly, True's smile fading while Orion's broadened.

"Wait, what?" True asked, blinking up at Orion. "You still think it was a spirit?"

"The EMF meter! The lights! The planchette practically impaling you!" Orion shook his head, still grinning. "You don't *really* think it was just an electrical malfunction, do you? Although I do think it's hilarious that we're on opposite sides of this . . . yet again."

The way he said it, as if he and True had some history, made her heart thrill. *No, stop it. Bad heart.* Pushing the thought away, True threw her hands up. "Of course I think it was an electrical malfunction!"

Orion cocked an eyebrow. "I thought that was just something you said to keep them calm."

"No!"

"I saw your face," he continued, obviously not convinced.

"There was a shadow of uncertainty there. You were thinking about it. After what you saw downstairs . . ."

"I didn't see anything downstairs," True countered quickly, wrapping her arms around herself. "Is it cold? It's freezing, right?"

Orion gave her a smug smile. Rolling her eyes, True began to walk to the end of the hallway, where she was pretty sure the movie theater was located. "Let me guess: you think the temperature is caused by the spirit instead of the thermostat."

"Oh, come on," Orion teased, falling into step beside her. "You're telling me there's *no* part of you that's wondering what else it could be? There's absolutely nothing in you that senses there's some magical *some*thing afoot tonight?"

True hesitated just a second. "My mom's an accountant's assistant, and my dad's an insurance agent, Orion. I was raised to believe in numbers. Hard facts."

Orion chuckled. "You didn't answer my questions, but I'll let that go . . . for now. Besides, the EMF meter *is* based on science. That should appeal to you."

They were outside the theater now, and True was glad she didn't have to respond. Putting a finger to her lips and pointing at the door, she reached for the handle and thrust it open quickly, hoping to take Bradley and crew by surprise.

🍁 🍁 🍁

Inside, two familiar faces looked up at her from cushy movie-theater-style recliners.

True's mouth fell open. She stepped into the vast, dimly lit room. There was a fifteen-foot microLED display screen on one end and an actual concession stand on the other. On the walls were dozens of framed movie posters—everything from *Die Hard* to *Moana*—and most of them were signed by the stars. But that's not what had floored her.

"Mom? Dad?"

Her parents were sitting in the front row, closest to her, their feet propped up on the recliner footrests. Her mom had even kicked off her shoes. Her dad, six inches shorter than her mom, had a neck pillow and looked halfway asleep. True was vaguely aware of Orion stepping in behind her and closing the door, but her attention was riveted to her parents. "What are you *doing*?"

Her mom's face lit up in a cheery smile. "Hello, True! We're just taking a break from the party."

Her dad, still drowsy, gestured to the empty seat beside him. "These midnight galas take forever, don't they? Come take a seat."

Her mom sat up a little more, peering in the low light. "Do you have a friend with you?"

True glanced over at Orion, her pulse thrumming for reasons unknown. Or unexamined. Same thing, really. "Oh. Um, this is Orion."

But he was already stepping forward, one hand outstretched, a pleasant smile on his face as he approached her parents. "Orion Parker, ma'am, sir. I go to North Pointe High."

True's mom and dad looked exceptionally pleased, probably by his manners (Bradley had been the type to honk from the driveway until she came out, which drove her parents nuts), and True felt she should do something to quickly correct the situation. "Yeah, we're not exactly friends. I mean, we just met tonight."

Orion's gaze flickered to her, hurt evident there, and for a moment True hated herself. Why had she said it like *that*? As if admitting Orion any deeper into her circle of trust would signal the coming of the apocalypse. It was just friendship. She could give him *friendship*, couldn't she?

"But, ah, he's cool, so, you know. We've been hanging out a bit."

Orion's eyes lit up again. It was so easy to make him happy. Again, so unlike Bradley, even early on in their relationship, when he'd been on his best behavior.

Refocusing her attention on her parents, True took a seat beside her dad. Orion sat on her other side. "But wait, how long have you guys been in here, taking a break?"

Her mom consulted her wristwatch, while her dad grazed on a bag of popcorn by his elbow, looking a lot like a disaffected goat. In spite of being rail thin, her dad was *always* eating. "Oh, only about fifteen minutes."

"And how long do you think you'll be staying in here?" When her parents made vague noises, she snorted. "Let me guess: until the party's over?"

Her dad gave her a reproachful look while he munched his buttery snack. "People are exhausting, True. You can only listen to tales of career trajectories and patio extensions for so long before you start to go very slowly but very surely insane."

True laughed and looked at Orion. "Is my antisocial nature making sense yet?"

He studied her for a moment, a smile hovering at his lips. The low lights glinted off his hair, turning it to gold. "I wouldn't say you're antisocial. More like . . . selectively social. You have to trust people before you talk to them, but when you talk, it's worth listening to."

True opened her mouth, but for once, she didn't have a solitary smart-ass comment to impart. Her cheeks were warm at the look in his eye.

The moment stretched out as they gazed at each other, neither speaking.

"Well! That's very nice." Her mother's booming voice sounded from the other side, making True jump. Right, she was in a room with Orion—*and her parents*. This was no time to get lost in those dreamy brown eyes. Jesus.

Her dad was suddenly regarding Orion very suspiciously over his bag of popcorn. "How old did you say you were, Orion?"

"I'm eighteen, sir." Orion smiled at him.

"*Hmpf.* He's *big*, though," her dad muttered, although to whom he was speaking, True didn't know. He pulled a box of his favorite candy—Whoppers—from his pocket to mix in with his popcorn, but his eyes stayed on Orion.

Awkward.

"So were you two coming in here to watch a movie? Were Ash or Onny going to join you, too?" Her mother's tone was smooth as river rock, but True knew what she was really asking:

Were you going to make out with this boy in your friend's home theater while Bruce Willis and The Rock looked on, True?

True felt her cheeks flame, and she hoped Orion couldn't see through her mom's not-very-subtle line of inquiry. "No, we were looking for a mannequin. Mr. Brightside asked me to keep an eye on it, and then Bradley and his friends stole it out from under our noses. We've been trying to track them down. They—" True looked from her mom to her dad—and then stopped short. Squinting at her dad's neck pillow, she gasped. "Dad! That's not a neck pillow; that's Wicked Wynona's scarf!" She reached toward him and tugged at it until he leaned forward and let her have it. True curled the green paisley monstrosity around her hand. "Where did you get this?"

Her dad held up his hands, one of which was covered in popcorn butter. "It was here when we came in, I swear!"

"So they *were* in here," Orion said from beside her. To her parents: "Did you happen to see where they went?"

"Oh no. But I did hear something that sounded like boys stampeding toward the turret staircase." Her dad waved his hand. Then, frowning, he added, "But you say *Bradley* has this mannequin? Bradley Morris?"

True knew what was coming. Sighing as she stuffed Wicked Wynona's scarf into one of her pockets, she said, "Yeah, Dad."

"That boy's bad news, True. You don't need to go chasing after him."

True rolled her eyes, but her face was hot enough to erupt into lava. *Not in front of Orion, please,* she tried to telegraph.

But her dad remained, as always, completely oblivious. "I'm not chasing *Bradley*, Dad. I'm going after the mannequin."

Her dad didn't look convinced. As if this situation wasn't hideously humiliating enough, her mom piped in, too. "The mannequin, the football game, the astronomy class you invited him to for fun. There's always something that sucks you into Bradley's orbit. But it always ends up the same way. With that boy hurting you and calling your interests silly. I still can't believe he fell asleep in that astronomy class."

"*Mom.*" True cut her eyes at Orion and then looked back meaningfully at her parents. "Not now, okay?"

But it was too late. "Wait, wait, wait." Orion sat up and angled his body so he was looking at all three of them. "You took Bradley to an astronomy class? On a date?"

True sighed, feeling more and more stupid with each passing moment. Clutching the skirts of her outfit, she said, "Yeah. I was taking it at the community college for fun, and I thought he'd enjoy sitting in on a session. But, um, as you can probably guess, he didn't."

"Dude!" Orion spoke so loudly that his voice startled them all. He was grinning. "That is such an *awesome* date idea! I tell you, True, if you surprised me with something like that, I'd die of happiness."

True and her parents froze. It took Orion a moment to understand why. And when he did, his face turned a rather endearing shade of flamingo pink.

He licked his lips. "Ah, not that you're my girlfriend. It's just, you know, a really neat idea. A nice thing to do for someone. Astronomy. I like stars."

Orion Parker *tongue-tied*? True couldn't stop staring. Orion was sweet, yes. Gentle, uh-huh. But he was also, True knew by now, confident and gallant and sure. Seeing him tongue-tied on her account was kind of . . . well, flattering. And hella cute.

True's mother spoke up, coming to his rescue. "I think so, too, Orion. But unfortunately, Bradley didn't. True was always showing him what she was interested in, and he was always making her feel bad about it. Just completely stomping all over her poor, sweet heart."

Oh god. The woman wouldn't stop.

"That's why I don't think True should be dating anyone at all," her dad put in, eyeing Orion rather viciously. "*Ever.*" He popped a Whopper in his mouth and crunched it with the menace he felt in his heart.

Her mom swatted at him. "Oh, Rohan. You don't mean that."

"Don't I, Emilia?" her dad asked, narrowing his eyes at Orion. "Don't I?"

Orion, thankfully, didn't run screaming from her crazy family. Instead, he turned to True. "Bradley's an assho—" Here he glanced at True's dad and amended hastily: "a jerk. He didn't appreciate you sharing yourself with him, which is one hundred percent his problem. It doesn't mean it was the wrong thing to do."

"Oh, I don't know about that." True pushed the toe of her boot into the plush carpet. "Being incessantly, unstoppably truthful about everything is one of my not-so-fine traits. It's why my parents nicknamed me True."

There was a tiny pause.

Her parents frowned in tandem and then exchanged looks with each other. It was like they'd memorized the moves beforehand: synchronized parental concern.

"That's not why we named you True," her mom said, still frowning. "Where on earth did you get that idea?"

"Yes, it was!" Their collective expression of utter confusion was throwing her a little bit. But she knew her own origin story. "Remember? It's that little anecdote you love to tell so much. I wasn't even three years old yet, and Dad brought that colleague of his with the halitosis problem home for dinner? Everyone was sitting around the table and saying how good the food smelled, and I proclaimed, very loudly, 'Food yummy. Him stinky.' And pointed right at that poor dude. You guys were so mortified you tried to tell him that I had a favorite bear named Stinky and I'd clearly just taken a liking to him and was calling him Stinky after the bear. You told him it was an honor." True snorted. "And ta-da, 'True' was born. Before that I was always and only Aria."

There was the synchronized parental concern again, mixed with a healthy dose of confusion. "That's not entirely accurate," her dad said. "I mean, yes, you did say that to my poor colleague. And we did laugh about how fitting your name was for you at that point. Maybe that's what you caught on to. But we were calling you True long before then. Ever since you were born, in fact."

It was True's turn to frown. "What? But that doesn't make any sense. Newborns don't spout brutal truths, do they?"

Her mom raised an eyebrow. "That's to be debated. Some of your dirty diapers felt very targeted. Regardless, what your father's saying is absolutely correct. You were True from the moment we set eyes on you." She smiled gently. "Do you know why?"

Completely thrown now, True shook her head. She saw Orion listening in interest. "No, why?"

"Because you were the product of true love," said True's dad. "You were the culmination, the perfect representation of how your mom and I feel about each other." Her dad reached out and put an arm around her and her mom. "You made us a family. You were everything that was true, and right, and precious about the world."

Her mom nodded, completely serious. "The name just came to me as I gazed down at you in the hospital and you gazed back. And it stuck."

True opened her mouth, but no sounds came out for a long moment. "Wow. I . . . I don't know what to say." It was like finding out you weren't descended from a line of Valkyries at all, but rather from a line of golden retrievers. It was . . . unsettling. Weird. And kind of . . . sweet?

"That's a beautiful story," Orion said softly, his eyes warm on her skin. "And it's much more fitting than the other one, I think."

True snorted. "I think you're the only one who'd say that."

"He is not," her mom said immediately, and her dad nodded in agreement. "I think Ash and Onny and the people who can really see to your core would all say the same thing. You're made of love, not hardness. No matter how much you might fight against *that* truth, ironically enough."

True glanced sideways at Orion. When they were tending the line to Wicked Wynona, he'd said it would be a shame if she lost herself. Did he feel real acceptance for her annoying need to speak her mind and assert her will? But maybe to him it wasn't annoying. Maybe, to Orion Parker, True wasn't too . . . True.

The thought made her dizzy. She wasn't sure what to do with that information.

So she stood abruptly, Wicked Wynona's green scarf fluttering to the floor. Bending down and snatching it up, True straightened again and turned to her parents, her tone brusque. "Well, okay. Thanks for that history lesson. But we have to be going." She turned to Orion, her face a mask of businesslike determination. "Right? We have a mannequin to take back."

"Oh. Yep." Orion arranged his face to mirror hers and stood. "It was really nice to meet you, Mr. and Mrs. Tandon."

"You too, Orion," her mom said, looking curiously between the two of them. Clearly her mother's intuition had picked up on True's inner turmoil.

Her dad, on the other hand, reverted to blissfully chomping on his Whopper-popcorn concoction. "See ya, kiddos. Close the door on your way out, would ya?"

Out in the hallway, True tried to push aside her million conflicting emotions and surveyed the path before them. Turning right would take them toward the main stairs that would lead them back to the first floor. But turning left . . . ? Tucked away by the window and around a corner was a spiral staircase that led to one of the turret balconies. "My dad said they were headed to the turret staircase, right? So they must be up on the balcony; that's why we haven't been able to find them. I really hope they're not planning something stupid. Come on."

But Orion caught her elbow and stopped her from running off. "Hey."

He came to stand in front of her. Something about his expression—focused and thoughtful and serious—made her heart tumble in her chest.

He pushed a hand through his thick hair. "I enjoyed meeting your parents. I know that's probably weird to say, but they're really kind of great. And it was cool hearing why they nicknamed you True."

"Oh, uh, yeah. Thanks."

Her response was too little. He was telling her, again—she thought—that he accepted all aspects, every dimension, of her. What Bradley had seen, he didn't care for. What Orion had glimpsed, he wanted more of. And there was something breathlessly momentous in the fact that he might accept every atom of who she was and what made up her universe: her family, her skeptic's mind, her passions.

Orion stepped a little closer, and True's pulse picked up. His eyes were like twin stars, twinkling down at her. If Bradley had been a craggy, icy, treacherous, mountainous terrain, Orion was a summery, wooded glen where she could listen to birds chirping and feel the sun kissing her skin.

What was he going to ask her? What would she say to him in response? In that moment, anything seemed possible.

But then True blinked, glanced past Orion—and saw *her*. The figure in the floaty silver dress was staring at True again with that eerie blue gaze. When True locked eyes with her, she dropped something that fell to the carpet with a soft thud and then rounded the corner and vanished.

Gasping, True hurried past Orion to whatever the figure had dropped at the end of the hallway. It glinted softly in the recessed lights, nestled into the plush carpet. "It's Wicked Wynona's ring!" True bent down and picked it up; it lay heavy and cold in the palm of her hand, the skull grinning up at her. She rushed to peek around the corner, but the figure was gone.

Turning to Orion, who'd caught up to her (and had a very "brimming with a hundred things I want to say" expression on his face that True tried to ignore—at least for now), she said, "I think she's leaving us clues. The scarf, the ring, and disappearing up to the balcony right here . . . she's trying to tell us to go up there. Come on."

Slipping the ring on her own finger, True climbed up the spiraling staircase, Orion at her heels. There was a small landing at the top, and, beyond it, French doors that led outside onto the spacious balcony. True plunged forward, ready to wrangle Wicked Wynona from Bradley's blunt-fingered hands.

But the moment she was actually outside in the cool night air, True realized that wasn't going to be possible. Bradley and two of his friends were laughing uproariously at what their fourth friend, Aiden, was up to—i.e., holding Wicked Wynona by her hair past the railing, dangling her twenty feet over the concrete patio below.

"Stop!" True yelled as Orion came up behind her, looking just as horrified as she felt. "What are you *doing*?"

Bradley turned to her, still laughing, one hand around a beer can. He walked over, his grin morphing into something malicious and nasty. "Ah, if it isn't the True-gooder, come to ruin our fun." His words were sloppy and he smelled like yeast, a fine mist of beer hanging around his face.

True took a step back, Bradley's words pinching at the softest, most vulnerable part of her soul, like they always did. "Just give me the mannequin, Bradley."

Hearing her, Aiden swung Wicked Wynona back and forth like a pendulum and hooted like a deranged owl. His floppy brown hair covered one eye. "Come and get her, or she's meeting a bloody fate on the concrete below!"

Orion stepped toward Aiden, leaving True behind with Bradley. "You don't have to do this. Just hand her over, man. Come on."

True wanted to laugh at the absurdity of the situation. Orion sounded like a hostage negotiator. Except, in this case, the "hostage" was an ancient pile of human hair and papier-mâché. But Bradley's leering, smug face took any little mirth she might find in the situation and flung it off the balcony.

She tried to appeal to a solitary shred of decency that might reside in him somewhere, assuming the beer hadn't washed it away. Speaking quickly—it didn't look like Aiden had the surest grip on Wicked Wynona's hair—True said, "Mr. Brightside asked me to look after it, and I can't give it back to him all damaged and broken. You understand, right? I mean, the mannequin's important to me, Bradley. This isn't some game I'm playing."

"Dude, just give her the mannequin." It was hard not to hear the hard edge of irritation in Orion's otherwise-soft voice.

Bradley grinned his horrible, twisted grin. "Aww, this is precious. I think this loser here thinks he has a chance with you, True. But take it from me, you're not even close to her type. She likes strong men who can reign her in. So run along. You don't want to be a pathetic try-hard who can't take a hint, do you?"

He was doing it again, hitting someone in the softest, most vulnerable parts of themselves. True could tell from the way the muscle in Orion's jaw jumped that Bradley's words had struck him as surely as a punch. She stepped in front of Orion. "Leave." She spoke coldly and unequivocally, her gaze pinned on Bradley. "Right now."

But he cocked his head. "See, now, I don't think you get to say that to me. I have as much a right to be here as you do." He stepped past her and headed for Wicked Wynona. "As a matter of fact, you don't have a right to tell me not to touch this thing, either. It doesn't even belong to you."

True and Orion speed-walked over to the mannequin, but the boys had already surrounded it.

"What's wrong with you?" True asked, throwing her hands up in the air. "If you're trying to show me you're not petty, this is not the way, Bradley."

His blue eyes glinted at her, hard and cold. "I'm not trying to show you anything, True. You're *nothing* to me."

True stepped closer to Wicked Wynona. "Good. Then step away and let me have her."

Bradley shook his head, and Aiden crossed his arms against his chest like some kind of goon. "You had your chance, little lady."

True wondered if there was actual steam coming out of her ears. "'Little lady'? What century do you think we're living in, you moron?"

Bradley snorted. "Says the girl in an eighteenth-century dress."

"That's *enough*." Orion's eyes flashed in a way True hadn't seen before. And his authoritative baritone was back. He looked down at Bradley, his face serious. "You will not speak to her that way."

"Don't tell us what to do, loser." Perhaps at the knowledge that he'd failed to intimidate Orion with his meanness, Bradley's voice wobbled, weak and unsure. As if this treachery by his own body angered him, Bradley pushed Orion on the shoulder, barely making the other boy move. Which was pretty impressive, considering Bradley was 99 percent muscle. This seemed to make him even angrier, because he shoved Orion harder.

"Hey!" True yelled, wondering if she could kick him in the shin.

But before she could move, Orion grabbed Bradley's arm and glared at him with an expression of absolute dislike that, until this moment, True hadn't been sure he was even capable of. "*Don't* touch me."

Aiden lunged at Orion, defending Bradley's honor, and True

lunged for Aiden. But then the other two boys lunged for Wicked Wynona, and True turned to save her from their meaty paws. Orion could take care of himself; Wicked Wynona was a hapless innocent who'd already been abused enough for one night.

But it was apparent almost immediately that this was going to be a quick fight, one not in True's—or Wynona's—favor. The boys, both football players like Bradley, were incredibly strong, fueled by mindless, self-righteous fury (and beer). True tried tugging on Wicked Wynona's arm, but she was afraid all she'd succeed in doing would be ripping the poor witch apart.

"Let her go!"

"No!" one of the guys yelled back.

"Yes!"

"No!"

Past the boys, True saw Orion grappling with Bradley and Aiden, both of whom were trying to pin his arms back. He had the upper hand currently, but how much longer could he hold out in an unfair fight?

True had barely finished that thought when Bradley's two friends went flying back and crashed to the floor of the balcony. True stood blinking at them for a moment, wondering if she'd begun putting out an energy force field using only her mind— seemed about right for tonight—when she realized what had actually happened.

The figure was back, looking down at the boys with contempt in her surreal blue eyes. There was a weird electrical charge on the balcony now, though it could've just been the storm due the next day. The two boys stared at True, their eyes wide and horrified. Wait, did they think *True* had pushed them? Couldn't they see the woman, standing right in front of them?

But there was no time to worry about that right now.

"Help Orion!" True called as she ran to his side, not even sure if the woman could hear or understand her. *What am I saying? Of course she can*, True thought, her body adrenaline-soaked and ready to fight Bradley and Aiden. Whatever was happening here, it was abundantly clear the woman knew exactly what was going on with True.

The figure was over by Orion's side in a flash. True wasn't sure exactly what happened next. One moment she was struggling to pull Bradley off Orion, and the next she was being pushed forward, though she didn't see who pushed her. A freezing cold spot spread across her back, and then she was propelled forward, her feet scrabbling uselessly on the ground. Afraid she was going to fall, True whirled her arms around, crashing into Orion, her hand—and Wicked Wynona's heavy skull ring—catching him in the face.

But before she could react to *that*, Bradley and Aiden were thrown through the air much as their other two friends had been, landing in a graceless heap on the cold tile floor of the balcony. They looked up at True as if she'd morphed into the Hulk.

"What the hell?" Bradley said, finding his voice first. "Are you on 'roids?"

"'Roids?" True scoffed. "That wasn't me who pushed you, though not for want of trying. It was her—" She stopped abruptly, her finger pointing at nothing. Once again, the woman in the silver dress had disappeared without a trace.

"Yeah, right, freak," Bradley said, though True noticed he said it quietly, to himself, as he brushed his clothes off.

"It wasn't!" True found herself insisting, though why she wanted Bradley to believe her, she didn't know. She gestured toward the empty space where the woman in the dress had been. "This is important—"

A sudden leering grin on Bradley's face got broader as he glanced over his shoulder at his two buddies, who were now also grinning back. Because True knew them, she could see the hint of uncertainty in their supposed-to-be-confident smiles. They'd gotten to their feet and were adjusting their clothes, too, but surreptitiously, as if they didn't want to show how unsettled they really were. Aiden wandered back over to Wicked Wynona and put his arm around her, as if eager to prove he wasn't at all cowed by what had just happened.

"See what I mean?" Bradley said to his friends, and they nodded enthusiastically.

Turning back to True, seeming empowered by her attention, he continued: "*Everything's* always important to you, True. Doesn't matter what it is—climate change, females in male-dominated careers, whether aliens are real, Fenrir's freaking Paradox. Everything's such a big deal. That's why I broke up with you. Guys don't like high-maintenance girls." He leaned down to her, blowing his beery breath all over her face as he spoke slowly, exaggeratedly. "Calm. Down."

It was like a red filter had been slammed down on the world. True was vaguely aware that Orion had turned to face her and Bradley and was opening his mouth to say something, probably in defense of her. But she didn't need him. She could handle this on her own.

Her words wanted to erupt from her like cannonballs, riddling Bradley with holes until he was nothing but a pile of smoking, shredded boy. But she forced herself to speak slowly, authoritatively, clearly. All the things he had failed at.

True held up one finger. "Number one: it's the *Fermi* Paradox. Unless a really big, scary wolf is confused about something." At his befuddled look, she continued: "Read a book sometime, Bradley. It might help. Number two: *I* broke up with *you*, and you know damn well that I did. And number three: thanks. Thanks for being a gigantic asswipe. Thanks for validating every single thing I've been marinating over since we broke up—that you're a toxic, vile, trash dump of a human. I'm so lucky I woke up when I did."

When she paused for breath, Bradley opened his mouth like he might begin to talk again. Hell, no. This was *her* time.

True plowed on. "And you know what I realized tonight? That I'm honestly a goddamn *hoot*. I'm a fun person to be around. Just because you're too stupid to realize it, just because intelligent women intimidate you, doesn't say anything at all about me." She stepped closer to him, making him back up in surprise. His eyes were wide, owlishly so, as if he couldn't believe she was actually talking back to him. "I will *never* calm down. Also, tell your goddamn friend to give me the goddamn mannequin back, or I will physically remove your balls with my bare hands."

There was utter silence on the balcony for a good four seconds, while all the boys processed everything True had said—and probably thought back to just a few minutes ago when "she'd" tossed them all around the balcony like a couple of rag dolls. Then Bradley blinked and cleared his throat, stepping back from her again. "Yo, Aiden," he called, not meeting True's eye. "Give her the doll back, man. We don't need this bullshit."

Nodding, Aiden slid his arm back from around Wicked Wynona and slowly backed away from the mannequin and True, his hands held up.

"Fucking psycho," Bradley muttered as he pushed past her and walked to the French doors, his friends flanking him on either side.

True and Orion watched them go in silence.

A cool breeze swirled across the balcony, making Wicked Wynona's red hair flutter. It seemed to break the spell; Orion turned to True, his eyes shining in the moonlight. "That was . . . wow." His voice held a hushed reverence.

True turned to look at him—and gasped. There was a gash on his forehead that she was just now noticing, and the front of his shirt was all spattered with blood. "Your head! I hit you with the ring earlier and oh my god, this is all my fault—"

But Orion waved her off, almost impatiently. "That can wait. I'm fine. I just . . ." He shook his head and smiled a little. "Can we first talk about what just happened here? True Tandon, I think you may be a bona fide badass."

He didn't *seem* to be in pain, and the look in his eyes was . . . She'd never been looked at like that before.

True tucked a thick strand of her hair back into its Marie S-curie bun and felt her face warm. Tipping her head back, she looked up at the sky. The solitary gold star next to the moon appeared to pulse, as if asking in Morse code where its companion, the other star, was. Another thing that baffled her. Tonight was full of them: the figure, the planchette, her *actual* origin story.

Looking back at Orion, True smiled a little. "I think all that had been building up inside me for some time. I just didn't know it." She shrugged one shoulder. "And, um, if I'm being totally honest, you had a small part in helping all those thoughts coalesce inside my brain tonight."

Orion shook his head, a small smile on his face. "Nah. That was all you; your inner fire."

True held his gaze. "Mostly, sure. But some of it was you. So . . . you know. Thanks, Orion Parker."

He stepped in closer, his face serious and handsome. Even the blood running down the side of his face didn't detract from his absolute beauty. "Anytime, True Tandon." And then he brought his face down to hers, brushing his lips against her mouth.

True's eyes fluttered shut. For just a moment, just one blissful moment, she let herself fall into this almost-kiss. Into this almost-moment. Into this almost-romance. And in the next, her eyes flew open again and cold reality came rushing in like frigid water. Gasping softly, she stepped back. "Wait."

Orion looked at her askance. "What's wrong?"

Cupping the back of her neck with a hand that had gone cold, True shook her head. She looked out over the balcony railing, at the softly lit reflective pool in the distance. "I'm sorry," she said, quietly. "I don't think I'm ready for . . . whatever this is."

"Oh." Orion's voice was barely above a whisper. The hurt in it hurt her heart. "Is it . . . Bradley?"

True turned to face him. "Absolutely not." Her voice was clear and strong. She saw Orion visibly relax. "Bradley has absolutely zero hold over me anymore. He's just a petty, misogynistic pig, and I should've kicked him to the curb a lot sooner than I did." The truth was, if Onny went out with a guy who treated her like Bradley had treated True, True would've immediately and without a doubt told her she deserved better. So what had taken her so long to do that for herself?

"But?" Orion prompted gently.

"But . . ." True took a deep breath, bringing her mind back to the present. She met Orion's eyes and found herself being completely truthful, completely vulnerable. "Why did I let myself get lost like that? Why did I let him get to the best parts of me? What does that say about me and my ability to be in a relationship?" She stuck her hands in her pockets and looked down at her feet, answering her own question. "I think it says that maybe I'm not meant to be in a relationship. Not everyone, not everything, is made to be in a pair." Craning her neck again, she looked at the solitary star. "Maybe sometimes we just end up alone . . . and that's okay. It has to be."

True brought her gaze back to earth, back to the balcony, and her breath caught in her throat. In the far corner stood a flickering figure in a long silver dress. Orion's back was to the figure; he didn't see her. The woman was staring right at True, though, with that unnerving blue gaze. But this time, she didn't look intense. This time, she looked sad. She shook her head slowly, as if disappointed in True.

True found herself staring back in silence; her mind wasn't

rushing to come up with a dozen scientific explanations for what was happening before her eyes. Right then, the only thought in her head was: *I'm sorry.*

A second later, the figure disappeared.

For a moment, True felt an immense, inexplicable sorrow in her heart. But then it fell away, bit by bit, carried off by the night breeze.

True looked back at Orion. He wasn't trying to hide the fact that her words had crushed him; his jaw was set, his eyes hollow with hurt. Seeing him like that, her own heart felt like there was an iron fist around it, squeezing and squeezing. She felt Orion's emotions echoing in her chest, but she forced herself not to retract everything she'd said. Orion was good; Orion was, in many ways, the perfect guy. The perfect guy who deserved someone else equally as perfect. Someone who was meant for him, someone who wouldn't mess it all up the way True *knew* she would.

"Okay," he said softly, stepping back from her, the space between them empty and cold. "I get it." Sticking his hands in his pockets, he said, "Ah, I guess this is it, then. I can help you carry the mannequin down, if you want?"

The remoteness in his words tugged at her heart. Suddenly, True realized she wasn't quite ready to say goodbye. "But first I'm going to help you dress that wound." She pointed to his head. It didn't look dire, but any head wound needed immediate medical attention, right? Right.

Orion looked a little surprised. "No, it's fine, really. I don't think it's serious. I just need some gauze or something."

"Yeah, and I know where the Diamantes keep all their first

aid stuff," True said matter-of-factly, taking his elbow. "Come with me."

Hoisting Wicked Wynona laboriously under one arm, she began to walk but soon realized Orion wasn't walking with her. He met her eye seriously. "You don't have to do this," he said, quietly. "I can take care of myself."

True set Wicked Wynona down. Wasn't that exactly what she'd thought before—that Orion could take care of himself? And it was true, she knew. He would be just fine without True. If they were to part ways right here, right now, he'd probably go on his merry way and never think of her again. But looking at him— that poor, bloody head, that ruined shirt, those soft brown eyes tinged with hurt—True realized she didn't want him to take care of himself. *She* wanted to be the one to tend to him, to minister to the wounds she'd caused, even if by accident.

What she'd said still stood, though. True wasn't meant for a relationship. Maybe she'd never see him after tonight, but at least it wouldn't be goodbye just yet. She could draw it out a little bit longer; she could delay the inevitable until she felt ready to walk away.

True smiled up at him even as she felt tears pricking at her eyes. "You don't know Onny's house like I do. Plus, I feel responsible. Come on."

After a beat of hesitation, Orion nodded.

True began to lift Wicked Wynona up again, but Orion beat her to it. In complete silence, he followed her down from the balcony, carrying the heavy mannequin easily in his strong arms.

It took a few moments for True to remember where the guest bathroom with the medical supplies was, but then the giant grandfather clock jogged her memory. "Ah, here's that vintage 1910 Stromwell Mr. Diamante loves so much." She paused, studying the clockface, her own face reflected in it. "Whoa. It's almost midnight." She glanced at Orion, feeling a pang of sadness. She remembered how, at the beginning of the night, she'd been desperate to get away from him. And now she'd do anything to wind back the clock, figuratively speaking, just to prolong their time together. "Ten minutes to go."

"The magical hour on a magical night," Orion replied, without much enthusiasm. The bloodstains on his shirt were drying to a muddy brown, but his forehead was still trickling. And Wicked Wynona probably wasn't getting any lighter.

"Right." Pushing her emotions aside, True bustled forward, two doors past the clock on their right. "Here's the bathroom."

Even for a guest bathroom, it was bigger than any True had ever used on a regular basis. The floor was a pale white stone threaded with gold, and there was a huge garden tub on one end. The counter and sink were shimmery pale with veins of gold shot through. The decor gave the impression of being suspended in a cloud. In fact, if heaven were a bathroom, True was pretty sure this would be it. *Okay, focus, True.*

Closing the door behind Orion, who set Wicked Wynona down in a corner, she began to rummage around in the cabinets under the sink. Sure enough, there was a box with a red medical cross on it.

True hauled it out and opened it on the counter with a satisfied grunt. "Have a seat. . . ." Looking around, her eyes lit on a beige tufted stool in the corner. "There."

Orion dragged the stool over, careful not to get any blood on it, and sat dutifully. "You know," he said, mildly, "what happened on that balcony, that was pretty nuts. You took on four football players and won."

They looked at each other.

"Uh-huh," True said finally, turning her attention back to the first aid kit.

"And you seemed to be talking to someone at one point. Who was that?"

True continued looking down at the kit, her face hot. "Dunno. Must've been the adrenaline."

"Of course. The adrenaline."

She darted a sideways glance at Orion, who was looking right at her, his gaze assessing. He was no fool, this boy.

Desperate to change the subject, True handed over a thick wad of gauze. "Here. Hold this over the cut and just sit there."

Orion did as he was told, but his characteristic mirth and openness were gone. He still looked hurt, distant. True knew it wasn't his bloody forehead. She'd built a wall between them he couldn't cross.

Truthfully, she didn't really need to be in here with him while he held the gauze over his wound. All he needed to do was apply steady pressure for ten minutes or so, put some antibiotic ointment on, bandage it, and be on his way. She should get Wicked Wynona back to Mr. Brightside before he decided True had absconded into the night with his witch and made a dark effigy of her out of deer gizzards or something.

True eyed Orion as if to memorize him, those big hands, those wide shoulders—and then noticed again his bloodied shirt. Yessss! "Hey, they have some hydrogen peroxide in here," she said breezily, pointing at the first aid kit. "That's a good way to get bloodstains out of clothes. If you give me your shirt, I can get it soaking."

Orion looked a little taken aback at this domestic overture. "Oh, you don't have to do that. I can take care of it when I get home."

"Are you kidding? This is fun for me." Smiling, True turned the brown bottle of hydrogen peroxide over in her hands, trying to be all casual. "It's like chemistry in real life." Her smile fell off her face with a splat. *Chemistry in real life.* If only the figure could save her from herself.

But Orion didn't seem to notice her lack of social skills, likely because she'd been displaying them all night. Shrugging, he set the gauze down for a moment and then slipped easily out of his shirt.

Holy hell. Even as she took the shirt from him, True's gaze remained on his abs. It was kind of hard *not* to notice them, considering that they were right there in front of her face (well, not *literally* in front of her face, although that would be . . . pleasant—very pleasant). His skin had a golden tint to it, as if he spent a lot of time outside in the sun, even this time of year. Her eyes traveled upward, to his smooth chest—and then stopped short.

Orion had no hair on his sculpted chest. Instead, right in the middle, on his breastbone, was a tattoo.

His shirt fell from True's hands to the bathroom floor, but she left it there. Her eyes were riveted on that tattoo. "It's a moon," she half-whispered, mostly to herself.

"Hmm?" Still sitting on the stool, Orion glanced down at his chest. "Oh, the tattoo. Yeah, I got it for my eighteenth birthday last month. The plan was originally to get a dragon, but at the last minute . . ." He shook his head, tossing the gauze into the trash can as he did. His cut had stopped bleeding. "I don't know, I just had this vision of a full moon in the night sky and changed my mind on a whim. It could've been a disaster, but I actually really like it." He shrugged and then noticed her expression. "What?"

For a moment, True couldn't speak. Onny's prediction kept echoing through her mind: *Your soul mate carries the moon on his chest.* At the time, True had laughed it off as Onny being Onny. What did that even mean, "carries the moon on his chest"? It was preposterous and ridiculous; it was actually, literally coming to pass right before True's astonished eyes.

Had she been completely wrong about love? Was it possible that, in this instance, some unknown outside force had brought True and Orion together? She thought about the woman in the old-fashioned wedding dress, shaking her head when True refused to admit her feelings for Orion on the balcony. The planchette practically skewering her when answering the question about who would be the next to be kissed. Onny's prediction and Ash's assurances. Orion dancing into her life, irrepressibly accepting of every aspect of her, in direct contrast to Bradley. As if he were an answer to a question she'd sent out into the universe, without even thinking about it.

True cleared her throat, forcing her eyes up to Orion's. With a shaking hand, she reached into one of the pockets of her dress and pulled out the love potion Onny had given her. *Only drink it with the one you're sure about,* she'd said.

True held out the fragile glass bottle to Orion, the pink liquid sloshing softly inside. "This is a potion Onny gave me," she said seriously. "I'm only supposed to drink it by midnight with someone I'm sure about. And if there's one thing I'm sure about right now, it's you."

Orion was studying her cautiously, as if waiting for her to burst into laughter or yell "Psych!" When she didn't, he stood up slowly, towering over her. "You're serious?"

True nodded once and gulped. "As deadly serious as radiation, like my friend Marie Curie would say. But you should only drink it if you . . . if you're sure about me, too. They say it'll bind us together. And, you know, after the way I've acted tonight, going back and forth like a pendulum . . . I'd understand if you didn't want to drink it with me."

Orion came to stand in front of her, his neck bent so he could meet her eye. "True Tandon, I'd love to drink that potion with you."

"Really?" she whispered, looking up at him.

He rubbed a thumb softly over her lower lip. "Really. I'm sure about you, too. It's completely wild and downright ridiculous, but you had me the moment you told me you were Marie S-curie."

"Maybe . . . maybe 'wild and ridiculous' aren't such bad things in this instance."

Her hands still trembling, True took out the silver stopper and put her lips to the bottle. She drank half of the slightly sweet liquid and then handed the rest to Orion. He didn't hesitate: tipping his head back, he downed the potion in one quick swallow. Setting the bottle down on the sink, he turned to True, bringing one warm hand to her cheek. "What changed your mind? You said you weren't meant for love."

True leaned into his hand, her eyes closing briefly. "So many things happened tonight that I can't explain. I kept bouncing from scientific rationale to scientific rationale. And I just realized . . . it doesn't matter. I can come up with a million reasons to turn down love if I want to. But there are a *million and one* reasons you're right for me, Orion. I'd be a fool to overlook all of those."

Smiling, Orion brought his mouth down to meet hers. "I've barely known you for an evening, and I'm a fool for you, True Tandon," he whispered. "I can't explain it and I don't really want to. Is that all right?"

"It's more than all right." True laced her hands behind his neck and pulled him even closer. "It's perfectly magical."

As their lips finally met, the grandfather clock in the hallway began to strike. It was midnight. True love had arrived.

EPILOGUE

$\mathcal{T}$rue hurried onto the balcony at ten past midnight, half
worried Wicked Wynona's ring would be gone. Once
she and Orion had finished their, um, kissing session, she'd realized she'd been too worried about Orion to realize that Wicked
Wynona's ring had flown off her finger in the scuffle with Bradley and crew. And she *knew* Mr. Brightside would not be happy
about his precious witch being divested of her accoutrements.

But her worry was for naught: True saw the ring on the bal-
cony floor right away, glinting in a beam of silvered moonlight.
She hurried forward to pick it up, not wanting to be away from
Orion an instant longer than she had to be.

He was headed downstairs to say goodbye to his friends; he
and True had decided to take a little romantic midnight drive
around Moon Ridge to get to know each other better. She was
going to show him the work she'd been doing on Hocus-Pocus.
True smiled at the thought. She'd expected to end the night
curled up in bed with some Netflix and buttered popcorn (with
some Whoppers thrown in for good measure; like father, like
daughter), but this was going to be so, so much better.

Bending down to get the ring, True noticed a piece of paper fluttering under it, as if the ring had been used as a paperweight. Frowning, True picked up both ring and paper, the latter of which turned out to be a note.

Three friends on this night
Have learned three lessons true:
1. Love does not bend to human will.
2. Love favors the brave.
3. The magic of love blooms in the air.
Now I return to the one who waits for me,
But remember dear friends, your lessons three.

~LOMR

"Truuuuuue!"

True turned to see Onny and Ash rushing onto the balcony. They'd both taken off their masks at some point, and their faces were glowing, their eyes feverish with bliss.

Onny cleared her throat and held up a solemn hand. "Announcement, and everyone brace thyself . . . but I think, no, I know, I don't hate Byron Frost's face. It might actually be on my list of favorite faces!"

"And Cassidy and I are together-together," Ash said shyly. "She told Logan she can't go to Sadie Hawkins with him, and then she asked me if we should make it official, since, you know, she and I are both already halves of the same painting." He gestured at his costume and blushed (the boy had no shortage of blushes when Cassidy was the topic of conversation).

True laughed, delighted. "Really?" She looked into her friends' shining eyes. "You guys, that's amazing!" She kissed each of their cheeks and pulled them to her for a group hug. "I'm so happy for you!"

"And what about you?" Onny pulled back, a sly smile on her beautiful face. "We ran into a certain Orion Parker downstairs, and he had a very interesting tale to tell, indeed."

Ash laughed. "You know, I actually met Orion when we were four years old, at a library story time. We both reached for the same stuffed elephant and then both insisted the other have it. Orion's really nice, True. Are you guys . . . ?"

True felt her cheeks heat up in spite of the cool night air. "I almost hate to admit it, but . . . you guys were onto something. I *think* Orion Parker may be my 'solid, mortal man.' And I may indeed prefer him to the centaur I was holding out for."

Onny and Ash both cheered, Onny attempting to lead her in a waltz across the balcony, but True laughed and resisted. "Wait, wait, wait. Before we go crazy with celebration, there's something you guys need to see." She handed over the note she'd found. "I found this under Wicked Wynona's ring, which I lost it up here for a while."

Ash held the note low enough that Onny could read it, too. They looked up at True a moment later, their eyes wide.

"Oh my god." Onny clapped her hand over her mouth. "It's *her*, isn't it? The Lady of Moon Ridge. I mean, we all saw her tonight! Even you, True."

True narrowed her eyes. "I mean, I saw some *stuff*, but was it the Lady? I don't know. . . ."

"The note's spot on about our three lessons," Ash pointed out in his gentle way.

Onny jabbed the bottom of the page. "And it's signed 'LOMR'! Lady of Moon Ridge!"

"Or Lisa O'Malley-Richardson," True countered.

Onny frowned. "What?"

"You know, *Lisa*. I saw her dressed up as a fortune cookie, handing out fortunes all night. This definitely could be one of hers." It sounded sort of implausible even to True, but was she really about to believe the long-deceased Lady of Moon Ridge had written this note? There were many things she'd ended up believing tonight, and she wasn't sure she wanted to add on a relationship-advice-giving ghost to the list.

Onny propped her fists on her hips. "So Lisa O'Malley-Richardson just happened to climb all the way up here in that giant outfit of hers, wrote this note that just happened to coincide with everything that's happened to us tonight, and left it here with Wicked Wynona's ring? For what purpose?"

True opened her mouth to respond, but Ash interrupted her. "Hey, look," he said, in a hushed, reverential near whisper. He moved to the balcony railing and pointed at the sky.

The full moon hung like a jeweled seed in the center. And beside it, *two* golden stars twinkled brightly.

"It's back," Ash whispered, as a gentle, fall-scented breeze tugged at True's hair. "The missing star."

"*She's* back," Onny corrected, shaking her head. "The Lady and the Gentleman of Moon Ridge are united again."

In spite of herself, True felt a lump in her throat. Much as she wanted to tell herself otherwise, she knew she'd never fully be able to explain what had happened tonight. Had a woman from centuries ago descended to earth to teach her and her best friends lessons about true love? Maybe, maybe not. But one thing True knew for certain: she was the luckiest girl in the world.

Linking arms with her two best friends, True sighed, a small smile at her lips. "I love you, Coven."

Her friends smiled back at her. "Love ya, too."

Then Onny said, "Let's get back to those significant others before they realize what they've been dragged into."

"Cassidy already knows you two are bananas," Ash said, raising his eyebrows.

True laughed and punched him lightly on the arm. "Wait till she gets to know you better."

True's friends walked with her back into the house, all three of them laughing and recounting the events of the night to each other.

In Onny's living room, Mr. Brightside stood with his arm around Wicked Wynona, looking like a proud parent, while Mayor Grimjoy sipped at his wine, saying in a beleaguered voice, "Whatever makes you happy, my love."

As The Coven walked past them, True reached into her dress pocket and then slipped the ring back onto Wicked Wynona's finger. Patting her head, she said, "Thanks for letting me be her keeper, Mr. B. She taught me a lot."

Mr. Brightside gave The Coven a collective wink, a knowing smile at his painted lips.

Out on the Diamantes' gigantic front porch, Byron, Cassidy,

and Orion were chatting in a small huddle, tendrils of mist wrapping around them.

"Hey, you." True slipped her arm around Orion's waist and watched her best friends greeting *their* true loves, a warm ember of joy glowing in her now-thawed heart. Behind her, cloaked in shadows, Igor chirped, his green eyes glinting in the moonlight, the only part of him that was visible. "Ready to go on that midnight drive?"

Smiling, Orion gestured out into the darkness. "Our chariot awaits."

"Ready?" Byron asked Onny, who nodded. True wondered what plans they had. Well, she was sure she'd hear about them soon enough.

Ash took Cassidy's hand, and they all walked down the stairs, out into the crisp autumn night that smelled of woodsmoke and glittered like jeweled secrets. As they went, the twin stars seemed to glow a little brighter, like watchful eyes shining in the dark.

ACKNOWLEDGMENTS

*T*his book has been pure joy to write, and we are so grateful to everyone who made it possible. Thank you to Thao Le, our agent extraordinaire, whose response when we told her we'd been secretly brewing a project together was to send us an ALL CAPS email with a giant mind-blown emoji. To Thao, Andrea Cavallaro, and everyone else at Sandra Dijkstra Literary Agency, we are thankful for your never-ending support and enthusiasm for our ideas, no matter how wacky they might seem.

Lots of love and thanks to our editor, Eileen Rothschild, who fell head over heels for Onny, Ash, and True from the moment she heard of our idea, and to the rest of the amazing team at Wednesday Books: Lisa Bonvissuto, Kerri Resnick, Brant Janeway, Alexis Neuville, Mary Moates, Carla Benton, Lena Shekhter, Kate Davis, and Devan Norman, as well as Mike Heath for the gorgeous cover art. There is no midnight gala grand enough to celebrate how awesome you all are.

We'd be nowhere without booksellers, librarians, teachers, and the incredible readers, bookstagrammers, booktokkers, booktubers, and bloggers that make up the YA community. Thank you for loving our books without even having to drink a love potion to feel that way.

And last but never least, thank you to our families for both inspiring and putting up with us. We know it's not the easiest thing to live with a writer—with all the talking to imaginary people or jumping up in the middle of dinner and shouting "aha!" when we've solved a plot problem—but thanks for loving us anyway. We're awfully fond of you, too.